continued . . .

String of Lies

Mary Ellen Hughes

BERKLEY PRIME CRIME, NEW YORK

THE BERKLEY PUBLISHING GROUP
Published by the Penguin Group
Penguin Group (USA) Inc.
375 Hudson Street, New York, New York 10014, USA
Penguin Group (Canada), 90 Eglinton Avenue East, Suite 700, Toronto, Ontario M4P 2Y3, Canada
(a division of Pearson Penguin Canada Inc.)
Penguin Books Ltd., 80 Strand, London WC2R 0RL, England
Penguin Group Ireland, 25 St. Stephen's Green, Dublin 2, Ireland (a division of Penguin Books Ltd.)
Penguin Group (Australia), 250 Camberwell Road, Camberwell, Victoria 3124, Australia
(a division of Pearson Australia Group Pty. Ltd.)
Penguin Books India Pvt. Ltd., 11 Community Centre, Panchsheel Park, New Delhi—110 017, India
Penguin Group (NZ), 67 Apollo Drive, Rosedale, North Shore 0745, Auckland, New Zealand
(a division of Pearson New Zealand Ltd.)
Penguin Books (South Africa) (Pty.) Ltd., 24 Sturdee Avenue, Rosebank, Johannesburg 2196,
South Africa

Penguin Books Ltd., Registered Offices: 80 Strand, London WC2R 0RL, England

STRING OF LIES

A Berkley Prime Crime Book / published by arrangement with the author

PRINTING HISTORY
Berkley Prime Crime mass-market edition / September 2007

Copyright © 2007 by Mary Ellen Hughes.
Cover art by Teresa Fasolino.
Cover design by George Long.
Interior text design by Stacy Irwin.

ISBN: 978-0-425-21767-2

BERKLEY® PRIME CRIME
Berkley Prime Crime Books are published by The Berkley Publishing Group,
a division of Penguin Group (USA) Inc.,
375 Hudson Street, New York, New York 10014.
The name BERKLEY PRIME CRIME and the BERKLEY PRIME CRIME design are trademarks belonging to Penguin Group (USA) Inc.

PRINTED IN THE UNITED STATES OF AMERICA

10 9 8 7 6 5 4 3 2 1

In memory of Mary C. and James J. Hughes
Always loving, ever giving

Acknowledgments

I am very grateful to the wonderful group at The Bead Shack in Crofton, Maryland, for introducing me to and guiding me through the fascinating world of beading. If any inaccuracies slipped in, it was entirely my fault and not theirs, for they know their craft inside and out. Thanks also to Susan Brown who generously shared her knowledge of the craft with me as well.

Many thanks to my editor, Sandra Harding, and the many hardworking people at Berkley for putting their fantastic skills to work on my behalf. I appreciate too the ongoing, generous support of my agent, Jacky Sach, without whom none of this would have begun.

Thank you, once again, to the members of the Annapolis critique group: Janet Benrey, Debbi Mack, Ray Flynt, Trish Marshall, Sherriel Mattingly, Marcia Talley, and Lynda Taylor, whose "tough love" always pushed me to do my best. I'm grateful as well to Stephen Hughes for his valuable automotive input, and to Suzanne Baker for her own very helpful knowledge of crafts and her unflagging support.

Last—but never least—my husband, Terry, who patiently played the part of my sounding board and who so often kept me from running off into a ditch: I couldn't have done it without you.

Chapter 1

Jo should have been tipped off when things began going much too well—always a danger sign in her life, but one she still somehow managed to ignore. She couldn't, however, ignore the huge "Closing Soon!" poster pasted in the window of Fantastic Florals by Frannie, just down the block from Jo's Craft Corner. Jo was on her way to pick up an order of sandwiches at the Abbot's Kitchen for Carrie and herself when she stopped dead in front of Frannie's shop, staring in disbelief at the sign.

Closing? But Frannie's place was always bursting with customers. Jo pulled open Frannie's door and called out without preamble, "What's going on, Frannie?"

Frannie, short and plump, and a regular dynamo of creativity with fresh flowers, looked down glumly from the ladder where she balanced on the third rung, holding a Teleflora poster that had previously hung on her wall. "I'm closing shop," she answered.

"Why? I thought your business was going great."

Frannie stepped carefully down the ladder, the top of her

head gradually sinking below Jo's until it ended about even with Jo's shoulder. She looked up at Jo, her expression both angry and resigned, and said, "We're being kicked out."

"But don't you have a lease?"

Frannie shook her head. "I was just about to renew it when I found out my landlord isn't my landlord anymore."

"Come again?"

"My landlord sold the building. He's not my landlord anymore."

"He can do that?"

"Yup." Frannie set down her poster and took hold of her ladder, sliding it sideways a few inches.

Jo automatically grabbed one leg to help. "But what about the new owner? Can't you rent from them? You've obviously been a great tenant."

Frannie looked at Jo with an expression of defeat on her face. Jo had never seen this feisty florist, a woman she had once overheard threatening a supplier with throat-constricting consequences if he didn't get an order of wedding flowers to her pronto, look so down.

"Parker Holt doesn't want tenants. Or this building. He wants the property, and all the other properties on this block, so he can tear them down and put up something brand-new and fancy. Mine's the first, or at least the first we know of. Who knows how many other properties he's gobbling up on the sly? Have you talked with *your* landlord lately, Jo?"

Jo felt her insides quiver. This conversation had taken a frightening turn. "Max? No, no I haven't."

"Well, I'd strongly suggest you do. Now, excuse me, dear. I've got some more dismantling to do."

Frannie reascended her ladder, and Jo numbly left the floral shop, looking dazedly about for signs of other businesses crumbling as she continued on her way to the sandwich shop. How could this be? She thought this neighborhood was solid as a rock, the perfect spot to set up a new business.

"Parker Holt made us a good offer," Ruthie Conway, co-owner with her husband Bert of the Abbot's Kitchen, admitted. She reached out one age-spotted hand over the counter to pass Jo her bagged order of turkey and bacon roll-up and tuna salad on wheat. "It's tempting, you'd better believe it. Bert and me, we're not getting any younger, you know."

"So you own your building?" Jo asked.

"Sure do. We bought it over thirty-five years ago, when nobody else wanted it, the condition it was in. But we fixed it up, little by little. It'd be hard to walk away from something we put so much work into. But with Bert's back acting up more, we maybe should be thinking of retiring. I don't know. Hate to do it, you know? We'd really miss our customers. They're like family, most of them."

Jo nodded. Ruthie had made her feel welcome in the neighborhood from her very first day last September. And their sandwiches, with Bert's special sauces, were more than worth coming out for on cold January days like today. What would Jo do for lunch if Ruthie and Bert sold out? She winced as the obvious occurred to her. What if she had no business to take a lunch break from?

Jo hurried back to the Craft Corner, clutching her sandwich bag closely to her chest as the cold wind whirled about her. "Carrie," she cried as she yanked open her shop door, sending the Christmas wreath that still hung there flying out perpendicularly. Time to replace that with something Valentiney, she thought as she rushed past.

"Carrie, who's Parker Holt and where's Max McGee's Florida number?"

Carrie looked up from the diamond-shaped yarn bins she was filling with newly arrived skeins. "I suppose the number's in your file somewhere. And why do you care about Parker Holt? Did he grab the last turkey-bacon roll-up at Ruthie's?"

"He might be grabbing more than that." Jo peeled off

her jacket on the way to her office cubicle at the back of the shop. She dropped the sandwich bag on her desk and her jacket on the chair, then pulled open a file drawer, rifling through it for her landlord's phone number.

"What's going on?" Carrie asked, unwittingly echoing Jo's very words to Frannie as she followed Jo to the back, still clutching a skein of heather blue wool.

"That's what I have to find out." Jo looked up at her longtime friend and part-time employee, dressed in a loose denim jumper to accommodate, she'd explained that morning with a woeful grin, her added holiday pounds. "Parker Holt bought Frannie's building out from under her. She's closing up shop."

"What!"

"And he's made an offer that might be too good to refuse to Ruthie and Bert. He's trying to buy up the block, according to Frannie, to tear it all down." Jo pulled her hands from the file drawer and looked at her friend. "Carrie, what will I do if I can't stay here?"

"But you have a lease," Carrie said, her tone hopeful.

"Only for six months, remember? I thought I was being so clever, not tying myself to the business in case it didn't work out. But after four months, and a surprisingly good Christmas season, my books are actually starting to show some black. I want to stay, Carrie. And with all the money I've sunk into the place, I *need* to stay."

"Oh, Jo." Carrie looked as woebegone as Jo felt. After her husband Mike's tragic death, Jo had come to Abbotsville mostly because of Carrie, who had suggested that Jo, with her art background, could make a go of an arts and crafts shop in the town where Carrie and her husband, Dan, had settled.

They had both helped scout out this location, and Dan, a home improvement professional, had stretched Jo's meager funds wonderfully by setting up the shop's interior—shelves, lighting, and everything else—for her. Carrie, with her vast needlework skills, had even volunteered to run that part of the shop, which Jo was convinced had made all the difference in drawing customers to her fledgling store.

Carrie and Dan, therefore, had good reason to feel as much pride in the Craft Corner's budding success as she did. And would take the blow of its demise as hard.

"Well, let's not panic until we have to," Jo said, trying to sound a little less worried than she was. "Maybe Frannie's landlord is the only one who's caved in to Parker Holt. Who is this guy, anyway?"

"He's a big developer." Carrie set down her skein of wool on Jo's desk and pulled up a chair. "You've seen Holt Meadows, haven't you?"

Jo nodded, remembering driving, on one of her early trips down here, through the winding roads of the impressive community just outside of town. She had drooled over the houses, but knew there was no way she could afford one, needing to sink most of Mike's modest life insurance payment into her business.

"Well," Carrie said, "Parker is the Holt behind it."

"Oh. Wow."

"And he's behind that new office building that's going up near the center of town, where the old library used to be."

"I've heard people complaining about that, how it's changing the character of the town, and all."

"And . . ." Carrie stopped, looking uneasy.

"What?"

"He's also Dan's employer, for the time being, anyway."

"*He's* the well-to-do homeowner that gave Dan the big remodeling job?"

"Uh-huh."

"And here I was, prepared to hate him. But I know how excited you were when Dan got the job."

"It's an important one, for what it could lead to as much as for what it's paying."

Jo nodded. Her old school friends Carrie and Dan had

made sacrifices to get Dan's business off the ground, including moving away from family and friends in tiny Glenn's Crossing to the broader possibilities of Abbotsville. It had been slow going, but Dan had gradually built a reputation for fine, honest work, and in his business, word of mouth was everything.

"Well," Jo said, "we at least know that Parker Holt has the good sense to hire the best."

Carrie grinned. "Yes, indeed. At least as far as his own home is concerned. Dan doesn't have much to say about the work on some of his other projects. 'Slapdash' and 'corner cutting,' I believe were words he used. But when it comes to his place, Parker Holt pinches no pennies. But he also checks every inch of the work with a magnifying glass, according to Dan. And interrupts him all day long with constant phone calls."

"A real control freak, huh?"

"Sounds like it."

"Oh," Jo said, glancing down, "duh! Here's Max's number. It's right here on my blotter, circled and everything. Let me call him, and we'll see just how much control Mr. Parker Holt actually has."

The shop's door dinged, and Carrie left to take care of the customer. Jo punched in the Florida number and waited. "Come on, Max. Climb out of that pool and answer your phone," she grumbled, drumming her fingers on her desk. But when the answering machine kicked in she calmly said, "Max, it's Jo McAllister," then hesitated, unsure what else to say. *Are you selling my business out from under me? Sending my life once again into a tailspin?* Tempting, but she added only, "It's very important. Please call me back," and gave her number. She hung up, feeling dissatisfied. Should she have explained her reason for calling? Would it get her a return call sooner? How soon should she try again if she didn't hear from Max?

Too many questions. Especially on an empty stomach.

Jo reached for the half-forgotten bag of sandwiches, and opened it up. The best answer to almost everything, at least for the moment, was turkey and bacon with Bert's special sauce. She unwrapped it and bit down, savoring the flavors that spread across her tongue, then groaned as yet another question popped up.

And if Bert decides to sell? What then?

By late afternoon, Jo had attempted to reach Max twice more without success, hanging up on the answering machine each time. She tried to take her mind off of it, telling herself the man was semiretired, after all, and wasn't sitting at a desk all day, taking calls. But the little bit of stock tidying she busied herself with between customers wasn't doing it for her. So when Carrie began to talk about Sylvia Ramirez and her tote bags, Jo welcomed the distraction.

"I told you about Xavier, didn't I?" Carrie asked, and when Jo nodded, continued. "Dan's been so glad to find him, says Xavier's the best worker he's had in ages, and so reliable. Anyway, Sylvia is Xavier's wife, and they're expecting their first baby soon, so she's recently stopped working. But she's been making these amazing handmade bags, quilted and beaded and such, for family and friends. I saw them the other night and thought how she could make a little money from them if she had the right outlet."

Jo caught where Carrie was going. "The right outlet such as Jo's Craft Corner?"

Carrie grinned. "Only if you like the idea, of course. Sylvia and Xavier have been having a tough time of things, ever since they lost everything in Hurricane Katrina. And I mean everything. They're still struggling to get back on their feet. Dan isn't able to pay Xavier very much yet, and they could probably use the extra income. But aside from that, the bags Sylvia makes are really quite beautiful. I think they'd be a terrific draw for customers."

"Let's ask her to bring some in, then," Jo said.

"Really?" Carrie looked delighted. "I could probably get her in today, have her bring a couple samples for you to look over."

"If you say they're good, Carrie, I'm sure they are." Jo thought it wouldn't hurt to put a couple bags near the needlepoint kits, and who knows? Maybe someone would be attracted by their novelty and actually buy one. She could see how much this meant to Carrie, who cared as much about her friends' well-being as her own. So Jo was happy to help Carrie assist Sylvia in this small way. At least, that is, as long as she had a shop to do it in.

Two customers walked in, and Jo took care of them while Carrie called Sylvia. The two had come mainly for scrapbooking supplies, and gathered a modest pile of purchases on the sales counter. But one, the slimmer of the two, hesitantly added a small kit Jo had packaged up for a bead-trimmed key ring as well.

"You shouldn't have any trouble with this," Jo assured her, "but come on back if you do, and I can help you out."

The woman's face brightened. "Oh, thank you!"

"Plus, we'll be starting a few beading workshops soon if you're interested in something a little more intricate." Jo slipped a flyer printed with information on the workshops into the woman's bag, and handed it over to her.

Carrie hung up the phone as the customers left and turned to Jo. "Sylvia said she can be here at four."

"Terrific," Jo said, taking in Carrie's happy face. She hoped she herself would be as pleased by 4:30 or so.

Pleased was not the word for it. It was as though Sylvia Ramirez was pulling rabbits out of a hat. The "hat" was a simple, white plastic trash bag Sylvia had used to transport her quilted bags, and her modest demeanor displayed none of a magician's flamboyance. But she might as well have cried "Abracadabra!" as she pulled out one handbag after another and placed them on Jo's counter. Even though the basics of handles, pouch, and zippers were identical, each bag was so different from the others. The uniqueness came from the designs Sylvia had stitched into them with her quilting and trims. One had a delicate flower pattern, another took on a charming animal face, and a third simply swirled with rainbow colors.

"I love them," Jo declared.

Sylvia, her dark hair pulled back and held simply with a white scrunchie, beamed, the smile rounding out her face to a near perfect circle.

"You think you can sell?" she asked.

"Definitely. How fast can you make them?"

Sylvia laughed, a light ripple that ran up half an octave. "Now, I have nothing else to do, mostly. I was cleaning houses, but with the baby coming, Xavier wants me to stay home. Our little place I can clean in two minutes. Rest of the time, I can make bags."

"Perfect. Let's figure out what a good price for them would be. What do your materials cost you, Sylvia?" Jo grabbed a clean sheet of paper and wrote down the figures the young woman pulled out of her head. Jo reached for her calculator to total the numbers up and work out percentages, and before long came up with a price that would give both the Craft Corner and Sylvia a reasonable profit.

"We're going to start a fad right here in Abbotsville, mark my words," Jo declared.

"A fad?" Sylvia looked puzzled. "What is a fad?"

"A 'fad' means every woman in town is going to want her own signature 'Sylvia' bag before long. They'll be pounding at the doors, money clutched in their fists, waiting for our next shipment to come in."

Sylvia spilled out her musical laugh. "No ships. I'll carry them over myself."

"Well, at least they're light. I wouldn't want you to over-burden yourself." Jo looked at Sylvia's rounded middle. "When is the baby due?"

Sylvia smiled, and ran a hand over her belly. "Two months. March fifth. But he is big already. Maybe he comes sooner."

Jo nodded, happy for Sylvia's expected joy, but at the same time selfishly hoping Baby Ramirez wouldn't rush to make his appearance. Jo wanted as many of Sylvia's bags as she could get, and she knew designer bags would be pushed aside once diaper bags came on the scene. Then she thought about Parker Holt, and her satisfaction in the moment faded away.

"Something wrong?" Sylvia asked. "You change your mind?"

"No, no," Jo reassured her. "Everything's fine. I just re-membered something I have to take care of." *Like making sure I have a business long enough to sell these bags for Sylvia, as well as support myself. Why isn't Max calling back?*

The phone rang, and Jo heard Carrie take it in the back. She waited, but when Carrie didn't call out, she turned her attention back to Sylvia, chatting until the young woman, bubbling her thanks, took her leave. Jo watched her buoy-ant exit, which, at this point in her pregnancy, was not ex-actly light-footed, but hadn't reached the dreaded "waddle" stage yet, either.

"Carrie," Jo called as she searched through a drawer for price tags to attach to the bags Sylvia left with her, "I'm so glad you—" A swooshing sound caused Jo to turn, and she saw Carrie pulling on her nylon parka in a hurry.

"You're going out?"

"That phone call—it was from the Abbotsville Play-house." Carrie's face was white. "Charlie was working there during rehearsals after school, and he's taken a fall. They're taking him to the hospital."

"Oh, no!"

"I don't know how bad it is, but I'm meeting them in the ER." Carrie was zipping up and pulling on gloves hurriedly as she headed to the door. "I couldn't get through to Dan. He's probably at the Holt house. Would you keep trying and tell him I'll call as soon as I know anything? And I'll call you too."

"Yes, of course. I'll get Dan." Jo couldn't get more out before Carrie was gone. She stared after her dazedly, thinking, Charlie's hurt? Her godson and most favorite fifteen-year-old in the world. How could it be? As alarmed as she was, though, she knew Carrie must feel ten times worse. This was Carrie's child, her firstborn, her son. But it was pretty awful for Jo to handle too.

"Mike," Jo silently said, speaking as she often did to her late husband, who, she was convinced, watched over her from his own particular heavenly spot. "How can this be? Bad things shouldn't happen to Carrie's family. I love them."

But you loved me, Jo, she seemed to hear, *and look what happened.*

"Exactly my point, Mike. Wasn't that enough?"

Mike didn't answer.

Chapter 2

The next couple of hours were a blur of hasty, worry-filled phone calls, and anxious pacing for Jo, all while handling the ongoing business of her craft shop. At Jo's suggestion, Carrie sent her eleven-year-old, Amanda, to the shop, leaving her one less thing to think about, and Jo had Amanda's favorite sausage and mushroom pizza delivered for their dinner. Instead of it being a fun treat, though, the pizza was nibbled at solemnly as each tried to put on a brave face for the other, with neither succeeding.

"When did Mom say she'd call?" Amanda asked, pushing a cooling, cheese-topped triangle around her plate.

"As soon as she's talked to the doctor who has looked at all the X-rays and test results. Honey, those emergency rooms can be a madhouse, believe me. I remember. Nurses and doctors are taking care of dozens of patients at a time. All anyone can do is wait for them to get to you."

"But why can't they just take care of Charlie first and then take care of the other people?"

"I know, we all wish that. Those other patients are wishing

it too, you can bet on it. But the hospital people have to do what they call a triage."

Amanda wrinkled her nose and Jo explained. "That means a kind of filtering, or sorting through the situation. The nurses and doctors do a quick check of everyone who comes in, then take care of the worst cases first, the ones that really can't wait."

"So maybe it's a good sign that Charlie's waiting?"

"I think it's a very good sign. Even though it's hard on the rest of us."

Amanda took a bite of her pizza. "It's yucky."

"The pizza?"

"No, the waiting."

Jo smiled at the girl who she remembered once insisting that Charlie was the most disgusting brother in the world because he had burped loudly at the table when Amanda's best friend Lindsey stayed over for dinner.

The Craft Corner's door opened, and Jo looked over to see Ina Mae Kepner coming in. "Any word yet?" Ina Mae asked.

"Not yet, but Amanda and I are taking that as a good sign."

The older woman looked over at Amanda and nodded. "Probably so." Ina Mae had seen Carrie drive off in a rush and rightly took it as an indication that not all was well. Though she'd been heading for the bank, she stepped into the Craft Corner and got an explanation from Jo.

For the few months Jo had known her, Ina Mae had been a rock of common sense, and Jo was always glad to share as much as she knew with her, unlike certain other individuals, such as gossipy Alexis Wigsley. Besides, as a retired elementary schoolteacher, Ina Mae still had an air about her that sometimes made Jo feel as though *all that is wrong would be made right because Mrs. Kepner is here*, and Jo was grateful for it, unrealistic though it may be.

"What exactly happened?" Ina Mae asked.

"Carrie said he had gone out on the stage to check on the

sound system when he got distracted, wandered too close to the edge, and fell into the pit. You know how those rehearsals can be. A million things going on at one time."

Ina Mae tsked. She was never one to approve of disorganization. But she managed to say, "Well, at least there were plenty of people there to help."

The phone rang, and Jo grabbed for it eagerly, but it was only a customer checking on Jo's closing time.

Ina Mae soothed, "You'll hear from Carrie soon. It can't be too bad, from what you said."

"I know, and I do expect good news." Jo sank onto her stool. "But I'm ashamed to say I'm also anxious to hear from Max McGee. I've been trying to get him all day."

"Your landlord? What on earth for?" Ina Mae glanced around as if looking for signs of a leaky roof or scuttling mice.

"To find out if he's selling this place out from under me." Jo dolefully told Ina Mae what she had learned that morning, and the tall, white-haired woman's lips pressed tightly as she listened.

"That man! It's bad enough Parker Holt is putting up an ugly office building where our beautiful old library used to be. What does he want? To turn this row of character-filled shops into some kind of T-shirt mall?"

"I don't know."

"If you can't reach Max—and who knows, he may be off on another one of those abominable cruises he loves to take—your best bet is to go right to Holt and ask *him*."

"You're right, I hadn't thought of that—that Max might ultimately be unreachable. But Parker Holt is certainly right here in town. There's nothing to stop me from finding Holt and demanding a straight answer from him, is there?"

"Nothing at all," Ina Mae agreed. "Of course, the man, from what I hear, is a master of evasion, so it might not be all that easy. But you're a capable woman," Ina Mae declared, looking Jo firmly in the eye. "You'll find a way."

The shop door opened, and the late-shopping customer who had called came rushing in. "Quick, I need a craft project for our Brownie meeting tomorrow. What do you have that will keep ten eight-year-olds occupied for half an hour?"

Ina Mae sniffed, and Jo led the woman to a few possibilities in the beading area. The phone rang, and Jo heard Amanda pick it up. She listened with one ear as her customer groaned into the other about the difficulties of handling a Brownie troop.

Amanda finally called out, "Charlie's got a cracked rib! But it's gonna be okay, and that's all that's wrong with him."

"That's fantastic, honey!" Jo called back.

"I imagine it'll be the last time he doesn't look where he's going," Ina Mae said, but Jo saw a little smile spread across her face.

"Tell your mom you can stay with me tonight, Amanda," Jo said.

"Yipee!"

"Do you have anything a little less expensive?" the Brownie mother asked doubtfully, oblivious to the excitement around her.

"Ma'am," Jo said, smiling widely, "I've just this moment discounted those beaded bracelet kits by 50 percent. Tell your Brownies, 'Happy New Year from Jo!'"

The woman blinked as Amanda ran over to give Jo a happy hug.

The next morning Jo dropped Amanda off at Abbotsville Middle School. She watched the girl hail her friends and smiled at her eagerness to share the excitement of Charlie's accident, now that he wasn't too badly off. Jo was relieved and happy about Charlie too, but she still had that other major concern hanging around ominously. She pulled out her cell phone and called Parker Holt's office number.

"Mr. Holt isn't in yet" was the cool answer she got to her inquiry.

"When do you expect him?"

"I really can't say. May I have your number and have him get back to you?"

Jo had had enough of leaving her number in the black hole of answering machines lately. "Perhaps I could just stop over. I only need a minute of his time."

"I can't guarantee when Mr. Holt will be in. He has several projects he's overseeing."

"I'd be happy to run over to one of those projects to see him. Can you tell me where he'll be?"

"May I have your number, and he can get back to you?"

Jo sighed and gave in, giving both her cell and store numbers. "Please tell him it's urgent, and I promise to be brief."

"Thank you for calling," the cool voice said, and hung up.

Jo grumped, and drove on to her shop, determined to keep on trying. However, as the day progressed and each call got her no further than that chilly, stonewalling voice, her frustration grew, and she began to picture the voice as coming from a thickly padded, robotic hockey goalie, poised to block any and all attempts by callers to score a point for their side.

"Parker Holt, please?" Jo would politely ask.

Zing, block, puck sent off.

"Is Mr. Holt in?"

Block, slap, smash.

"May I—"

Zip, slam!

Parker Holt had clearly trained his office staff well in the art of courteous but effective obstruction. It grew increasingly exasperating, but Jo was determined to get around such slipperiness. After all, she had dealt with masters up in

New York when working to place her handwrought jewelry for consignment, and here in Abbotsville she had team-mates to bring in. With their help she could surely work out a circumventing screen shot. All those hours of watching Wayne Gretzky surely should be worth something.

Never mind that she'd always been lousy on skates.

Chapter 3

Jo waited until her latest customer left, happily clutching a bag of newly purchased beading supplies, then picked up the phone and speed-dialed.

"Carrie, it's me. How's Charlie doing?"

"Fine, though he's pretty sore, pain pills or not. He's sleeping most of the time and really doesn't need me here. I could easily come into the shop for a couple hours."

"Don't even think of it. That isn't why I'm calling at all. But tell Charlie when he wakes up that I'll come visit as soon as he's up to it, and I'll bring something special."

"Oh, Jo, don't—"

"Carrie," Jo interrupted firmly, "he *is* my godson. But don't worry, I'll try to make it educational. Maybe a book on theatrical soundboards?"

"How about," Carrie's voice turned wry, "*How to Ogle Pretty Girls and Not Kill Yourself at the Same Time*?"

"Oh-ho, so it wasn't just the sound system at the playhouse! He was checking out a few other things of interest as well?"

"Sometimes pain pills make you babble, say things you wouldn't normally mention to your mother."

"Let's hope for his sake that little revelation disappears into the amnesia of pain control. Carrie, is Dan back working at the Holt house today?"

"Yes, he went over with Xavier this morning."

"Great. Do you think he'd mind me calling him there?"

"If he answers his phone, it's because he can talk for a minute. What's up?"

"I'm having trouble catching hold of Parker Holt. I thought, control freak that he is, that he might call Dan to check on things there, and Dan could let me know where he is. Or better yet, he might stop at the house."

"You'd close up the shop to run over?"

"I'm getting desperate, Carrie. It's becoming clear that the only way to talk to the man is to do a screen shot."

"A what?"

"You know, that sneaky thing they do in ice hockey. An ambush."

"You've been watching too much late-night TV. But good luck. I only hope if you catch up with Holt you're not unhappy with what he'll have to tell you."

"Me too, Carrie. Me too."

Dan answered on the first ring and promised to do what he could to connect Jo with Parker Holt. "Have your running shoes on, though. The man doesn't stand still for two seconds, and he has his cell phone to his ear the same time he's talking to you face-to-face."

"I'll be prepared. How's the work going there?"

"Not bad. Carrie probably told you we're redoing his basement into a game room–party room. We put the wet bar in place yesterday—luckily finishing before I got the call about Charlie—and today we're framing up the bathroom."

"Sounds like a big job. Carrie said you're really happy to have Xavier working with you."

"Yeah, it makes a big difference to have a good worker

like him. Only thing," Dan's voice dropped slightly, "he seems really bugged by Holt, whenever the guy stops by to check up on things."

"Oh? Is Holt that abrasive?"

"No, mostly just annoying, poking into everything we've done as though we need close watching. But as I see it, he has the right. He's writing the check. But Xavier really, well, never mind. He'll be okay. I hear you've worked out something with his wife."

"Yes. She's a real sweetheart, and her bags are already flying off the shelves."

"That's great. I'll pass that on to Xavier. It should cheer him up. And I'll call you about Holt."

"Great. Thanks, Dan."

Jo was replacing her phone when Ina Mae popped in, on her way, she explained, to the senior center.

"How's Carrie's boy doing?"

"He's home, taped up, and resting under his mother's care."

"Good," Ina Mae said. "Let's hope he doesn't miss too much school."

Jo smiled. The woman may have left the classroom, but the classroom had not left Ina Mae.

"How about that other problem of yours. Hear from Max yet?"

"No, and you're right about Parker Holt. He's proving to be about as hard to pin down as a," Jo paused, thinking Ina Mae probably wasn't much into ice hockey, "as a school board member with budget cuts in mind."

"Hmph.

"But I'm working on it. However, since troubles, as they say, always come in threes, I've discovered another problem. This one, though, is very minor compared to the other two."

Ina Mae raised her eyebrows, waiting.

"The last time I went into my storeroom, I noticed one

of the shelves is seriously buckling. I wouldn't dream of asking Dan to take care of it for me now, what with Charlie's accident and probably getting behind on his own work. But I'll have to unload everything from that shelf before it breaks, which will make it difficult to get around the storeroom until the shelf is fixed."

Ina Mae thought a minute. "You could try Randy Truitt."

"Who's that?"

"He does odd jobs about town. Fixed up Patsy Holcomb's back porch after a big tree branch fell on it last summer, and she was happy with his work. If the job's not too involved or time consuming, he's good for it, I'd say."

"What is he, a retiree, filling in his time?"

"No, Randy's a young man, or relatively so. Couldn't be more than forty, I imagine. I used to buy fresh eggs from his folks, Bill and Myrtle Truitt, when they had their farm out along Route 23. They're gone—dead, I mean—and the farm's gone too. Randy," Ina Mae paused, frowning, "never seemed able to quite pull things together for himself. At least not yet. There's always hope. If you like, I could get his number for you from Patsy."

"I'd appreciate that."

"By the way, I heard you're handling that young Ramirez woman's handmade bags on consignment."

"You did? We only arranged that yesterday."

Ina Mae smiled as if to say Jo still had a lot to learn about how quickly news traveled in a town like Abbotsville.

"As a matter of fact," Jo proudly added, "I sold all three bags she left with me, this morning."

"I'm glad to hear that. For her, but not for myself. My daughter-in-law's birthday is coming up, and I'd hoped to pick one up. Let me know when she brings more in." Ina Mae began pulling her gloves back on. "Well, I'll head on to the senior center. It's quite possible I'll run into Patsy there, in which case I'll get Randy Truitt's number for you. But I also intend to sign up for that next yoga session."

The older woman briskly exited, and Jo watched, impressed once again with her level of energy—both mental and physical. In addition to all her other activities, Ina Mae was one of Jo's most constant craft workshop members. She'd retired, but obviously never slowed down. Jo began to wonder what she would be like at that age. Then it occurred to her if she didn't get some straight answers soon regarding the future of her craft shop, she just might, at age thirty-six, find herself retired and living on the kindness of strangers.

More customers drifted in, and many asked after Charlie, as well as how soon Carrie would be back so they could get advice on knitting projects. Around four o'clock, just as Jo had bagged up a purchase of scrapbooking supplies and handed them over, Dan called.

"Jo, we're taking off for the day here. Have to pick up things for the bathroom that came in, before the place closes. Holt just called, but I don't know from where. He wasn't happy to hear we were calling it a day. But he said something about coming home around six to look over what we've done. You might be able to catch him here, if you want to try."

"That would work out great, Dan. There's no workshop tonight, and I can close at six. What's the address?"

Jo grabbed a pen and scribbled down Parker Holt's address. "I should be able to find that. Thanks for the heads-up. And wish me luck!"

From then on, Jo watched the clock impatiently. For a day that had been fairly busy, things suddenly quieted down, and the minutes dragged like a sable brush through a half-dried blob of paint.

Ina Mae called with Randy Truitt's contact number. "It's for Otto's," she explained. "That bar and pizza place over on Borne Avenue." Jo knew the place. She had stopped in on one of her early days in Abbotsville, for a take-out pizza, and could barely communicate over the blare of a basketball game on the television. "Apparently," Ina Mae continued, "Otto takes messages for Randy."

Jo remembered seeing a handful of men at Otto's bar that day, looking glued in place, half-full glasses of beer before them as they gazed up at the television cheerlessly. Randy Truitt might have been one of them. Not a totally re-assuring image, but Ina Mae wouldn't recommend an in-competent. And it was a small job.

"Thanks, Ina Mae. I'll give him a try."

Jo punched in the number for Otto's and asked for Randy.

"Not here," a not-unfriendly voice barked into her ear. Jo heard droning motor noises in the background and pictured a NASCAR race on the bar's television, captivating—or perhaps hypnotizing—its patrons.

She left her message and wondered when she'd hear back from Randy, grimacing over how her days seemed to be turning into ongoing searches for men who uniformly kept one step beyond her. Hopefully Randy, with the prom-ise of payment, would come within her reach.

Finally, after only one more customer stopping in—at five minutes before six, of course—Jo closed up shop. She pocketed the slip of paper with Parker Holt's address writ-ten on it, clicked off the last light, locked the final lock, and headed for her not-so-trusty Toyota in the small lot next to her shop.

What exactly would she say to Holt? she wondered as she turned the key in her ignition and listened to the slow grind of the cold motor working hard to start. He might not be too happy to be cornered at his home. How should she begin, in order to put him in a more comfortable frame of mind and therefore more apt to answer her questions? In-troduce herself first as a friend of Dan's? No, that might put Dan in an awkward position.

The engine caught, and she let it warm a bit while she thought, then put the car in gear and headed out Main.

She should probably be open with Holt as to her purpose for coming, but nonconfrontational. Simply seeking information.

That was it. To the point and brief. And if Holt told her he had arranged with Max to buy her store's building, and planned to tear it down so that she'd better start looking elsewhere for accommodations, so be it. She would nod and thank him for his time and leave.

And go straight home to cut her throat.

No, not quite, though the urge would definitely be there. But she shouldn't think about that yet. First things first. And right now, she needed to concentrate on finding the house. The address Dan gave her was on Foxwell. Which, he had told her was off of Old Stagecoach Road. Ah, there it was. Okay, had Dan said take a right turn? Yes.

Jo turned and drove down Foxwell, checking the numbers on the houses, which were spread apart and set much farther back from the street than in the parts of town she was used to. Larger too. The address numbers were at the ends of their long driveways, on lighted pillars or artistically stacked rocks: 241, 239. There it was, 237. Jo stopped and looked over at the house.

It was old, but beautifully so, well maintained and full of character. Interesting, she thought, that a man who made his money erecting new, flashy, and according to some, flimsy structures, chose to live in a solid, stone-fronted, traditional home such as that. The landscaping, lit by outside lights and dusted with snow, was attractive and not overdone. No see-how-many-expensive-shrubs-I-can-afford extravagance, but tasteful, graceful arrangements separated by wide spaces of lawn.

Was this a good sign? Did it mean that Parker Holt was a man who would not ruthlessly ruin others for his own profit? Or was it, perhaps, simply a sign that he had married a woman with good taste, to whom he had given carte blanche? Jo hadn't thought about a wife. Would Mrs. Holt answer Jo's knock on the door and run interference for her husband just as his goalie secretary had done? Only one way to find out.

Jo drove up the driveway, which split in two near the top, one part leading to a three-car garage, partially blocked by a silver Lexus, the other to the front of the house. Jo chose the front. She parked, stepped out, and walked up the porch steps, admiring the look of the house, close-up. The front door was framed by sheer-curtained sidelights, through which she barely made out a wide, slate-floored foyer. She lifted the brass knocker and tapped it three times, then waited.

Nothing seemed to stir within the house. Jo checked the edges of the sidelights and found a door bell, which she pressed, hearing the musical chime play inside. Again, no response. Had she arrived too early and beat Parker Holt home? But someone's car was here, possibly his, and the house was brightly lit. What should she do? She hadn't counted on just being left at the door. She didn't like it much, either.

Jo lifted the door knocker again and let it fall heavily on its base, several times. When this brought no response, Jo stepped back off the porch and looked up. No windows on the upper floor were lit, though most of the downstairs seemed to be. Then she caught sight of light glimmering through a basement window. Perhaps Holt was in the basement, checking on Dan and Xavier's work. Maybe he couldn't hear her knocks.

Jo looked over to where the silver Lexus was parked. Perhaps there was an entrance there? Maybe Holt would hear her if she banged on that one. She trotted over to that side of the house and saw it as soon as she rounded the house's corner: a door, set next to the garage doors, with light showing through its high window. Jo ran over and knocked. Again, no response. She knocked harder, and this time the door eased open an inch, apparently not having been firmly shut. Should she go in? The cold wind whipped around the corner of the house, lifting her hair to chill her ears, urging her to go ahead. She pushed the door farther open and leaned in.

"Hello? Mr. Holt?"

No response.

"Hello?" Jo took one step in and called again. She spotted stairs over to the right, leading obviously to the basement, light coming from them. Was he down there? But it was quiet. So quiet. No sound of movement, or of Holt talking on his ever-present cell phone. Nothing. Jo felt a sudden chill, aware it wasn't from the wind this time. Something wasn't right.

She called out once more and moved to the head of the stairs. Then she saw him.

A man—Parker Holt?—lying head first at the bottom of the steps.

Jo froze.

No sound came from him, no movement, no intake of breath. If this was Holt, she feared he was the late Parker Holt

Jo fumbled for her cell phone.

Chapter 4

Lights flashed from emergency vehicles, giving Jo a sickening sense of déjà vu: first Mike's horrible accident in New York, then that bizarre death scene she'd encountered in her own shop only four months ago. Apparently that last one also came to the mind of Lieutenant Morgan when he arrived at the house and spotted her sitting in her car.

"You again," he'd said, exhaling a puff of condensing air.

Jo managed a weak smile, her concern at the moment more for Dan, whom she'd called immediately after 9-1-1. Dan had arrived, grim faced, shortly after the emergency responders and was in the basement with police at the moment. The man on the stairs, Jo had learned, was indeed Parker Holt, confirmed for her by several of the rescue personnel who recognized him.

How would this affect Dan's remodeling business, she worried, with a homeowner dying in the work area? Had something been left so carelessly and in such a dangerous spot that it somehow caused Parker Holt's death? Jo could hardly imagine that. Dan was extremely meticulous; she knew that for a fact. He would never overlook anything deadly, especially knowing that Holt would be poking through the area later on. So how did it happen? Jo had seen a crowbar on the floor near Holt's body. But what that had to do with anything she couldn't begin to guess. From the position of his body, he seemed to have fallen down the steps. But why?

Lieutenant Morgan disappeared into the house, then other, nonuniformed people arrived. A portly man wrapped in a heavy dark overcoat emerged from a black Lincoln and blustered in along with a younger man, both unchallenged by police. Was that Warren Kunkle, the mayor of Abbotsville? Jo had seen only photos of him in the *Abbotsville Gazette*, but she thought it might be. What would the mayor be here for, she wondered? But before she had time to consider, another car pulled up and a woman wearing high-heeled boots and fur-trimmed coat and hat got out. She conferred briefly with an officer, then hurried to the front door.

Jo hadn't seen her face, but the manner in which the woman had entered the house told Jo it was her own, that this was Parker Holt's wife. Jo's heart instantly went out to her. She understood better than most what she would be going through on hearing the devastating news that her husband was dead. The memory of her own experience flashed once more, and Jo sucked in a deep breath, then opened her car door and got out. Better to move around, even in the cold, than sit alone with painful memories. She went up to a patrolman standing beside his car.

"I was asked to wait so Lieutenant Morgan could talk to me. Any idea how soon that might be?"

"No ma'am. They're probably still working the scene. Did you want to wait inside the patrol car?"

"No, but thanks."

Jo's cell phone rang. She knew who it was before checking the caller ID. "I haven't heard anything more yet, Carrie," Jo said, answering, and stepping away from the red-nosed patrolman.

"Jo, I'm just so worried. And it's awful of me, I know, for feeling worse about what this means to Dan—and us—than I do about that poor man."

"Carrie, you've never even met Parker Holt, right? Of course you should feel that way. But try not to, anyway. I mean, don't worry. We don't know what exactly happened yet. Holt might have simply tripped on his own shoelaces. Or maybe he had a heart attack. Do you know if he—oh, wait." Jo caught sight of someone heading to the garage side entrance. "I think Xavier's here. Youngish, with a mustache, wears a dark baseball-type jacket?"

"That sounds like him. Poor Sylvia. She'll be worried to death. I should give her a call."

"Why don't you do that." Jo knew Carrie would wring her hands less if she focused more on Sylvia. "I'll call you if I learn anything."

"Mrs. McAllister?"

Jo turned to see a sandy-haired uniformed officer. "I've got to go," Jo said to Carrie and hung up.

"Lieutenant Morgan would like to talk to you."

Jo pocketed her cell phone and followed the officer into the house. He led her through the foyer, turning left, and Jo trailed behind, glancing over at the living room on the right. She saw no sign of the woman she'd assumed to be Holt's wife but did hear muffled voices coming from somewhere farther back, possibly the kitchen. Agitated voices.

The living room, from her quick look, had exuded an air of quiet opulence—polished cherry, brocades in bright colors. The door that the sandy-haired officer opened for her, however, led to a smaller room with a cozier feel. Plump armchairs flanked a round table that held a reading lamp and a small pile of books. Built-in shelves were filled with more books, framed photos, and a small television. A Queen Anne–style desk took up one end of the narrow room, and behind it sat Lieutenant Morgan, looking, Jo thought, less than comfortable on the delicate chair.

"Mrs. McAllister," he said, greeting her with a half-rise, "please have a seat."

Since the only choice was one of the oversized chairs, Jo took the nearest one and perched on the edge of its puffy cushion as she tried to meet Morgan's gaze in a businesslike way. The chair's softness, however, swallowed her and she sank backward ungracefully.

"Sorry about that," the lieutenant said, as Jo struggled. "This was the only available room with any privacy."

Jo nodded, and found that once she gave into it, the chair was amazingly comfortable. Images of it replacing her own broken-springed sofa ran wistfully through her head.

Morgan got down to business. "Tell me how you happened to come here tonight." He flipped pages in a notebook, which, Jo was sure, held the information she had already given to the first responding officer. She hadn't seen Morgan for several weeks, and once again it unnerved her how the sight of him brought flashes of Mike to mind, though there was little actual resemblance between the two men beyond their dark coloring and build.

Jo remembered having spotted the lieutenant during a break at the Abbotsville Country Club's craft show last fall. She had watched him then, meeting an attractive woman for lunch and greeting her with a kiss on the cheek. What did that kiss indicate? she had wondered at the time, and continued to wonder. Was this woman still in his life?

Jo suddenly became aware of how she must look, knowing how she tended to run her hands through her own dark hair under times of stress. And her nose, she was sure, must be as red as the patrolman's outside. But as Lieutenant Morgan looked up expectantly, and a bit impatiently, Jo straightened up, annoyed with herself for letting her thoughts wander so frivolously. This was not, after all, a social visit. She launched into her answer to Morgan's question, explaining about her unsuccessful attempts to reach Holt all day, and finally coming to his house.

"So he wasn't expecting you?"

"No. I thought my chances of talking with him were better if I caught him by surprise."

"But Dan Brenner knew you would be coming."

"Yes, as I said, Dan gave me the address and told me when Mr. Holt would likely be here."

"Did Mr. Ramirez also know you were coming?"

Jo thought it an odd question. "I don't know. He might have heard Dan talking on the phone to me, I suppose. Or Dan might have mentioned it to him. Why?"

"Tell me what you found when you arrived at the house."

Jo described knocking at the front door and eventually spotting light at the basement window.

"You didn't see or hear signs of anyone in the house at that point?"

"No, which is why I went around, looking for another entrance. I thought maybe Mr. Holt hadn't heard my knocking on the front door if he was in the basement."

"Uh-huh. And then what?"

Jo told about the side door moving open at her touch, then walking in and seeing Holt at the bottom of the stairs.

"And did you go down those stairs?"

"No. I called 9-1-1. On the slim chance he was alive, I didn't think I should try to do anything in case moving him at all would be dangerous. But he looked dead."

"Yes, I guess you, better than some, would pick up on that."

Jo had been expecting a comment like that. In the past she might have bristled, but now she searched for a glint of humor lurking in the lieutenant's eyes, and found it.

"Believe me, it's not something I'm happy to have

expertise in," she replied. "What happened? Did he trip?
Hit his head? I didn't see blood."

"We're still looking into that." The veil of officialdom
slipped back down, covering the glint, and Morgan returned to his notebook. "Well, that about covers everything, Mrs. McAllister."

"You *can* call me Jo, by now. I'd say it's been long
enough."

Morgan opened his mouth to respond when a patrolman
stuck his head in the door after a single knock.

"Excuse me, sir, but the mayor wants—"

"Tell him I'll be there in a minute."

Morgan stood and came around the desk, and, as Jo
worked at climbing out of her soft chair, held out a helpful
hand.

"I thought I recognized that man as Warren Kunkle," Jo
said, taking Morgan's hand gratefully and pulling herself
upright. "What does the mayor have to do with this?"

Morgan guided her out the door.

"Thank you for your help," he said, adding with a small
smile, "Jo." He opened the front door for her and stepped
back. "And Mrs. Holt is Warren Kunkle's niece."

"Oh," Jo said, as the door closed behind her.

Jo left the Holt property with some difficulty, maneuvering
her Toyota past the clusters of vehicles clogging the drive,
grateful that the simplicity of the Holt's landscaping allowed her to veer onto the hard, snow-dusted ground as
needed. Once back on the street, she sighed with relief,
glad to pull away from the flashing lights and crackling radios, wondering how those whose job it was to regularly
function under such conditions could bear it. The lieutenant seemed as calm and in control as he always had,
which in the past had often been maddening but tonight felt
comforting. It brought back memories of how Mike had

been able to soothe her far simpler worries with his usual reasonableness.

Carrie's worries, however, Jo quickly reminded herself, were not so simple, and she gave her friend a call before heading over to her place. Carrie was waiting at the door as Jo pulled up.

"Charlie's sound asleep on his pain medication in the family room, and Amanda's finishing her homework upstairs," Carrie said. "You probably haven't had any dinner yet, right? Come on back. I've been keeping a pot of stew warm on the stove."

Jo peeled off her jacket and gloves as they walked through Carrie's work-in-progress living room whose sparse sheet-covered furniture shared space with paint cans and tools. Never waiting on ceremony in her long-time friend's home, she deposited her things on a chair before entering the warm, welcoming kitchen. Carrie lifted the lid on a large pot and stirred at its contents, releasing aromas that set Jo's mouth to watering. As she dished out the stew, Carrie peppered Jo with questions, most of which Jo was unable to answer.

"I'm sorry, Carrie. Lieutenant Morgan was playing it very close to the vest. All I managed to learn from him is that Parker Holt's wife is the niece of Mayor Kunkle. I saw Kunkle arrive while I was waiting."

"That's right. I'd forgotten she was his niece." Carrie set Jo's steaming bowl in front of her on a bright placemat. She frowned. "I wonder what his coming there means to all this."

"Probably nothing," Jo said, tucking into her food. "I'm sure he was simply there to offer support and comfort to his niece. She apparently wasn't home when this all happened. I saw a woman who I presume was her arrive shortly after Kunkle did."

Jo speared a gravy-soaked potato chunk, then asked, "Did you talk with Sylvia? How is she?"

"She's nervous, doesn't like the idea of Xavier being questioned by police, even though I assured her it was just routine, that they had to talk to everybody with any connection to the situation at the house so that they can write up all the proper reports." Carrie's brave tone faltered as she sat down across from Jo. "But I just don't understand what's taking so long. Dan's been there over two hours now. What could he have to tell them that would take more than five minutes?"

"Carrie." Jo set down her fork to reach for her friend's hand. "He's probably waiting all this time for them to get around to him. All things official, by definition, move at glacier speed."

"I know, I know. I'm just so afraid that if it somehow reflects badly on Dan's work, it could damage his business. What if they say he must have left something on the stairs, an extension cord stretched across it, or something? And that's the reason Parker Holt tumbled down them?"

"They won't, because Dan would never do that. And he would double-check to make sure Xavier didn't either."

"Then why call Xavier over there at all?"

Jo frowned. "I don't know. And Morgan brought up Xavier in his questions to me, which struck me as odd. Something about whether Xavier knew that I was planning to come to the house."

Carrie leaned her face into her hands, worried eyes looking at Jo over her fingertips. She seemed about to say something when a voice from behind Jo startled them both.

"Mom? Aunt Jo?"

"Charlie! Did we wake you?" Carrie jumped up from her chair to go to her son. "How do you feel? Do you need another pain pill?"

Charlie shook his head, looking only half-awake, his hair spiking in several different directions, his too-small robe drooping over pajama bottoms and a T-shirt.

"Is that stew? Can I have some?"

"Of course! I didn't want to wake you when Amanda and I had supper." Carrie bustled over to the stove. "Shall I bring it to you in the recliner?" she asked, filling a fresh bowl.

"Nah, I'm okay." Charlie shuffled over to the kitchen table, and Jo hurried to pull out a chair for him, which he eased onto in slow motion.

"Looks like you got yourself out of shoveling any snow for the next few weeks," Jo said.

Charlie grimaced. "I think I'd rather shovel snow."

"Yeah, I would too."

Carrie put his supper before him, and Jo watched Charlie work at getting as much food into his stomach with the least possible amount of movement. It didn't look easy. As the level of food lowered, though, Charlie's eyes grew increasingly clear. Eventually he released his fork and leaned slowly back in his chair.

"So, what's going on?" he asked.

Getting only surprised silence from the two women across from him, he continued. "Aunt Jo's here, Dad isn't, and Mom, you look pretty darn worried."

"I'm not . . ." Carrie began to protest, then stopped. "Well, yes, I am, but I'm probably just being silly. There was an accident tonight. Mr. Holt—the man whose basement Dad's been working on?—took a bad fall. Aunt Jo found him, and Dad's over there right now talking with the police who are trying to figure out just what happened."

"A bad fall. You mean a really bad one, right? Not like mine?"

"No, not like yours. Mr. Holt is dead."

"Whooo!" Charlie thought a moment. "So—what? They're thinking it might be Dad's fault or something?"

"We don't know what they're thinking right now, Charlie," Jo said. "As your mom said, I discovered Mr. Holt lying at the bottom of the stairs, but I have no idea what happened. They have to talk to everyone, and it all takes time. We'll just have to wait."

Charlie nodded. His gaze wandered about the kitchen, but Jo had a feeling he wasn't thinking about what more he might find to eat. This was a fifteen-year-old who already had experience with police investigation and violent death, though thankfully only at arm's length. She sincerely hoped that remained to be the case. But having one's father being questioned on the circumstances of his present employer's death had the potential of bringing that arm in closer than she cared to see.

The phone rang, and Carrie jumped up to answer.

"Dan! Where are you? What's happening?"

Jo could only guess at Dan's response by reading Carrie's face, which wasn't encouraging. Carrie's expression grew more worried as the moments went by.

"Oh! Oh dear. But why—? Oh! Oh!"

She ended by saying, "Yes, I'll call Sylvia. Yes, yes, of course. No, certainly not. All right."

Carrie hung up, turning to Jo and Charlie with a stunned look.

"Dan's at the police station. He went there for further questioning, and now they're talking with Xavier. They've been talking with him for a very long time."

She drew a deep breath. "Dan said things don't look good."

Chapter 5

Jo paced through the Craft Corner's maze of shelves the next morning, unable to sit still for more than two seconds at a time. She had stayed late at Carrie's the night before, but as midnight approached and Dan still hadn't come home, Carrie shooed her off, insisting Jo should go home and get some sleep. She had gone home, but as for sleep, well . . . She reached for her coffeepot and filled another mug. Jo had already called Carrie's twice. The first time, Carrie answered, sounding rushed.

"I'll call you back," she'd promised. When Jo didn't hear back after a half hour, she tried again, this time getting Charlie, who sounded groggy.

"No one's here. I was kind of out of it when Mom left, but I think she said she was going to Mrs. Ramirez's, and that Dad got home late last night and went out again early."

"Thanks, Charlie. Sorry if I woke you."

"It's all right. Hey, if you find out what's going on, ask someone to let me know, okay?"

Jo promised, and hung up, then considered trying Carrie's

cell phone. She decided not to, though it was torture to hold
off. She knew Carrie would have called her if she could.
Whatever Carrie was doing must be far more important than
keeping Jo updated.

A figure crossed in front of the shop's windows, catching the corner of Jo's eye, and she whirled, hoping it might
be Carrie. She recognized, instead, Alexis Wigsley and
groaned, knowing exactly what the woman was coming
for. A middle-aged woman, Alexis's well-to-do family, Jo
had learned from Ina Mae, left her with a large house and a
highly developed interest (Ina Mae used the word "nosi-
ness") in her fellow townspeople.

Jo had been lucky enough not to have encountered
Alexis during the stressful days following the Craft Corner's grand opening, since Alexis had been confined with a
bad case of poison ivy. She remembered that there had
been more than one speculation at the time that Alexis
might have been slipping about in places she shouldn't
have, and more than one joke concerning the setting of that
noxious plant at the boundaries of one's property.

"Hi, Jo," Alexis sang out as she walked through the door
looking deceptively nonchalant, a red scarf tied jauntily at
the neck of her navy jacket. "Oh, I see you've put out some
Valentine things. Goody!"

Alexis headed for the new display of red papers and
white lacey doilies, looking for all the world as though they
were all she had on her mind. But Jo knew better, having
listened to the woman's prying gossip—always camou-
flaged as neighborly concern—on more than one occasion.
She braced for what was sure to come.

Alexis oohed and aahed over various items, picking them
up and setting them down, tossing out innocuous comments
on the weather, then finally said, "Wasn't that a shame what
happened to Parker Holt?"

Jo considered pretending ignorance but doubted she could

ever be a good enough actor to fool Alexis, whose hawk-like eyes watched closely.

"Yes, it was," Jo agreed, walking away toward the back of the shop, aware at the same time that any attempt at escape was fruitless. As the Craft Corner's proprietor, she was essentially a captive audience to whoever decided to drop in. Plus Alexis had timed her visit well, in the quiet, early morning hours when few distracting customers appeared.

"I heard you found him," Alexis said, following behind.

Jo sighed. Of course Alexis had heard that.

"Yes," Jo said, then, to head off the next question she knew was coming, added, "but I have no idea how it happened. I'm sure the police will let us all know as soon as they've figured it out."

"I just hope it doesn't turn out that it was due to some fault, totally inadvertent, of course, on the part of Dan Brenner, which would certainly be bad for him. You know, like maybe a heavy light fixture fell from the ceiling because it wasn't secured properly. Something like that." Alexis's eyes locked on Jo.

"I didn't see anything of that sort, Alexis. In fact, I saw very little. Just enough to know I should call for help. Then I kept out of the way."

Alexis frowned. "You didn't overhear anything, I mean, after the police came? Surely there was plenty of talk going on. And you were there for quite a while."

Alexis knew that? Jo immediately pictured the woman hovering as close as she could weasel herself to Parker Holt's house, probably frustrated at the garble of police-radio talk rendered unintelligible by distance, and enviously spotting Jo up close to the action. Jo was surprised Alexis hadn't followed her to Carrie's place and demanded an immediate accounting. What a restless night this gossip must have spent, waiting hours to pry for information.

"I don't know anything, Alexis," Jo repeated. "I'm waiting to find out, the same as everyone else."

Alexis's brow puckered and she wandered off among the Craft Corner's shelves. She spotted the sign Jo had made for Sylvia's bags that sat next to an empty space waiting for the next batch to arrive. "Ramirez!" she said in an *ah-hah!* tone. "Wasn't that the name of the man working with Dan Brenner?"

"Yes. It's his wife who's making these bags. They're becoming quite popular," Jo added, hoping to turn Alexis's thoughts in a different direction. "I should be getting more in very soon. They're being snapped up so quickly that if you're at all interested I'd suggest—"

"That poor woman," Alexis plowed on, sticking firmly to her track, and not looking particularly sympathetic despite her words. "She must be worried sick, just as Carrie must be, what with their husbands being questioned by the police, and all."

Yes, but darned if I'll let you in on that. Jo set down a picture frame she had picked up, and faced Alexis. "Knowing Carrie," she said, "she's probably just as anxious about Parker Holt's widow. Wouldn't you say that's where the concern should be right now?"

Alexis stared back at Jo through narrowed eyes, her face telling Jo she had caught the message. She wasn't, however, going to go down without a fight. "Why yes," she said, "normally that would be the case."

Jo's eyebrows shot upward before she could stop them, and Alexis's lips curled in satisfaction. She turned and sauntered back to the front of the shop. "I wouldn't say Mallory Holt is your normal widow. Whatever grief she'll be feeling, she'll have plenty of consolation. And I'm not just talking about the money."

The shop's door jingled, and Ina Mae walked in. Jo saw the two women's eyes meet, and felt the temperature of the store drop ten degrees.

"Why, good morning, Ina Mae," Alexis said, her voice a tad less confident.

"Alexis." Ina Mae gave a brisk nod.

"Oh my, look at the time!" Alexis exclaimed, glancing at her watch and quickly pulling on her gloves. "I have at least a dozen stops to make before lunchtime. Good day, ladies."

Alexis bustled out of the shop, Ina Mae watching her progress with a look of one whose acid reflux had suddenly returned. When the door closed, Ina Mae turned to Jo.

"Trying to get information?"

"One of her better efforts," Jo acknowledged.

"Phhht," Ina Mae blew disgustedly. "A dozen stops to make. I can guess what their purpose is." Ina Mae shook herself. "I came by thinking you might want to run over to be with Carrie. I'd be happy to watch the shop for a while."

"Thanks, Ina Mae. But I'm not even sure where Carrie is right now. I'll just have to wait til she lets me know."

"Well, best she keep active, I suppose. Her boy's doing all right?"

"Charlie won't be jumping hurdles for a while, but I think he's able to manage on his own reasonably well."

Ina Mae nodded, then shook her head. "Let's hope nothing more befalls that family."

"Amen to that."

"By the way, are you still planning on running that beading workshop? I've signed up for it, and Loralee too, but we'd understand if you want to postpone."

"Oh, the workshop! I'd almost forgotten that it's tonight. But that's fine. I have my lesson plan ready." Jo picked up the sign-up sheet near her cash register to see who had signed up. The first few names were her regulars: Ina Mae, Loralee Phillips, Javonne Barnett.

"Who's that last one?" Ina Mae asked, peering over her shoulder. "I can't quite read it. Verna something?"

"No, that's Vernon. Vernon Dobson."

"Vernon? The man I used to buy my standing rib roasts from?"

"I imagine so. He said he was a retired butcher and that he's been looking for a more creative hobby. He said he tried woodworking, even making a dollhouse for one of his granddaughters. But it didn't do it for him."

"Well, isn't that interesting."

Jo smiled, remembering what Carrie had said when she first heard of Vernon signing up for beading: "Could be there's a whole new customer base waiting to be tapped, Jo. Maybe you should offer workshops for things like handmade tie clips and belt buckles."

Jo had quickly countered with, "How about you teach a 'Crochet Your Own Motorcycle Cover' class?"

They'd then tried to top each other with, "Beaded Rearview Mirror Frames," and "Macramé Fishing Lures," "Stamp-Decorated Golf Scorecards and Bowling Score Sheets," their fun ending only when two sober-faced customers entered the shop.

Jo sighed. She missed having Carrie around already. The craft shop without Carrie, she was finding, was too much like a necklace missing half its beads—still colorful, but definitely unbalanced.

"Well, give me a call if you need me," Ina Mae said. "You have my cell phone number?"

Jo didn't, not having ever had a need to reach Ina Mae in a hurry. She dug her own cell phone out of her purse and entered the number in as the older woman recited it, mainly to be polite since she didn't foresee a need for it. But one never knew.

Ina Mae took off, and other customers drifted in. Jo took care of them, glad to keep busy, and even happier that few mentioned Parker Holt. During a lull, a man tentatively entered the store, coming over to Jo who was refilling her craft paints.

"Mrs. McAllister?"

Jo looked up to see a slim man dressed in a worn quilted jacket and work pants. He pulled a knit cap off his head.

"Otto said you had a job for me?"

"Oh, you must be Randy Truitt!"

The man nodded, his pale blue eyes moving uneasily from her face to the floor and back.

Jo held out her hand, saying, "How do you do?" apparently surprising him since he hesitated a moment before taking her hand and giving it a shake.

"Yes," Jo said, answering his question. "I have these shelves in the back room that are sagging badly." She led the way back to show him the problem. "I've been storing fairly heavy boxes on them, which apparently became too much. Do you think you can shore them up somehow? Or maybe replace them?"

Randy stepped carefully around Jo's stock, which had been unloaded from the worrying shelves and now covered much of the floor. He made a quick examination. "Sure. Just this section here?"

"I think so. The others seem okay."

Randy looked around, tested a few, then nodded. "Yeah, they seem all right. This shelf here I'll have to replace, but a couple of the others just need better bracing. I can get what I need and start work on them tomorrow afternoon. That work for you?"

"That works just fine for me. Now about the cost . . . ?"

Randy threw out a few numbers and discussed the necessary materials, which, as it demonstrated his familiarity with the subject at hand, raised Jo's confidence level. Her immediate impression of the man had been, despite Ina Mae's referral, not exactly stellar. He added on his labor cost and gave her a very reasonable total. Jo nodded.

"That sounds fair. We'll see you here tomorrow, then, Randy." Jo held out her hand once more, and this time

Randy took it with more assurance. Then he pulled his cap on and strode out the door, his posture noticeably straighter than it had been on entering.

Jo smiled, relieved to have one of her problems on the way to resolution. She wondered what Randy's situation was, exactly. Ina Mae had said something about his being unable to quite get things together, which to Jo meant his life had had its ups and downs, and not all due to things beyond his control.

Well, she'd see how he did on this job, and if she was satisfied, might throw a little more work his way as her finances allowed. Dan, with his "almost-family" free labor was obviously the easiest on her budget for skilled jobs, and Charlie, at his teenaged rates, for the simpler ones. But both were definitely unavailable for the time being, so she was grateful to have connected with Randy.

Jo was still nodding over this little satisfaction when the door opened and Carrie came in along with a burst of cold, January air.

"Oh, Jo!" Carrie said, stopping just inside the door. Her face, normally so serene, was flushed and strained. Jo had only seen it this distressed one other time—after Mike's accident, when Carrie had rushed to New York to be with her.

Jo drew a quick breath. "What? What is it?" she asked, hurrying over to Carrie, and fearing the worst.

"Jo, it wasn't an accident at all. Parker Holt was murdered!"

Jo's first reaction of shock was immediately followed by a guilty feeling of relief. Surely this let Dan off the hook? Terrible as it was, at least it didn't have anything to do with him. But Carrie obviously wasn't sharing that feeling.

"Tell me the rest."

Carrie took a deep breath, shaking her head over the wrongness of it all.

"They're looking at Xavier."

Chapter 6

Jo flipped the "Closed" sign on the Craft Corner door, turned the lock, and drew Carrie to the back of the shop.

"Okay, what's this all about? First of all, why do they think it's murder?"

Carrie sank into Jo's desk chair. Now that she'd spilled the worst, she seemed at a loss for words. Jo poured out a mug of coffee and put it into Carrie's hands.

"Here, drink."

Carrie did, pulling off her gloves and opening her jacket in between sips, her head continuing to shake with disbelief. Jo leaned against her desk and waited.

"Oh, Jo. It's so awful."

"Start from the beginning, Carrie. What exactly happened to Parker Holt?"

"He walked into a trap." Carrie took another sip, then choked on a new thought. "Jo! It's so lucky you never went down those steps after him. You might have been killed too!"

"What! Why? What was going on?"

"Holt was electrocuted. It was all set up, waiting for him."

Jo was trying hard to be patient. "What was, Carrie?"

"I'm sorry. I know I'm being incoherent. It's just so . . ." Carrie cleared her throat, possibly with the hope of straightening the distressing jumble in her head as well. "The handrail, along Holt's basement stairs. It was metal. Wrought iron. Someone stripped one end of an electrical cord and wrapped the bare copper wire around the lower part of that rail. Then they plugged the other end of the cord in."

Jo winced.

"Dan explained it to me," Carrie continued. "He said that alone wouldn't have been enough to kill the man. But there was also a crowbar on the stairs near Holt. The crowbar had a battery jumper cable attached to it that ran to a nearby copper water pipe. The police are speculating that the person who set this up planted the crowbar on a lower stair. Holt probably reached down to move it out of his way, while automatically holding on to the wired metal railing for balance. The electricity would have surged right through him, killing him instantly."

The image Carrie presented was chilling. "And that could have killed me too?" Jo asked.

"Well, I suppose only if you'd grabbed hold of both things, the rail and the crowbar. It's something to do with grounding. The electricity needed the connection to the water pipe to run all the way through the body. The paramedics, though, were lucky. One of them spotted the wires right away."

Jo pictured the danger she might have blundered into, shivering, but had a question. "Why wouldn't Holt have spotted the wires?"

"Dan wondered about that too. But he said there was a rag near the crowbar. It could have been thrown over the end of the crowbar where the wire was attached, covering it. Even then," Carrie said, looking up questioningly, "Holt probably wouldn't have been looking for something of that sort, would he? I'd think he would've just seen the crowbar left sloppily in his way as he was trotting down the steps, and would have grabbed at it in annoyance."

Jo nodded. She could envision the man who had been described to her as a perfectionist reaching impatiently for the tool and thinking only of the blistering earful he would later give Dan and Xavier. Which reminded her of the major cause of Carrie's upset.

"Why do they suspect Xavier particularly?" Jo asked. "From all you've told me, he doesn't sound like anyone that evil."

"No, absolutely not! He's the gentlest person you'd ever meet. It's completely ridiculous."

"But they have some reason?"

Carrie sighed. "They do, but if they really knew Xavier they'd know it just doesn't work. I should be glad they're not suspecting Dan—and believe me, I am! But Xavier—"

The handle of Jo's front door rattled as someone obviously didn't believe Jo's "Closed" sign, and Carrie looked over at it worriedly.

"Never mind," Jo said. "They'll come back."

"I hope so." Carrie shifted out of her jacket. "I just came from Sylvia's place. She told me the whole story. The poor thing's trying really hard to hold it together, and in her state—the baby and all—I'm really worried about her. Anyway," Carrie said, clearly trying to hold it all together herself, "as far as why the police are concentrating on Xavier: I don't know if I mentioned Sylvia used to clean houses?"

"Actually, I think Sylvia mentioned it."

"One of the houses," Carrie said, "was Parker Holt's. Remember Dan said Holt popped in a lot to check on his work in the basement? Well, he also managed to stop in a lot when Sylvia was scrubbing and vacuuming too, and it wasn't just to check on her work."

"Uh-oh."

"Right. Mallory Holt was seldom around when Sylvia came. If she was, she usually took off within minutes. She was involved in things like the Junior League and such. Parker obviously knew his wife's schedule and Sylvia's too." Carrie paused and gave Jo a significant look.

"So he thought he could set up a little fun with the maid during the day," Jo filled in.

Carrie nodded. "Sylvia said she tried her best to discourage his advances, but she ended up having to quit altogether. She was in her early stages of pregnancy and she told Mallory Holt she was feeling too ill, though she continued working at her other homes. Mallory Holt had paid well, though, and Sylvia didn't know how to explain leaving there to Xavier. When he questioned her she became upset, and it all came out.

"He was furious, of course, and she had to beg him not to confront Holt. Sylvia finally convinced Xavier that a fight with Holt might jeopardize their chances of bringing Xavier's younger brother here from Mexico. They saw Holt as a powerful man who could make more trouble for them if he chose to."

"So that was the reason for Xavier's dark mood whenever Holt came by."

"Dan told you about that? Yes, poor Xavier. Dan had no idea what he was forcing him to do, refurbishing the home of the man who had sexually harassed his wife."

"I don't know about forcing, Carrie. After all, Xavier could have said no, couldn't he?"

"That's probably what the police are thinking, Jo. That Xavier worked the job solely for the chance to take his revenge on Holt. They don't see that he really didn't have much choice in the matter. Xavier needed the income. His wife is having their baby soon. The only other construction jobs around here were with Holt's own crew, which would have meant encountering Holt even more—long term. At least Dan's job was short term."

"That's true."

"Plus Dan, who knows Xavier pretty well, says if he were inclined to murder at all—which we know he wasn't—he wouldn't do it in this underhanded way. He would go face to face, giving Holt a fighting chance."

"They haven't actually charged Xavier, though, have they?" Jo asked.

"No. But I'm afraid it's only a matter of time, unless they come up with a better suspect."

Jo thought for a while. "If Holt was behaving that way toward Sylvia, I'll bet she wasn't his only victim. I imagine there might be a few other husbands, or angry women, with motives just as strong as Xavier's."

Carrie's face took on its first glimmer of hope. "I'll bet there are."

"And who knows what other enemies he might have had from other areas. Don't give up hope yet, Carrie. I suspect that with a little shaking, a few beads just might fall off the string."

That evening, Jo was reminded of her brave words to Carrie as she set her boxes of beads about the table for the earring workshop. She had thrown out the probability of other suspects for Carrie's sake, with little idea if it had any weight to it. But she hoped so.

Though she'd never met him, Jo felt nearly as bad for Xavier as Carrie did. He hadn't been charged and was free to be home with his wife. But that freedom, as Jo well knew, would be far from worry-free while the axe still hovered over his neck, ready, at the first signal, to fall. Xavier and Sylvia, she was sure, must be going through hell.

Was Lieutenant Morgan convinced Xavier was the one?

Jo wondered. Should she try to talk to him about this? No, she'd better talk to Xavier first. While Jo couldn't imagine Sylvia choosing to marry a man who would step on an ant, much less commit homicide, and Carrie and Dan were no slouches at judging character, nevertheless, she wanted to see for herself.

Jo thought of the mind-jarring turn of events. Just a few short hours ago her worries had centered on the effect Holt's death could have on Dan's small business if the death was caused by his negligence. Dan's professional reputation would certainly be shredded, and his and Carrie's income severely diminished.

But the effect could be just as devastating if Xavier were charged with murder. Xavier was Dan's employee, and they had worked together closely for the time leading up to the murder. The collateral damage to Dan and Carrie was undeniable. Jo hoped that a murder charge would never come, but the fact remained that the longer Xavier was considered a "person of interest" the harder the mud would stick—to everyone concerned.

Jo went back to her storeroom to get the Vellux work pads for the group. As she pulled them out of their box, surrounded by her myriad crafting supplies, she was reminded that the question about her shop's future still remained, though temporarily buried beneath this rock slide of events. What would Parker Holt's death mean to her shop? She still didn't know if he had in fact bought her building, since Max had never returned her calls. For all she knew he was sailing out of reach somewhere in the Caribbean sipping margaritas.

If Max *had* sold out, how did Holt's death affect things? Would whatever plans he had for her building still be carried out? Jo needed to track down the answer to that question in addition to the others that had rolled onto her doorstep.

But for the moment, she thought, as she tossed the work

pads about the table, her central question needed to be how to teach her novices the techniques of beading. So she'd best set these concerns aside.

The shop's door opened, and Javonne Barnett sailed in. "Hey, Jo! Wow, isn't that a shock about Parker Holt?"

So much for setting anything aside.

"You're early, Javonne. No late patients tonight?"

Javonne worked with her husband Harry, a dentist, and Jo was used to seeing Javonne dash in late for workshops, full of legitimate excuses involving last-minute dental emergencies. Usually dressed in medical whites, Javonne looked particularly chic this evening as she pulled off her coat to reveal a burnt orange and tan outfit that complimented her mocha complexion nicely.

"We actually had time to go out to dinner!" Javonne exclaimed. "Harry's mom is watching the kids, and Harry went off to Baltimore to give a seminar. Dental implants. Sounds like fun, huh? So what about all this with Parker Holt?" Javonne dropped her wrap on the "coat chair," so designated because of the two wobbly legs that made it a less desirable seat. She pitched in to help Jo open the bead boxes spread over the table.

Jo drew a breath to speak, but then the shop's door flew open once more, ushering in a draft of January chill countered by the warm smiles of Loralee Phillips and Ina Mae Kepner.

"Jo, dear," Loralee said, hurrying up to Jo, her ever-present large tote on her arm, "are you sure you're up to this? You must have had a terrible couple of days, not to mention poor Carrie. She's not here, is she?" Loralee looked over to Carrie's knitting area with motherly concern. A petite, white-haired woman, not much bigger than her outsized bag, Loralee always seemed on the verge of pulling out jars of homemade chicken soup and checking foreheads for fever.

"No, Carrie's home tonight," Jo said.

"Good," Ina Mae pronounced. She pulled off her long coat and pushed up the sleeves of her blue velour warm-up jacket, ready to get down to work. After greeting Javonne, she glanced around. "Vernon's not here yet?"

"Vernon?" Javonne asked. "Vernon who?"

"Vernon Dobson. Former proprietor of Dobson's Meats. Ever go there?" Ina Mae asked.

"Lord, yes, all the time. But that sweet man who kept my family in excellent steaks and hamburger is coming tonight to make beaded earrings?"

Ina Mae didn't need to answer as the "sweet man" himself appeared, red-cheeked and blinking as he paused inside the shop's door.

"Good evening, Vernon," Ina Mae called. "How nice to see you."

Vernon Dobson pulled the baseball cap off his balding head and joined the group, unzipping his jacket. "Mrs. Kepner," he said, nodding.

"Oh, we're all on a first-name basis, Vernon," Jo said. "I believe you know Javonne. And Loralee?"

"Yes indeed," Loralee said, bobbing her white curls.

"Drop your things over there," Jo said, pointing to the pile of coats, "and grab a seat at the table. We're just about ready to begin."

Vernon settled in along with the others, folding his hands over the purple and white Raven's sweatshirt stretched over his well-fed middle as he placidly waited. Jo noticed that Javonne seemed unable to keep from staring, as though still struggling to fit her former butcher with this beading workshop classmate. Jo smiled to herself and got down to business. She picked up a silver pin, about two inches long, and held it up for them to see.

"This, ladies—and gentleman—is what we will use to build our first earring," she said. "It's sterling silver, and it has, as you see, this little flat head at one end to hold the beads on.

"Spread over the table are boxes of beads, separated by color, size, shape—you name it—as well as spacers, bead caps, and such. Just about everything you could want to put on this pin to create your drop earring."

"Oh, my, they're beautiful, but there's so many," Loralee cried. "How do we know what to use?"

"I know!" Javonne agreed. "Look at all of them. They're all gorgeous! What are these black ones, Jo?"

"Those are black agate. And over here are turquoise, then amber, and cat's eye, all the gemstone beads. Then these," she moved to another large group, "are the crystals, in so many beautiful colors. Here," she said, pointing out yet another group, "are the metals—sterling silver, gold, pewter, and cloisonné."

Jo picked up a box of beads she particularly liked. "And aren't these wooden beads wonderful? Just look at the carving on them."

The women oohed, agreeing.

"I realize it's overwhelming at first," Jo said. "But for now, just try to keep it fairly simple. Pick your color scheme for your earrings, as well as the size of beads. Play around with them until you find a combination you like. I'll show you the basics, but then go with your own taste. Now, to begin . . ."

Jo demonstrated how to slip a round bead onto the head pin, then a spacer and a second larger bead. She made a wrapped loop above her second bead by bending the wire with her chain nose pliers, looping it, and twisting her wire tail around the wire stem above the bead, clipping the excess and pressing the end tightly to the stem with crimping pliers. She attached an earring wire—the little hook that would slip through a pierced ear—by opening the loop at the end of that wire, slipping it onto her wrapped loop above the beads, then closing it securely. The group watched, transfixed.

Jo held it out. "There you go. One beaded earring. What do you think?"

"I think I'll never be able to do that," Javonne said. "You're going to have to draw me a few pictures, Jo."

"It's lovely!" Loralee cried. "And you made it look so easy."

"It really is easy, once you get the hang of it. I'll go through it a few more times, guys. Don't worry, you'll pick it up. And tonight you'll be going home with your very own, custom-designed earrings." Jo noticed that Vernon was already quietly picking through the bead boxes.

"My plan is to make a pair for one of my daughters," Ina Mae stated, looking over the selection.

"Not me," Javonne said, shaking her head. "I'm aiming to have earrings to match all my outfits. How about you, Loralee? You making these for yourself or your daughter?"

Jo looked over at Loralee and was surprised to see a pained look cross her face, which was quickly replaced with a weak smile to Javonne. "Oh, I don't know," she said. "I'll just make them and then decide what to do with them. You have so many lovely beads here, Jo! I don't know how I'll narrow it down."

"Vernon's not having any trouble, I see," Ina Mae put in. The women all turned to look. Vernon had transferred several oval-shaped beads and silver spacers to the Vellux work pad before him and was busily lining them up in a striking combination.

"Ooh, I like that," Javonne said.

Vernon looked up. "Evelyn—my wife—likes blue. And silver," he added matter-of-factly.

"Yes, but the ones you picked . . ." Javonne's voice trailed off, clearly impressed. "Do you think you could choose a combination for me? To go with what I'm wearing tonight?"

Vernon glanced over, took in Javonne's outfit, and said, "Sure."

Jo smiled. It appeared she had a natural in the class. She watched as Vernon's stubby fingers hovered over the myriad of bead boxes, pausing, dipping, moving on, selecting,

until he had several in the palm of his hand that he was satisfied with. He handed them over to Javonne, saying simply, "Here you go."

Jo caught Ina Mae's eye, which twinkled back at her.
Who would have thought, she seemed to say, such talent
lurked in the heart of the man who had cut her chops and
trimmed her roasts each week?

The group got busy, trying to manipulate the wires as Jo
has shown them, a silence settling over them as they focused. Eventually, though, conversation returned, and it
centered on Parker Holt.

Jo listened to their comments on what they clearly still
thought of as an accident, uncertain about passing on what
Carrie had told her. But memories of how the group had
aided her in the past by tracking down useful information
when she needed it most, helped her decide.

"Guys," she said, when their chatter came to a pause,
"there's something I'd like to talk to you about."

Chapter 7

All heads at the workshop table tilted upward at Jo's words, and all fingers, whether poised to slip a spacer on the pin or squeeze chain nose pliers on a wire, froze in mid-action. Jo spilled out the details of Parker Holt's murder, including Xavier Ramirez's grim situation as prime suspect, and saw the faces before her reflect many of the emotions she herself had felt, all resolving into "solemn."

"Murder!" Javonne said. "I thought Parker Holt had broken his neck falling down the steps."

"This certainly puts a whole new light on things," Ina Mae said.

Loralee's hand had flown to her mouth, but slid away as she said, "That poor man."

"Holt?" Jo asked.

"No, I mean Xavier. Parker Holt's troubles are over. Xavier Ramirez's are just beginning."

"That's the truth," Javonne said.

"Carrie and Dan," Jo said, "are positive Xavier would never have done what the police suspect him of. But the trouble is he seems to be the only one in their sights. Can any of you come up with other possibilities? Someone who might have wanted Holt dead?"

"And had the opportunity too," Ina Mae added.

"Of course."

"And the means," Loralee put in. "That person would have to understand wiring and electricity."

"Yes, the setup Carrie described to me sounded fairly complicated," Jo agreed.

"A person on Holt's work crew? An electrician?" Javonne offered.

"It wouldn't have to be an electrician," Vernon said, speaking for the first time on the subject. The ladies turned to him in some surprise as though they had forgotten he was there. Jo noticed his earrings lay finished on his work pad and were quite well done. "I mean," he said, "*I* know that much about grounding and all, and I'm not a licensed electrician. I just learned enough working around the house and on my car to keep from killing myself."

"A good point, Vernon," Ina Mae said. "And we all know how easily things can be picked up when needed, nowadays. The Internet is filled with information and instructions— even for making bombs, I understand. Someone like Loralee or me, for instance, could probably teach ourselves how to do just what Jo described."

"Assuming," Loralee added with a rueful smile, "we knew how to work the Internet in the first place."

"Well, that opens up the possibilities, doesn't it, Jo?" Javonne said.

"Too wide," Jo agreed. "Can we narrow it down to people who might have a good reason to want Parker Holt dead?"

"He was making money hand over fist, from what I heard," Javonne said. "That could make a few enemies along the way, wouldn't you say?"

"Definitely," Loralee agreed. "But which one of them would strike against him in this way? In Parker's own home? It seems more personal, doesn't it, I mean rather than a business sort of enemy."

"Plus there's the question of getting into his house," Ina Mae said. "How many people would be able to do that? A pricey home like that must have had security protection, which I assume Dan and Xavier would have been able to turn off as needed in order to come and go. Xavier, I'm sorry to say, Jo, fits the bill very well what with having a personal grudge against the man as well as easy opportunity, not to mention the knowledge and tools available."

"Yes, and that's clearly why the police have zeroed in on him. What we have to do is find someone else who could get into the house somehow."

"Mrs. Holt could." Again, everyone turned to Vernon with surprise.

"*Mallory* Holt?" Ina Mae asked. "Yes, of course she could get into her own house."

"But I saw Mallory Holt arrive home when I was waiting outside the house, after the police had come," Jo said.

"But you don't know where she was at the time of the murder setup," Loralee pointed out.

"No, I don't. That would be between four and six—after Dan and Xavier left the house together, and before I got there. As far as where Mallory Holt was during that time, I might be able to find out. I imagine she's been asked that by the police too. But do we know of any reason she'd want to kill her husband?"

The women looked blankly at each other. Then Vernon spoke.

"Maybe." He paused, squirming uneasily on his chair.

"What?" all four women asked at once.

"Well, when I had my butcher shop, most of my customers were women, and you know how two ladies running into each other like to talk?"

The four ladies in the room nodded.

"I couldn't help overhearing things, of course, standing right there. But I always made it a point never to repeat what I heard. Customer confidentiality, you know, like with a lawyer, or, as Evelyn tells me, a hairdresser. I knew it could only cause trouble if I ever started, although the temptation often was there, I must admit."

"Highly admirable, Vernon," Ina Mae said, "and we certainly understand your reluctance to break that rule now. However, I'm sure you understand the present circumstances are quite special. Sharing what you know with us would be for the purpose of saving a man from being falsely charged and is far from the realm of idle gossip."

Vernon nodded, agreeing. "Mrs. Holt," he said, sucking in a long breath, "seems to have been unhappy in her marriage to Mr. Holt."

"Oh!" Four reactions came out, with varying degrees of surprise and interest.

"Well," Javonne said, "that doesn't exactly knock me over, I'm afraid, Vernon. I mean, if Parker Holt behaved the way Jo says he did with Sylvia Ramirez and who knows who else, Mallory Holt must have picked up on it."

"And," Loralee said, "surely divorce would be her option, not murder."

"Unless," Ina Mae pointed out, "money was a factor. She could have wanted all of it instead of just half. Or she might have feared she would end up with much less than half if Parker got a better lawyer than she did."

"A good possibility, then," Jo said. "So I should learn more about Mallory Holt."

"She's been a very active member of the Abbotsville Women's Club, president of it, lately," Ina Mae said. "The other women in it would likely know her quite well. And," she added, giving Jo a significant look, "Alexis Wigsley is also a member."

"Why is that important?" Vernon asked.

"Alexis," Jo explained, "was in the shop this morning, looking for gossip to spread. She dropped the hint that Mallory Holt wouldn't be your typical grieving widow."

"Well, there you go, Jo," Javonne said with a grin. "Just go to Alexis and find out all you need about Mallory Holt."

"But I'm afraid you can't trust everything that woman says," Ina Mae cautioned. "She likes a good story more than the truth. Whatever she tells you, Jo, you'll need to find a second source to back it up."

Jo nodded.

"Jo," Loralee said, "please be very careful when you ask people about Mallory Holt. She could very well be innocent, and if so she could be genuinely grieving. We shouldn't assume too much just yet."

"You're quite right, Loralee. I promise not to stir up false rumors."

"Her uncle's the mayor," Javonne reminded them. "Another good reason to tread lightly."

"Ah, yes. He showed up at the house even before Mallory Holt did. What is Warren Kunkle like?" Jo asked the group. "Would he be likely to put pressure on our Abbotsville police to solve this murder quickly?"

Ina Mae nodded. "Warren and Lucy fairly raised Mallory, because her own mother was a widow and an invalid. Mallory was, I believe, fifteen when her mother finally died, but had been living with the Kunkles long before that. Warren thinks of her as his own daughter. He will want to see this case settled quickly, and he might easily convince himself that Xavier is guilty."

"All the more reason to find other likely suspects," Loralee said. "And soon!"

"There might be a possibility or two right around here." Jo told the group about Parker Holt's plans to buy up properties that housed the small shops in the area, including the likelihood that hers would be among them.

"Oh, that man!" Loralee cried. "He probably wanted to tear down all these beautiful old buildings and put up something ugly and high rent! Why do people always want to change things so drastically? Why can't what's been working fine be left in place?"

Loralee spoke with such surprising vehemence that Jo noticed the others giving her startled looks. Loralee had taken the news that Parker Holt had been murdered much more calmly, and had been sad and concerned over Xavier's situation, but hadn't ranted about the injustice of it. Something about Holt's wanting to bring about change in Abbotsville, however, had struck a chord with Loralee. Jo looked to Ina Mae for a clue, but Ina Mae had begun examining her earring project closely.

"So," Javonne asked somewhat tentatively, after a glance at Loralee, "your other possibilities, Jo, are the people who might be losing their businesses because of this buy-up?"

"Yes, exactly, although I hate to even mention it since these are my neighbors, and all good people as far as I know."

"Everyone has a breaking point," Ina Mae said as she clipped off the end of a coiled wire on her earring. "I think you're quite right, Jo, to include these businesspeople as possible murder suspects."

"Well, good luck, Jo." Javonne began packing up after a glance at her watch. "I don't know if we narrowed down the list much for you. I'd sure hate to be someone who had so many people wanting to kill me. But," she added, "if I don't get home soon to relieve my mother-in-law of my kids, she just might start a list of her own—for *me.*

"Thank you, Vernon," she said, holding up her new earrings. "I love them. And I bet you didn't know what all you were getting into when you signed up for this workshop. Beaded Earrings and Murder 101."

Vernon smiled, looking a bit dazed.

"I really didn't plan to go into all this," Jo hastened to explain to her newest student. "It's just that Ina Mae, Loralee, and Javonne were a great help to me with my last problem."

"With Jo new to this town, she needed our inside information," Ina Mae said as she stood up and reached for her coat. "Xavier and Sylvia are newcomers too. You don't mind pitching in to help them out, do you Vernon?"

"When I had my shop," Vernon said, "I might have been asked for a 'Free Hamburger' coupon for their welcome basket. This is a whole lot different. But I'm glad to help if I can."

"That's the spirit!" Ina Mae patted his shoulder and handed him his jacket.

Vernon told Jo he looked forward to the next beading workshop, raised his hat to them all, and left with new jewelry to present to his wife. Jo glanced back and saw Loralee taking the time to close up and stack the boxes of beads for her.

"Thanks, Loralee," she said, and the petite woman looked up and smiled sweetly. Loralee was always so considerate, Jo thought to herself. Then she remembered Loralee's little outburst and how she hadn't seemed quite herself that evening. With only Loralee and her good friend Ina Mae left, Jo decided to bring it up.

"Is anything wrong, Loralee? I mean, besides what we were all discussing tonight?"

Loralee, who had reached for her coat, paused for a moment, then slipped it on. "You have enough on your mind, dear. It's really nothing."

"It's more than nothing," Ina Mae said, "if it's causing your stomach to bother you again. You've been chewing on quite a few Tums lately, I've noticed."

Loralee flapped a hand. "That's just because I've been eating too much takeout."

"Because you're too distracted to cook your own good food. Tell Jo about it. She won't mind."

Loralee looked at Jo, who nodded encouragingly, then took off her coat and sat down. "If you're sure you have a minute."

Chapter 8

Jo watched as Loralee fiddled silently with the chain nose pliers on the workshop table and worried about what she would hear. Was Loralee ill? Did she have money problems? Jo didn't have much experience with the first, thankfully, but she couldn't offer much help with the second either.

"It's Dulcie, my daughter."

Ah. Jo thought of the pained look crossing Loralee's face when Javonne casually brought up her daughter.

"She wants my house."

"What?"

"And I don't blame her. It makes perfect sense, in a way."

"Perfect sense to *her*," Ina Mae put in. "She's not thinking what this means to you."

"Why does Dulcie want your house, Loralee?" Jo imagined herself demanding the same from her own mother, who was comfortably settled, since Jo's father's death, in Florida, and knew exactly the response she would get: *Why Jo, dear, what an interesting idea. Let me think on that a bit.* And the "bit" would, of course, last for the rest of her life. As well it should.

"Dulcie and Ken want to move back to Abbotsville, which I'd dearly love too! Having my grandchildren all the way across the country in Seattle and being able to see them only a few days a year is terrible! They've all missed living here too and want to come back, but Dulcie explained that the only way they could afford to settle here is if I sell them my house at a very reasonable price. Dulcie hasn't been working since the new baby, and they've had quite a few unexpected expenses gobbling up their savings. Plus Ken wants to start his own tax service and accounting business, which would take time to get off the ground. My house has this nice basement room he could use as his office, saving him the expense of renting one."

"But where do they think you would live?"

"Dulcie thinks I should take one of those new seniors' condos. They both insist keeping up my house is too much for me at my age, and I have to admit it's becoming harder and harder. And my knees *are* starting to give me trouble with the stairs. But, oh, Jo!" Loralee looked at Jo with an expression that tore at her heart. "I love my little house!"

"Of course you do, Loralee."

"And I love working in my garden, sore knees or not. How could I live high up in a condo with no tomatoes to grow in the summer or crocuses to watch for in spring?"

"Then don't. Tell Dulcie you can't sell them your house."

"But I really want them all to come here!"

"It's a dilemma," Ina Mae said, nodding.

Jo looked at Loralee's sad face. There had to be some kind of solution. "Have you thought about building an addition? A mother-in-law suite?"

Loralee nodded, her expression turning even more forlorn. "I looked into it, dear, but it can't be done. My property isn't big enough. An addition, where we'd have to put it, would come too close to my neighbor's property and zoning won't allow that. Alice and Walt, my wonderful neighbors, have said they're fine with the idea. Their garage is on that side, so it wouldn't be at all like we'd be overlooking each other's windows. But the zoning board was firm. It can't be done."

"I'm so sorry, Loralee," Jo said. "I certainly see why you're upset, and I wish I had a solution for you. How soon do you need to decide?"

"They want to know by the end of the month. I promised Dulcie I'd look at the seniors' condo, and I've spoken to the manager there about stopping in tomorrow. But I'm dreading it. I feel as if it would be my first step toward the nursing home."

"Don't be silly," Ina Mae scolded. "Pheasant Run is an active adult complex, not assisted living. I know a few people living there who love it. I'd go with you, Loralee, except for an appointment for my annual physical, which was set up weeks ago."

"The Craft Corner's closed tomorrow," Jo said. "I'm planning to go see Sylvia and Xavier, but I'd be glad to go with you to the condo afterward."

Loralee brightened. "Oh, would you? Maybe you could give me a young person's perspective on it. May I go to the Ramirezes' with you? I have some lovely homemade vegetarian chili in my freezer I'd be so happy to take them. Do you think they'd like vegetarian chili?"

"If you made it, Loralee, I'm sure they'll love it."

Loralee perked up, and the worry lines in her face eased for the moment, which cheered Jo. Taking Loralee with her to Ramirezes' would work very well too, Jo thought, since her presence would help distract them from the fact that Jo was looking Xavier over carefully, to judge for herself if he was capable of murder.

* * *

When she got home that evening, Jo fixed herself a hearty ham and tomato sandwich and speed-dialed Carrie's number.

"How are things?" she asked when Carrie picked up.

Carrie sighed. "Dan's been getting job cancellations."

Jo winced but said, "Tell him to hang in there. This will certainly be cleared up, and those people who cancelled will be begging to get back in line."

"I hope so. Jo, you know how normally I'm glad when Dan has a little free time, since it means he can work on all the unfinished projects around here. But when it's for a reason like this . . ." Carrie's voice trailed off. "I know Dan's worried sick about being able to keep up our mortgage payments now, not to mention all the other bills that will keep coming."

"Carrie, I'm going to talk to Xavier and Sylvia tomorrow. Plus, the workshop ladies—and Vernon—have given me a couple leads to look into and maybe point the police in another direction."

"Oh? Like who?"

"Like—and keep this to yourself for now—Parker Holt's wife Mallory. We have hints that she might have wanted out of their marriage. Maybe she chose the quickest way."

"That would be great, ah, I mean, well you know what I mean."

"I do, and I agree, not knowing Mallory Holt yet. Maybe Dan would feel better if he were out looking around too. Do you think he might talk with some of Holt's employees? Maybe he could dig up dirt on someone with a grudge bad enough to do Holt in."

"I think that's a terrific idea, and I'll suggest it. Much better to be out and active than sitting and worrying."

Jo agreed, aware of how her search for an alternative suspect to Xavier had, to some extent, taken her mind off her own worry about the future of her shop. It didn't, however, do anything toward making her own problem disappear. If

Dan, on the other hand, found someone who would interest the police a lot more than Xavier, Dan's problems—as well as Xavier's—would be solved.

"On another subject, how is Charlie doing?" Jo asked as she picked up her sandwich and bit into it.

"He's improving. Fifteen-year-old bones heal faster than yours or mine would. He'll be moving carefully for a while, but he might be back to school in a couple of days if he feels up to it. Either way, he doesn't need me around 24-7, so I'll be back in the shop on Thursday."

"That'd be great. The place misses you." Jo didn't mention anything about Randy Truitt coming in the next day to fix the storeroom shelves, because she knew Carrie would insist Dan do it. The deal with Randy was set. Plus, Dan would be much better off working to resolve his own problem rather than taking care of her little repairs.

"Let me know what you learn tomorrow," Carrie said.

Jo promised and rang off. She polished off the rest of her sandwich, then mentally scoured her kitchen for anything good she might follow it with. Cookies? A bit of ice cream left in the freezer? The extra calories shouldn't worry her, she thought. With all these problems piling up—Carrie and Dan's, Xavier and Sylvia's, and now Loralee's—her shoulders could use a little bulking up.

Not quite as much as Atlas's, perhaps, but who knew what else might be coming?

Chapter 9

At nine o'clock on a cold Wednesday morning, a traveler's mug of strong coffee beside her in the console, Jo pulled up to Loralee's house. *Just beep, Jo. I'll be ready,* Loralee had insisted, so Jo beeped. The door to Loralee's pretty Cape Cod swung open, and Loralee, bulging tote bag in hand, stepped out and waved. She turned to fiddle at some length with what must have been more than one lock, so Jo took the moment to scan the property. It was definitely well kept. The siding was white, the shutters bright, and the windows sparkled in the pale January sun. Loralee's gardening skills weren't evident yet, but the rhododendrons edging the house's foundation looked healthy, with light frost accentuating their dark green leaves.

The property wasn't large, though, and Jo thought she could see the zoning board's problem with allowing an addition, though if Loralee's neighbors were okay with it, it seemed like a moot point. The ins and outs of zoning boards, however, were areas Jo had little knowledge of.

"When we come back," Loralee said as she pulled open

the car door and leaned in, "I hope you can stay for a cup of tea. I took a nice pound cake out of the freezer last night when I brought out the chili to thaw."

"That sounds great, Loralee. I'll see how things go. Randy Truitt is coming to the shop to fix some shelves for me later on, and I'll have to be there to let him in."

"Oh, Randy!" Loralee said, settling her bag carefully beside her feet and buckling herself in. "How is he?"

Jo hesitated. She had no idea if he was in better or worse shape than he had been before she met him. "He's fine, I guess," she said, putting her Toyota in gear and pulling off. "Ina Mae suggested him for the job, and he showed up promptly enough after I called. He seems to know what he's doing."

"He's fixing shelves? He'll do fine. I always thought Randy had more ability than he gave himself credit for. It's sad that he's wasted a lot of it, but there's still hope."

"That's pretty much what Ina Mae said. I take it he's gone through some tough times?"

Loralee sighed. "It was very unfortunate that both his parents died so early—Bill first, from a terrible farm accident, then Myrtle of cancer. Randy was an only child, and I think it was more than he could cope with. He sold the farm, then frittered away the money drinking too much and living foolishly. I think he's finally seen the error of his ways, but there's still a lot of pieces to pick up to get his life back on track."

Jo turned onto Albion Street, which led to the Ramirezes' apartment. "My only way to reach Randy was to leave a message for him at Otto's," she said. "Do you know what his living situation is?"

"He might still rent a room at Tillie Watson's place, in the older section of town. Tillie won't take messages for her roomers. She keeps a clean place, though, I've heard."

Jo pulled up to the Manor View Arms, a place whose

name was much grander than its appearance. A solid-looking sandstone building that may have been attractive in the sixties or seventies, it had an air, Jo thought, of an old man who had greatly relaxed his grooming rituals and leaned toward home haircuts and too-often-worn flannels.

"I think this is it," Jo said. "Their address is 8147, that entrance over there." Jo undid her seat belt. As Loralee worked at releasing her own belt and gathering up her bag, Jo asked, "Randy grew up on a farm, then? Where was it?"

"Oh," Loralee said, checking the plastic lid on her chili for leakage, "I'm sure you've seen it." She unhooked her belt and pushed open the car door. "It's not a farm anymore. It's where all those big houses went up. Holt Meadows."

Jo knocked on apartment 303. Its door, unlike most of the others she and Loralee had passed on the way, was scrubbed clean, although the paint showed signs of peeling. Jo had called Sylvia that morning to say she wanted to see them both, and Sylvia had been politely, though quietly, agreeable.

A far different Sylvia than the bubbly woman Jo had first met opened the door. She had dark-circled eyes and a somber air, though her hair had been brushed back neatly and her maternity clothing was crisp and clean. "Mrs. McAllister," she said, stepping aside to welcome them in. "So good to see you."

"Please call me Jo, Sylvia. Do you know Loralee Phillips?"

"We met at St. Adelbert's, dear," Loralee said, "at the newcomers' coffee. But I'm sure you won't remember; there were so many people. I asked Jo if I could come along. I hope you don't mind. And I brought you a little something." Loralee held out her vegetarian chili. "Just heat it up whenever you don't feel like cooking. And don't worry, I don't make it very spicy. Your husband can add more pepper if he likes, but for you right now, with the baby, well, you know."

Sylvia took it from Loralee, then nodded. "I remember, from the church. You were very nice." Her voice trembled as tears threatened. "And you *are* very nice."

"Oh, sweetie, it's nothing, believe me." Loralee bustled about, pulling off her coat and taking Jo's, giving Sylvia time to compose herself. "These don't need hanging up. We can just leave them over here. What a lovely place you have! I'll bet you made this throw, didn't you? The colors in it are beautiful."

"Yes, I make," Sylvia said, smiling for the first time. "Please, sit down. You like coffee? I have it ready."

"That would be great," Jo said. "Is Xavier here?"

"He be out in a minute. He was up late last night." A shadow passed over Sylvia's face and she turned away, heading to her kitchen for the coffee. As she crossed her small hallway Jo heard her call softly in Spanish, apparently notifying Xavier that their visitors were there.

Jo glanced around as she joined Loralee on the sofa, seeing a room that was achingly tidy, though furnished with what might well be flea-market finds. Wood surfaces, while scratched, gleamed with polish, and the worn upholstery was well brushed and fresh smelling. Sylvia, Jo saw, had managed to add brightness in what could have been a drab décor, with beautifully made paper flowers and simply framed colorful prints, most with a Mexican theme. Jo saw no sign of the quilted tote bags and assumed Sylvia's work area was somewhere in the back of the apartment.

She heard noises coming from the room down the hall, and soon footsteps headed their way. The man Jo had glimpsed arriving at the Holt's house the night of the murder stood before them.

"Senoras," he greeted them, bowing slightly.

Xavier Ramirez was slim, but his muscular arms were

apparent below the rolled sleeves of his denim shirt. About five foot eight and dark haired, Xavier had a full mustache that could have easily made him appear intimidating, but the brown eyes that looked at Jo were soft. Despite his young age, Jo found herself reminded of her Grandpa Wagner, who had talked little but had never shown up at her house without a fresh roll of cherry Life Savers for her in his pocket.

Sylvia did the introductions, and Xavier nodded gravely to both Jo and Loralee as he held out his hand. Loralee twittered, explaining in detail once again where they had already met, and Xavier nodded solemnly as though Loralee were telling him information of such importance that he was storing it carefully in his memory bank.

As Sylvia handed around coffee, Jo dove into her reason for being there.

"Carrie Brenner told me what you've been going through with the police."

Xavier was silent for a moment, seeming reluctant to discuss his problem. Finally he said, "It's very bad to be suspected of killing a man."

"Yes," Jo said, "believe me, I know. I had the bad luck to be in the same position not too long ago."

Xavier's dark eyebrows shot up.

"It's true," Loralee said. "Poor Jo here was new to our town, just as you are. Someone was killed the very day she opened her shop—*in* her shop. Jo was their only suspect until she could prove to the police who really did it."

Xavier turned to Jo. "So you understand."

Jo nodded. "I do. And I also understand how important friends are at a time like this. Carrie and Dan are your good friends, as they are mine. They're upset about this situation, and they've told me—which I hope you don't mind—about the legitimate anger you had toward Parker Holt, reasons that lead the police to think you would have wanted him dead."

"Oh, no, no, no!" Sylvia cried. "Never dead, never dead."

Jo looked at Xavier, who only pressed his lips together tightly and shook his head. "But you can see their reasoning," she said, "can't you? That you had been there in the man's house, that you certainly knew how to set up the trap that electrocuted him, and that you would likely be happy he was dead?"

Xavier crossed himself rapidly and shook his head. "I didn't like the man, that is true. But I never be happy that anyone die like that, no matter how bad he is. He was bad; he deserve to be punished, but not in such a way."

Xavier said this with quiet vehemence, and Jo felt his sincerity.

"It's a terrible thing," Loralee said, jumping in. "For you, for the Brenners, and for everyone concerned. The police are doing their job, trying to get to the truth, but please know there are people here in Abbotsville who care. We will do all we can to help. We want this to be cleared up so you can have a peaceful home to bring your baby into."

"Thank you!" Sylvia said. "That is so much what we want also. I want to have our baby with a happy heart. I want to make my quilted bags for you, Jo, and I want everyone to know that my husband is good man. He is honest man who work hard. And he would not hurt anyone."

Sylvia reached for Xavier's hand. He clasped hers and patted it, giving her a small smile.

"I imagine," Jo said, "a lot depends on who had the opportunity to set up that trap for Holt. Xavier, you left the house with Dan at four o'clock, isn't that right?"

"Yes, we go to pick up the sink and toilet for the new bathroom. We couldn't do anything more until we got those things, so we stop work early."

"And I came to the house shortly after six. Were you with Dan those full two hours?"

Xavier's gaze shifted slightly. "No, we load everything in Dan's van, then he drive home I think around five."

"And then you came right home?"

"No. I went to store first, to buy food. Sylvia shouldn't carry heavy things now, so I do it."

"You told the police that?"

He nodded.

"Does anyone at the store remember you were there?"

"I don't know. I didn't talk to anyone because I don't know people there. I just fill basket, get in line, and pay. When I come home, I see neighbor. We talked. I tell police that."

"So your neighbor is the only one who knows when you came home—besides Sylvia, I mean."

"Yes. A little past six."

Xavier's demeanor seemed to have changed just a bit as he told Jo about going to the store. He hadn't looked at her quite as firmly nor sat as still as before. "It would be very good for you," Jo said, "if there was some way to verify you were at the store. A credit card receipt?"

"No, I pay cash."

"I show police what Xavier bring home," Sylvia said. "I show them cereal, milk, apples, everything. All fresh."

"Did you have the store's receipt?"

Sylvia's face fell. "I look. We both look through all the trash. We could not find. Xavier thinks he might have dropped it coming out of store."

"That's too bad," Jo said. "That would have made a big difference."

"You think they will arrest Xavier?" Sylvia asked, her face filled with worry and fear. Xavier reached out and grimly rubbed at her shoulder.

"I hope not. They haven't yet, and that might be a good sign."

"Don't you worry," Loralee said. "You just take care of yourselves. Get ready for that baby. Jo's going to talk to people for you, and she's very good at finding out what's really going on. Everything will be straightened out."

Jo heard this with dismay. *We can't promise that!* she

wanted to cry. But she saw the spark of hope that had leapt to Sylvia's dark-circled eyes. And the gratitude in Xavier's. They needed help so badly. They needed friends beyond Carrie and Dan.

Jo nodded, swallowing anything that might dampen their tiny spark of optimism. "I'll do my best."

Loralee was quiet as Jo drove away from the Manor View Arms. "You okay?" Jo asked as she pulled up to a red light.

"Yes, dear. I'm just thinking about that nice couple and how they're going to need a little practical support too if Xavier isn't working. There's a group of ladies at St. Adelbert's who pitch in with meals and such when there's an illness or death in a family. I'd say this nearly qualifies, wouldn't you? We could call it a little preemptive care—to ward off those two falling sick from worry."

"That's a good idea, Loralee," Jo said, meaning it, but knowing at the same time that it would only be a Band-Aid on the Ramirezes' problem. The way to really fix it would be to find out who wanted Parker Holt dead and took those lethal steps to guarantee it.

"Am I heading the right way to Pheasant Run?" Jo asked. Loralee had told her generally where the active adult community they were going to see was, but Jo wasn't familiar with the particular roads that led there.

Loralee sighed, not at Jo's ignorance, Jo was sure, but at what lay ahead. "Yes. Just keep going straight, and you'll turn left after you pass Hanson's Garage. I'm so glad you'll be with me, Jo. I'm dreading this."

"We're only looking, Loralee. Nobody's going to force you to sign anything."

"I know. Don't mind me. I just sink into one of these moods whenever I think about moving. But I'm going to try very hard to face this with an open mind."

"That's the spirit. And—" Jo was going to say "You

might actually like the place," but, sensing that was not what Loralee wanted to hear at the moment, she changed her comment to: "And it's a nice day just to be out and about." "Nice" stretched it a bit, as the temperature hovered around freezing, and clouds had moved in to turn the sky gray. But no wind howled nor sleet flew, so "nice" it was.

Jo made a few more turns at Loralee's direction and finally pulled up to a long building with multiple rooflines that stretched beyond view. A large sign identified it as "Pheasant Run Active Adult Living."

"This is it," Jo said.

"Pheasant Run," Loralee sighed. "What an appropriate name. Just looking at it makes me want to run."

"Where did that 'open mind' run off to?"

Loralee smiled. "You're right. And I'm trying very hard to be positive."

"Maybe focus on the 'active' part of it. That doesn't suggest anything near an assisted living or nursing home, does it?"

"No, but who knows if they don't have a section in the back named 'Cooked Goose.'" At Jo's wry look, Loralee smiled and shrugged. She reached for her door handle. "Might as well get started."

Jo opened her own door, feeling no need to call out, "Wait for me," what with Loralee's attitude definitely that of a woman being dragged kicking and screaming. Her ever-perfect manners, however, would never permit such a rude display. They managed to make their way into the building and to the open office door of the building manager, Angie Palmer.

"You must be Mrs. Phillips." A cheery, red-haired woman of about fifty bounced up from behind a desk to greet them.

Loralee solemnly admitted that indeed she was, and shook the woman's hand. She introduced Jo.

"How nice of you," Angie said to Jo, "to bring your mother."

"No." Jo hastened to correct her, catching the fleeting troubled look that crossed Loralee's face. "Loralee's daughter is in Seattle right now. I'm just a friend."

"A very *dear* friend," Loralee added.

"Wonderful. Well, let me show you around, and then I can answer any questions you might have. All right?"

Jo and Loralee both nodded and dutifully got behind their enthusiastic guide. She led them through the model one-bedroom "Cardinal," then opened up a folder showing sketches of the two-bedroom "Blue Jay" and the super-sized three-bedroom "Oriole."

At one point, when Angie took a quick call on her cell phone, Loralee whispered to Jo, "I'm really hoping she doesn't say something about building a little nest here."

"I'm wondering about the nest *egg* it might take to buy one," Jo whispered back, smiling. She had been impressed with features such as hardwood floors, marble vanities, and deluxe appliances.

"Now let me show you our wonderful amenities," Angie said, leading them briskly out of the "Cardinal." Loralee and Jo agreeably followed behind.

"This is our state-of-the-art fitness center!" Angie announced as she opened the door to an impressive array of treadmills, exercise bikes, and a few other machines for which Jo had no name nor any idea as to their function. A single gray-haired man worked a rowing machine near the back as he gazed upward at a television tuned to CNN.

Jo could picture Ina Mae making use of the place, but she wasn't all that sure about Loralee. Loralee didn't look all that sure herself.

Angie, perhaps sensing the disinterest, said, "And then, we have our Great Room." She took them to a large bright room with scattered tables and chairs, a wall of shelves filled with books, and an unoccupied bar with stools. A few people relaxed around the tables, and Jo thought it all looked very pleasant.

"Our residents use this for a variety of things. It's great for the occasional large party, but as you see it has its quiet times too."

"Loralee Phillips! Is that you?" A round-shaped woman seated at one of the tables with three others, all holding cards, called out.

"Why Betty Kidwell!" Loralee cried. "I had no idea you lived here."

"Bought a Cardinal last May," Betty said proudly. "Last winter's heavy snow just about did me in. I couldn't get my own car out of my garage what with always needing someone to clear the driveway for me. You looking to buy, Loralee? If you do, you won't need your car anymore. I got rid of mine. The shuttle bus takes us anywhere we want to go."

But I love my car! Jo could almost hear Loralee thinking, but what came out of her mouth was a polite, "I'll remember that." Loralee introduced Jo to Betty, and Betty in turn named her table companions.

"You're that arts-and-crafts lady, aren't you?" one of the women asked. Thin, with unnaturally dark hair, she'd been introduced to Jo as "Donna."

Jo confessed that she was.

"Angie," Donna said enthusiastically, "you should have Jo come and teach a few craft classes. They'd go over big! I always wanted to sign up for one of your workshops, Jo, but I always seem so darn busy. If you came here, though, I wouldn't have any excuse, would I? I could just walk over and plop myself down."

"Jo gives wonderful workshops," Loralee said. She pulled back her hair to show her earrings. "I made these at her last one."

The ladies oohed over the earrings, impressed.

"I've been dying to try beading," Donna cried. "Angie, let's get her over here!"

"We'll definitely look into it," Angie said, smiling at Jo.

Jo was mentally running over her schedule, wondering if

she could fit another workshop in, when Betty said, "Angie, I've been meaning to ask you. Is Parker Holt's death going to change anything with our condo management?"

"Parker Holt?" Jo asked. "Is he connected to Pheasant Run?"

"Why, he built the place!" Betty said with some surprise.

"It shouldn't affect us at all," Angie assured Betty. "Parker Holt turned over care of the property to C & A Management. Everything will continue on smoothly, don't worry."

"More smoothly, I hope, than what went on with that first management company," said a third woman at the table, Celia, who had been silent until now. All eyes turned toward Celia, and she explained. "Ralph and I were one of the first to move in here. I remember hearing about some terrible rows between Parker Holt and the woman who first managed here. There were even threats of a lawsuit, which, as far as I know, never materialized."

Celia's tablemates' eyes bugged with interest, but Angie Palmer looked highly uneasy. "I haven't shown you our swimming pool yet," she said to Loralee and Jo, moving coaxingly away from the table.

Loralee agreed that she hadn't, and, as she and Jo took their leave from the table of card players, Jo decided she could definitely find time in her busy schedule to come back to Pheasant Run.

Chapter 10

"Well, Loralee, what do you think?" Jo asked as they drove away from Pheasant Run. She thought she knew what the answer would be, not having seen any increased interest from Loralee toward moving there, despite her admitting at one point that it had very pleasant living conditions and that she enjoyed encountering old acquaintances.

Loralee shook her head. "That place is just not *me*!"

Jo nodded, almost understanding. That, however, didn't solve Loralee's problem of wanting her daughter to return to Abbotsville.

"Could your daughter and her husband just find another house?" Jo asked.

"Nothing the size of mine at a price they could afford," Loralee said. "And Dulcie says she has such happy memories of growing up in this house that she wants her children to have the same. I can't fault her for that, can I, Jo? It's a wonderful compliment from your child to be told she loved her childhood."

Jo agreed that it was, but it also seemed that Dulcie was

exacting a high price for her compliment. Jo couldn't tell Loralee what to do, though. She could only support her in whatever she decided. She dropped Loralee off at her house and declined her repeated offer of tea and home-made cake with sincere regret.

"I'd love to, Loralee. But it's grown late and Randy will be waiting for me." Jo then drove off, Loralee's profuse thanks for accompanying her to Pheasant Run ringing in her ears. When she turned onto Main, Jo saw Randy sitting in a battered tan pickup in front of her store, boards of lumber visible in the back. As she pulled up behind him, he hopped out holding his toolbox.

"I hope you weren't waiting long," Jo said, greeting him.

Randy shook his head. "Just a couple of minutes."

Jo unlocked the shop's door and held it open as Randy brought in his supplies. The increased level of assurance she had noticed at the end of their first meeting seemed to have dipped, as Randy showed a certain nervousness. She hoped it was simply his lack of social skills making him uneasy once again, not a lack of carpentry skills. Loralee had been confident of his ability to do the job, and Jo crossed her fingers that she was right.

"We'd better move these boxes out of the way," Jo said as they entered the stockroom, referring to the boxes of beads, papers, dried flowers, and other supplies that she had taken down from the sagging shelves.

"Where do you want them?" Randy asked, instantly reaching for a large, heavy-looking box.

"Out front is the only place, for now," Jo said as she be-gan making space in the shop area. She carried out what she could herself and watched carefully after the lighter, more crushable items as Randy rushed boxes out, perhaps in an effort to demonstrate efficiency. She hoped he would be able to settle down. She wanted shelves that would last, not ones put up slapdash.

But fairly soon, as Randy began measuring and marking wood, Jo saw that he had found his focus. He promised the job would be done in time to move everything back to the storeroom before her shop reopened the following day, and Jo nodded, glad to be reassured in more ways than one. She settled herself down at her desk to work on her bills while hearing the thumps, bumps, and the occasional whine of an electric saw in her stockroom.

When her stomach signaled it was past lunchtime, Jo called out, "I'm going to run down to the Abbot's Kitchen, Randy. Can I get you something?"

After a short wait she heard, "I'm all right. Well, maybe just a Coke or something."

"I've got that right here and should have offered it. Want one now?"

"Yeah, great. Thanks."

Jo pulled a Coke out of her small refrigerator and carried it into the stockroom. Randy set down his level and took the can, popping it open.

"How's it going?" Jo asked. She could see at least one freshly cut shelf set in place.

"Pretty good." Randy took one long drink, then looked like he wanted to get back to work, so Jo left him to it. She pulled on her warm jacket and headed out the door.

On her short walk down Main, Jo came to Frannie's floral shop, which stood dark and empty. Frannie had apparently vacated during the busy-ness of the last couple of days and taken off for parts unknown. Blank windows looked into a dim, flowerless interior, and a phrase Jo had read somewhere popped into her head: *like dead eyes looking out of a soul-less body*. Jo shivered at the bleak thought. Would her own shop look like that once her lease ran out?

She continued on to the Abbot's Kitchen, checking around for signs of other business mortalities and thankfully finding nothing more. Jim Wald's little bookstore displayed a fresh supply of best sellers in its window, though the windows of Lily's Dress Shop looked somewhat dreary. That, however, was not unusual for Lily's, whose styles leaned toward last-decade funereal. At the Kitchen, after giving her order to Ruthie and adding, on second thought, a ham and cheese for Randy, Jo asked, "Have you and Bert made any decisions about selling?"

Ruthie shook her head. "We don't know, now, who we'd be selling *to*, do we? I mean, who's going to take over his business now that Parker Holt is dead, and what will their plans be?"

"I presume Mallory Holt inherits the business," Jo said. "But I don't know if she'll hold on to it. I'm not having any luck finding out if Max McGee sold my building to Holt's corporation, but I'm not sure if Mallory would know. Has she been involved in the day-to-day operations?"

"Mallory was involved with a lot of things," a voice behind Jo said, startling her. She hadn't been aware of anyone coming in. Alexis Wigsley, who was clearly very good at creeping up on people, smiled slyly at Jo. "But making money wasn't one of them. Now spending it . . ."

"Good afternoon, Ms. Wigsley," Ruthie said, somewhat stiffly. "May I take your order?"

"Shrimp salad on a croissant, Ruthie."

Jo remembered what Ina Mae had mentioned, and said to Alexis, "I've heard one thing Mallory Holt was pretty involved with was the Abbotsville Women's Club."

"Oh, yes," Alexis agreed. "She's been our president these last few months. Mallory's the one behind our club's decision to purchase red, white, and blue flowers to plant about the base of the statue of General Jeremiah Boggsworth in the park. Quite an exciting idea, isn't it?"

Unsure whether Alexis was being sarcastic, Jo simply nodded.

"In fact," Alexis continued, "I was at the committee

meeting with her Monday to discuss that and other things when she got the call about Parker."

"You were?" This was one thing Jo had wanted to look into—the whereabouts of Mallory Holt that afternoon.

"Didn't I mention that at the shop yesterday? Yes, Mallory asked Sally Robinson to hold the committee meeting. Very inconvenient, I thought, even though Sally lives in Mallory's neighborhood. Sally's driveway, though, is being repaired, and we had to park on the street a good distance away and then dodge slush puddles to get to the house. But Mallory said she couldn't hold the meeting herself because she would be coming from a shopping trip in Baltimore with her aunt, Lucy Kunkle, and wouldn't have time to get anything ready.

"Interesting, isn't it? I mean, who knows what might or might not have happened if we'd all been at Mallory's place instead of Sally Robinson's?"

Jo nodded. It *was* interesting. "Your meeting was all afternoon long?"

"Oh, no. Mallory didn't get back until three."

So Mallory, according to Alexis, was with her committee members from three until the time she got the police call, and with her aunt before that. Much too occupied to slip into her basement after Dan and Xavier left, to set up the deadly trap for her husband.

"Turkey and bacon, and ham and cheese," Ruthie announced, and Jo took her order and paid for it.

"You and Carrie are working at the shop today?" Alexis asked, eyeing the two sandwiches.

"No, the shop's closed on Wednesdays as usual. But I'm getting some repair work done in the stockroom."

"Oh. Dan's doing it for you?"

Jo shook her head and had no real reason not to explain further, but she was just as glad when Ruthie called out, "Shrimp salad on croissant."

"Enjoy your lunch," Jo said, and turned toward the door.

"Oh, I will," Alexis said, "just as I'm sure Mallory will be enjoying her lunch at Hollander's with Sebastian Zarnik." At Jo's surprised, and, she was sure, blank look, Alexis's lip curled, and she elaborated. "Her artist friend. Mallory always admired his art. Perhaps," she said, her eyes innocently wide, "they're getting their heads together to design a really nice tombstone for Parker."

Jo headed back to the Craft Corner, clutching the carryout bag and thinking about Alexis's final comments. Clearly they were dropped with the intention of stirring gossip. Was it credible, though? Ina Mae had warned that Alexis was more interested in a spicy story than an accurate one. At the thought of Ina Mae, it occurred to Jo that the senior center was located fairly close to Hollander's, a fine restaurant Jo knew about but had never dined in. With all the classes Ina Mae took at the senior center, maybe she was currently within quick checking distance? Jo pulled out her cell phone and punched in Ina Mae's cell number—the one Jo had been so skeptical of ever needing.

"Yes?"

"Ina Mae, it's Jo. Where are you?"

"Waiting for a lecture on vitamin supplements at the center. Do you need me?"

"Yes, but not for the shop." Jo explained what Alexis had told her, and heard disapproving noises coming across the distance from her friend. Ina Mae's personal book of proper behavior clearly did not include a widow of only two days lunching alone with a single man.

"Do you feel like running over to check on the story?" Jo asked. "Maybe Alexis forgot to mention that Lucy Kunkle was also along. Or possibly she, ah, *created* the whole story."

"I'm on my way," Ina Mae said, and Jo heard the line go

dead. She pictured Ina Mae sprinting out of the senior center in her blue warm-up, white hair flying, and smiled to herself. Ina Mae was never one to waste words—or time.

Jo tucked her phone into her purse and entered the craft shop. She heard Randy thumping the walls of her stockroom, and headed on back there. "Time for a break," she announced, holding up the lunch bag. "I brought you a ham and cheese. Hope that's what you like."

Randy stared at her. "Ham and cheese. Uh, yeah, that's great."

"Set your tools down and come on out. We can eat at my workshop table. Want another Coke with it?"

"Uh, I, ah, I guess," Randy stuttered out. "Thanks."

"No problem. It's always been my opinion that a hungry workman is, well, a hungry workman. I imagine Tillie Watson isn't big on packing lunches, huh?"

Randy grabbed a rag and wiped at his hands, then finger-combed his hair out of his face as he came out of the stockroom. "How'd you know I'm at Tillie's?"

"I was out with Loralee Phillips this morning and told her about the job you'd be doing for me today. She mentioned it." Jo set the sandwiches on the table and pulled a Coke out of her refrigerator, handing it to Randy. She poured a mug of coffee for herself.

"Mrs. Phillips," Randy said, nodding. "She's a nice lady."

"Yes, she is." Jo unwrapped her turkey and bacon, and passed a couple of paper napkins to Randy. "But sometimes a little *too* nice for her own good, in my opinion."

Randy looked over his sandwich at Jo as he took a huge bite of his ham and cheese. He worked at it a few moments, gulped, then asked, "Too nice?"

Jo wiped at the corner of her mouth. Bert's sauce was delicious, but definitely oozy. "I guess I mean that if you're making yourself unhappy because you're trying to please other people, you're being too nice. Right now Loralee is considering selling her house in order to make someone else happy. But I'm afraid doing that will ultimately make Loralee miserable. Her home means a lot to her."

Randy nodded, chewing on that thought as well as his ham and cheese. "We had a nice house on our farm," he said. "I miss it."

"Yes, I heard you grew up on a farm."

"Yeah," Randy said. "We grew tobacco, some corn, kept cows. I even had a couple goats for a while." He looked up at Jo with a face fluctuating between pleasure and pain at the memories.

"I guess that was a great way for a kid to grow up, huh?"

"Yeah. But then my pop had that tractor accident. I was off picking up seed when it happened. It was tough. My mom, she was never the same after that. I think that's probably why she got sick and died. But I know she felt bad about leaving me on my own, even though I was out of school and everything."

"How long out of school?" Jo asked.

"Almost a year."

So Randy was only about nineteen when he was orphaned. Old enough, some would say, to stand on his own two feet. But to Jo it seemed terribly young. No wonder he'd stumbled around, with the rug being yanked out from under him like that. When Jo's own father died, her jewelry-design career was already off to a good start and she was on the brink of being married. Losing her father had been traumatic, but it hadn't derailed her life like losing Mike had.

"So you sold your farm then?" Jo asked.

"Yeah. But I didn't want to, really. It had been in our family for, uh, since my great grandfather bought it, way back."

"You didn't think you could run it alone?"

"I don't know. Maybe. There was a lot of, well, stuff going on then. And I was just a kid, you know?"

Jo nodded. Her cell phone rang, and she said, "Excuse

me," and got up to retrieve the phone from her bag. She saw from the display it was Ina Mae. Jo walked toward the front of the store to take the call, wondering what this senior sleuth would have to tell her.

Chapter 11

Jo heard voices in the background, along with a soft clatter of dishes and tableware and realized Ina Mae must be calling from inside Hollander's restaurant. The older woman spoke in a hushed tone. "They're here. Just the two of them." Ina Mae's voice suddenly rose, startling Jo. "No, just coffee's fine, thank you," then, after a brief pause, she resumed her conspiratorial tone. "I walked past their table as slowly as I could manage without looking like an utter fool. What I picked up sounded like they were talking about an art show, maybe his. And I caught mention of Los Angeles."

Jo heard Randy get up from the table and drop his sandwich wrappings and Coke can in the wastebasket. He walked toward her and continued on out the door, heading for his truck.

Jo asked, "How does this lunch strike you? Business or social?" She could see Randy through the window, rooting around in his truck bed. Jo edged toward Carrie's yarn bins, idly reaching out to stroke some of the softer skeins stacked there.

"Oh, social, definitely," Ina Mae said. "Mallory Holt has been known to patronize the arts, and I suppose this Zarnik fellow qualifies as an artist, though I've seen some of his work and it wouldn't hang on *my* wall. But the look on her face—she's facing me—is what we used to call moony-eyed."

"Hmm. So this confirms what Vernon said, that Mallory Holt was unhappy in her marriage. And she seems to have found her happiness elsewhere."

"Hmph!" Ina Mae snorted. "Happiness! If that's what you want to call it. And," she said in the same disdainful tone, "this *relationship*, as people also like to term these things now a days, certainly didn't develop overnight. It's been brewing for a while. Sitting here, out in the open with her husband not even in his grave yet, says a lot."

"Does it say she had a motive for murder?"

"It does to *me*."

"Me too," Jo said, squeezing a skein of supersoft pink baby yarn. "Unfortunately it doesn't look like she had the opportunity." She told Ina Mae what Alexis Wigsley had said about Mallory being off in Baltimore with her aunt, then at the committee meeting from three until six. As she did, Randy reentered the shop and headed on back carrying a small rubber mallet.

Ina Mae asked, "Have you had a chance to confirm Alexis's story yet?"

"No."

"I'll give Sally Robinson a call, though it might mean getting roped into a committee I have no interest in. Have to have some pretext for calling, though, don't I?"

"You're a trooper, Ina Mae," Jo said with a grin. Volunteering to discuss flower choices for three hours over tea and cookies would probably be, for this dynamic ex-teacher, as excruciating as seeing a class of third-graders run through a museum at top scream.

"They're getting up to go now," Ina Mae whispered. "I'll call you later."

Ina Mae disconnected, and Jo closed up her own phone. She heard Randy back at work banging at her stockroom walls, and headed back thoughtfully to her desk. Ina Mae might be able to establish that Mallory Holt was definitely with others the entire time Parker Holt's murderer was setting up his death trap. Mallory had motive, but she may not have had opportunity. Someone new, however, had appeared on the radar who had the same motive as Mallory: Sebastian Zarnik.

What, Jo wondered, was *he* doing between three and six?

Jo had settled back at her desk and was pulling out an order sheet for stamping items when she heard a tapping noise coming from her front window. Surely Ina Mae hadn't rushed over from Hollander's, had she? Or could it be Carrie? Except Carrie had her own key and wouldn't be tapping. Curiosity caused Jo to stand up impulsively, which she quickly regretted as she spotted Alexis Wigsley peering back at her, hands cupped around her eyes, nose pressed against the glass.

"Yoo-hoo! Jo," Alexis called, waving.

It was too late to hide, but Jo walked to the window instead of the shop's door, hoping to limit this interaction.

Alexis, however, asked, "Can I come in, Jo? Just for a minute? It's important."

Jo groaned inwardly, but how could she say no? She went to the door and turned the lock, stepping back to let Alexis—and a chilly wind—in.

"It's so *lucky* I ran into you at the deli and found out you'd be here. I suddenly realized that I *have* to get some of that rainbow-colored wired ribbon I saw here the other day. You don't mind, do you, Jo? After all, a sale's a sale, isn't it? I'm having guests for dinner tonight, and I know I can make darling bows for my napkins with that ribbon. Won't that be pretty?"

"Yes, it will," Jo agreed, and she headed to the shelves that held her wired ribbon.

Alexis's interest, however, turned toward Jo's stockroom, from which Randy's hammering reverberated. "How's the repair work going?" she asked, following Jo.

"Fine. You wanted rainbow-colored?" Jo asked, running her finger down the rolls of solids, polka dots, and plaids.

"Yes. Pastels."

Jo found a roll of ribbon with lovely pastel washes of color and pulled it out. When she looked up to show it to Alexis, however, the woman was no longer beside her. Jo leaned around the end of her shelf and saw Alexis heading for her stockroom.

"Oh, it's you, Randy!" Alexis cried at the stockroom doorway. "So you're fixing Jo's shelves."

Jo hurried over, anxious to keep Alexis out of Randy's way.

"Hello, Ms. Wigsley," she heard Randy say, but not too happily.

"Well, I seem to be running into you all over the place lately, don't I Randy?" Alexis said.

"Was this the ribbon you wanted?" Jo asked.

Alexis looked over at Jo, then at the ribbon. "What? Oh, yes, that's the one. Can I have two spools, please?"

"Of course. Come on over to the checkout counter. I'll pick up another on the way."

But Alexis was not so easily budged. "Yesterday," she said to Randy, "I saw you changing a flat tire for Mrs. Bauman as I was driving to my friend Christi's. Did you see me wave to the two of you?"

"Uh-huh."

"I wonder how Mrs. Bauman got that flat? Was there a nail in the tire? Seems to me she just bought those tires."

Randy shrugged, looking a bit bewildered. "I didn't see a nail."

"And the day before that," Alexis went on, "where was it? Oh, yes, I saw you cutting up that tree limb that fell on the Schillings' front lawn. And here you are now. You certainly do keep busy, don't you Randy?"

And Alexis certainly did too, keeping tabs, apparently, on everyone in the town, from Mallory Holt, to Carrie and Dan, all the way down to Mrs. Bauman and Randy Truitt. What else? Jo wondered. Did the woman lurk in the aisles of the Food Lion, noting what suspicious items her fellow Abbotsvillians might be slipping into their shopping carts, or check their recycling bins for the number of beer bottles?

"Randy's a hardworking man," Jo said. "We'd better let him get back to work so he can get home in time for his dinner." She took Alexis firmly by the arm and led her away from the stockroom, grabbing the extra spool of ribbon on the way and heading for the cash register to ring up the sale.

Alexis dug through her pocketbook for cash, searching for stray quarters and dimes to add to the bills she'd pulled out. "So, Dan must be too busy to do your shelves for you, huh, Jo?" she said as she lined up her change. "This murder situation hasn't affected his business, then?"

"Dan's doing fine," Jo said carefully, thinking, however, of Carrie's worried mention of job cancellations.

Alexis lowered her voice to a whisper. "You might not have had much choice hiring Randy, Jo, but I'd suggest you keep a close eye on him. He has a drinking problem, you know."

"Randy's been fine," Jo said, annoyed. Did Alexis really think Jo wouldn't notice if her workman staggered about and hung shelves helter-skelter?

The thumps from the stockroom stopped, and Randy

came out, heading once more for the front door. "Forgot a couple braces," he explained as he lumbered by.

Alexis smiled and nodded until the door closed behind him, then she leaned toward Jo. "I only mention it because I know you're fairly new in town. Unlike that Williams woman who should know better. She's actually dating Randy! With his history!"

"From what I've learned about Randy," Jo said, "his history is exactly that—history. I'm happy with his work today, and that's all I care about."

Randy pushed the door open, braces in hand, and Alexis quickly changed her tone, shivering at the cold air that followed him in. "My, doesn't it feel like snow is coming?"

Randy didn't answer as he continued on, obviously assuming the question wasn't aimed at him, and Jo murmured something noncommittal. She wanted to get Alexis out of the shop and briskly handed her the few pennies of change along with her bagged ribbon.

But not surprisingly, Alexis had more to say. "I'm so glad to hear," she said, dropping her coins in her purse, "that Dan's business is surviving this trouble, since I highly doubt the salary Carrie makes here would be able to support their family—if that's all they had coming in, I mean. And, come to think of it, there's the possibility you might not even have a shop for her to work in, isn't that right? If Parker Holt bought your building, that is?"

So Alexis had overheard Jo discussing Holt's possible buyouts with Ruthie. "I'm hoping for the best for my shop, Alexis," Jo said, then decided to ignore her exasperation and put this snoop to some use. "If you know of a way to track down my landlord, Max McGee, let me know. So far I haven't been able to reach him."

"Hmm." Alexis's eyes sparked interest. "Let me think on that, Jo."

"Great." Jo quickly moved from behind the counter and led her to the door. "Good luck with your dinner tonight."

Alexis nodded absently, clearly already working busily on her Max McGee assignment. Jo wondered whether the woman was actually holding a dinner party or if it was simply a silly ruse to get into Jo's shop. No matter. At least she was finally going out. Jo locked the door behind her with a firm click. If she'd had a shade, she would have snapped it down. She put it on her mental list to get one.

Jo returned to the stockroom. "Sorry about that, Randy," she said, sincerely hoping he hadn't picked up any of Alexis's whispers.

"No problem."

"I won't open that door to another soul, I promise. Even if they sob on their knees that their child's project requires purchasing my poster board and paints immediately or all chances of making it into Harvard will be destroyed."

Randy grinned. "I'm almost finished here, anyway."

"It's looking really good, Randy."

"I'll clean up the mess before I leave and stack your boxes back in here if you'll show me where you want them. And don't worry, these shelves are good and strong. They'll hold what you had stored here before, and then some, without any trouble."

"Terrific." Jo went out to her desk to get Randy's check ready, thinking that his modest fee had been well earned. Alexis may not be willing to overlook the man's past stumbles, but Jo was more than happy to help him steady himself. And if her payment added a bright spot or two into his possibly drab life, such as maybe sharing a nice meal with his girlfriend, all the better.

As Jo pulled out her shop's checkbook, she checked her watch. It was going on four. How long would Russ Morgan be at the police station, she wondered? She had decided, after meeting Xavier, that she wanted to talk to the lieutenant about the importance of looking elsewhere for a murder suspect.

Jo searched through her Rolodex for the police head-quarters number, thinking that Morgan's attitude toward her had improved significantly since their first encounter. Had he become more open-minded in general, though? There was, she decided, only one way to find out.

Chapter 12

Jo wound her way through the maze of desks to Lieutenant Morgan's office, aware that, unlike preceding times, she was looking forward to this visit. Once their adversarial relationship of the past had been resolved, albeit with some difficulty, Jo had been seeing the lieutenant with clearer eyes. She liked what she saw: an intelligent man—and, she had to admit, an attractive man, which was, of course, beside the point. What she needed most now was a man who would pay attention to and act on what she had come to tell him. The future of several innocent people depended on it.

Jo stopped outside Morgan's door and slipped off her jacket, then straightened the rose-colored turtleneck she had donned that morning. It was one of her favorites; Jo always felt the color added a bit of bloom to her too-pale cheeks. Now, as she prepared to see the lieutenant, the sweater's flattering quality popped into her mind, but she chided herself. How well she looked sitting across from Russ Morgan certainly wasn't going to automatically win him over to her side. She raised her hand to knock at his door, then paused and smiled. It couldn't hurt, though. She tapped.

Morgan's voice called out a brisk, "Come in."

"Thanks for seeing me," she said, entering the familiar spare, utilitarian room.

Morgan rose from behind his steel desk and waved her to a seat. "What's this about?"

"Parker Holt's murder," she said, pulling up her chair.

"You remembered something you forgot to mention the other night?"

"No, nothing like that." At the lieutenant's quizzical look Jo plunged into her explanation, hoping he would take it the way she wanted him to. "Russ," she began, using his first name deliberately, and caught a twitch of one eyebrow, "I know the police are focusing on Xavier Ramirez as the murderer of Parker Holt, and I understand why. But I think you're making a mistake."

"That's interesting—Jo." Morgan laid a slight emphasis on her name, and Jo wasn't sure if he was teasing or showing annoyance. "Do you have a reason for this opinion?"

"For one thing, Carrie and Dan know Xavier quite well, and they are both certain he would never do something like this. I also met with the man and came away convinced of his sincerity when he says he's innocent. He disliked Holt, was angry with him, but he didn't wish him dead."

"And your experience with interrogating subjects is what?"

"I know, you're the professional. I'm not. Although you have to admit I do have some experience in your field."

"And almost got yourself killed because of it."

"This is an entirely different situation. I'm not confronting a murderer; I'm simply trying to keep a man from being falsely charged. A decent man."

"A man who can't prove where he was at a very critical time."

"Yes, he told me that. But how many people can come

up with concrete evidence of their whereabouts twenty-four hours a day?" As she said that, Jo's mind flashed back to Xavier's uneasiness as she questioned him about his grocery store trip. Surely, though, it was simply worry on his part. "A person," she said, "shouldn't have to prove he's innocent, should he?"

"It would certainly help."

Jo had a sudden inspiration. "What about the grocery store?" she asked. "Do they have security cameras? Perhaps you could find Xavier standing in the checkout line on one of them."

"They have cameras," Morgan said, and Jo's hopes leaped. "Unfortunately," he continued, "they weren't in good operational order that day. Or for several days before that, either. Nobody had checked on them for a while, and the images they recorded are indecipherable."

Jo groaned. "But I still believe there are others you need to look at besides Xavier."

"Such as?"

"Such as Mallory Holt. She apparently has a romantic connection to a man named Sebastian Zarnik. Parker Holt wasn't a model husband, which I'm sure you know. It's possible his wife may have decided on a quick way out, isn't it?"

Morgan scowled. "Sounds like you're poking around into other people's business."

"Which I wouldn't normally do, believe me, except for the dire situation Xavier Ramirez finds himself in."

"I would advise against harassing the victim's widow, or anyone else. Stick to your knitting needles and paints."

"I'm not *harassing*, Russ. I'm simply gathering information. And trying to stick to my craft affairs doesn't work, as you might remember. Problems don't stay away just because you stick your head in the sand. Russ, if the police continue to regard Xavier as a suspect there will be irreparable damage done to his life as well as that of Dan

Brenner's. Dan is already losing business over this, which of course impacts Xavier's income. People will never think of either of them in the same way. Then there's all the pain it's causing to Sylvia, his wife."

Russ Morgan scowled again, but Jo couldn't tell whether it was from uncomfortable awareness of the effects of his investigation or anger at her bringing it up.

"I'm sorry," she said, "I wouldn't—"

"Jo, you're really getting into something you should leave alone. I understand your concern for your friends, but this is a police matter, a serious police matter, and you're going to have to trust us to deal with." Morgan looked at his watch and stood up. "Now please, go back to your shop, be patient, and be assured the police are doing everything possible to get to the truth of the matter."

It was Jo's turn to scowl. "You sound like one of those police spokespersons talking to the press."

"Simply because a statement is used often doesn't mean it's untrue. Trust us, Jo."

Jo stood up. "I will if you'll promise to keep an open mind."

Morgan gave a crooked half smile and opened his door for her. "Always." He ushered her out courteously, but Jo couldn't help feeling pushed out. She stood for a moment outside his closed door, wondering if there was more she should have said, something that would have caught his attention. Failing to come up with anything, she wound her way back through the desks, hearing phones ringing and computer keys clicking. A couple of faces glanced up at her and nodded cordially, but Jo left feeling dissatisfied, as though Russ Morgan had simply gone through the motions of hearing her out. His advice to stay out of police business could be interpreted as *don't waste my time with things I'm not really interested in.* Had she made any positive impact on him at all? she wondered.

Jo pushed out of the building and paused a moment to

pull on her gloves against the cold. As she did so, a black car pulled up at the curb nearby, and the driver got out to hold open the back door for a familiar figure in a dark overcoat. Mayor Kunkle. Was he coming to see Lieutenant Morgan as well? Kunkle climbed out, then paused to straighten his coat before striding into Abbotsville's police headquarters.

Jo remembered Ina Mae's description of Mallory Holt as being like a daughter to Kunkle. Warren Kunkle, as mayor, obviously had power in Abbotsville. Was he using some of that power to influence the murder investigation of his niece's husband? If so, how open would Russ Morgan be to such pressure? They were two worrying questions to which Jo had no answer.

Jo intended to stop in at Carrie and Dan's, but didn't want to walk in at their dinnertime, even though she always felt welcome to join them. She decided instead to grab a quick meal at TJ's, a restaurant whose food and service was a step up from fast-food burgers but still well below pricier fine dining. Jo felt in need of the comfort food they offered, and a mental check of her own cupboards came up with nothing even approaching that.

As she was heading for an empty booth near the back of TJ's, she passed one holding two men in casual attire, one middle-aged, the other much younger. They both munched on nachos and each grasped a mug of beer. Pausing a moment by their booth to allow a tray-laden waitress to pass by, Jo caught mention of Parker Holt's name. She immediately slipped into the vacant booth behind the men. Maddeningly, as soon as she sat down, their conversation switched to basketball.

Jo ordered the home-style meatloaf with sides of mashed potatoes and green beans, and as she waited for it, she sipped at her water and mulled over her busy day. The conversation that floated over the top of her booth was sprinkled with college-team names and basketball stats, and Jo tuned them out as she decided which of her day's happenings she would share with Carrie and Dan. When the waitress brought her food, one of the men in the next booth asked for more nachos and a second round of beer. About the time Jo had reduced her potato volcano by half, she overheard: "So, you think she'll forget about suing Holt?" from the booth next door. Her fork froze in midair.

"Hard to sue a dead man," a deeper voice, possibly belonging to the older man, answered.

"Yeah, but can't you sue his estate?" Jo pictured the younger one asking this.

"I don't know. She always said she didn't have a strong case to begin with. Pretty much her word against Holt's, I guess."

"But Holt fired her from Pheasant Run for no good reason!"

"He claimed her work wasn't up to par. She said it was because of, well, you know."

"But that sucks! He lies, and she's got a black mark on her résumé."

The younger voice had risen with that last remark, but he had obviously had been shushed with a gesture, because he suddenly lowered his voice and Jo could distinguish no more words.

Jo chewed her food as silently as she could, but all she managed to hear from then on had to do with car engines and gas octane. She waited, but the men eventually called for their bill, paid it, and got up to leave. Jo peered around her booth as they walked away, seeing only the backs of two jacket-clad men, the younger of the two slipping a baseball cap onto his buzz-cut hair.

When the waitress brought her coffee, Jo said, "The two guys that were in the next booth. I think I know them, but I'm not sure."

"Who, Jim and Gary? You've probably been in their hardware store. Price's, over on Mulberry?"

"Right, that must be it. Thanks."

Jo took her coffee and stirred at it, thinking over the few remarks she had overheard and felt, despite the hearty meal of meatloaf and two sides, hungry for more.

Chapter 13

"Hi, Aunt Jo," Amanda greeted her at the door. "We just finished dinner, but there's tuna casserole left. Want some?"

"No thanks, honey," Jo said, giving her a quick hug. "I'm fine. How's it going?"

"Okay. We're going on a field trip tomorrow, up to the State House in Annapolis, while the senate's in session. No school all day—yea!"

"Sounds great."

"But you still have that book report to turn in, Amanda." Carrie's voice sailed out from the kitchen. "Better get working on it."

"I will."

Jo followed the voice and found Carrie wiping off the kitchen table. "Have you had dinner?" Carrie asked, looking up. Her friend smiled, but Jo saw worry harbored deep in her eyes.

"Yes, a hearty meal at TJ's, along with a teaser of an appetizer."

Carrie's eyebrows rose, and Jo said, "I'll tell all in a minute. How's everything going here?"

"Not too bad."

"Hi, Aunt Jo!" Charlie's voice came from the family room along with the sound of a *Seinfeld* rerun.

Jo poked her head through the doorway. "Hey, Charlie. How're you feeling?"

Charlie was stretched out in the battered recliner. He muted the television with the remote in his hand. "Gettin' there. Good enough to go back to school tomorrow. No PE though." He grinned.

"Which means you better turn off that TV and hit the books too," Carrie called from the kitchen.

"I will, right after this. It's almost over."

"What," Jo asked, "you found a *Seinfeld* you only saw nineteen times instead of the usual thirty?"

"Maybe only five. It's one of their real early ones. Everyone looks a little weird in it."

"I'll leave you to the weirdness," Jo said, smiling. She was glad to see Charlie looking—and sounding—better than he had a couple of days ago. She rejoined Carrie.

"Coffee?" Carrie asked.

"No, thanks." Jo pulled out a kitchen chair and sat down. "What do you know about Jim Price?"

"Jim Price? Of Price's Hardware?"

"That's him. He and someone named Gary—is that his son? Anyway, they were sitting in the next booth at TJ's tonight." Jo told Carrie what she'd overheard.

"Well, that's interesting." Carrie pushed her dishwasher's On button, waited a moment for it to start chugging, then sat down across from Jo.

"When I was at Pheasant Run today," Jo said, "one of the residents there mentioned having overheard fights between Parker Holt and his former manager—a woman."

"You didn't get a name?"

"No, and I didn't hear one mentioned tonight, either.

But I'm betting it's the same person. I think I'll go back to Pheasant Run and see what more I can learn."

"Why were you there in the first place?" Carrie asked. "You're not thinking of moving, are you?"

"No," Jo laughed. "I wouldn't qualify for two major reasons—age and income." She explained about taking Loralee to the active adult community after first stopping in at Sylvia's.

"I wanted to meet Xavier myself, and now that I have I agree with you wholeheartedly, Carrie. He is not the kind of man to arrange that trap for Parker Holt. But he has a major problem in trying to prove it." Jo told Carrie about his hour spent buying groceries just about the time Holt's trap was being set.

"Oh dear. No receipt, and no witness he can bring forward?"

Jo shook her head. "And nothing recorded on the store's security cameras, either. Just his word, which won't be enough for the police. Unless we can come up with a better suspect for them." She was about to tell Carrie about Mallory Holt when she heard Charlie's television snap off and a major groan erupt as he eased out of his recliner. Charlie shuffled into the kitchen.

"Got any more of those cupcakes, Mom?"

"Yes, and one will be in your lunch bag tomorrow. If you're still hungry after the huge dinner I just saw you eat, you can take an apple upstairs with you."

Charlie appeared to think this over, then shook his head. "That's all right. Is Dad going to be on the computer long? Mrs. Thomas was going to e-mail me some stuff to go over for American history."

"Dad's working on bills, but I'm sure he'll let you have the computer for a while."

"Okay. See you later, Aunt Jo." Charlie lifted a hand in farewell, his other arm bracing his middle as he walked carefully through the kitchen.

" 'Night, Charlie. Hope it all goes well tomorrow."

Carrie waited until Charlie could be heard making his way carefully up the steps, then said, "Dan got another cancellation today. It was just an appointment for an estimate, but it was on a sunroom addition and would have been a significant job. I know he's up there trying to juggle our finances again and probably tearing his hair out with worry."

"I'm sorry to hear that. I spoke with Russ Morgan, by the way, trying to point him in other directions than Xavier's. But I'm not sure I succeeded."

"What other directions?"

Jo told her about hearing of Mallory Holt's lunch with Sebastian Zarnik from Alexis and sending Ina Mae to check it out.

"So Ina Mae thought it made Mallory a good suspect?"

"Yes, and she's also going to double-check on the timing of Mallory's presence at the committee meeting Alexis told me about."

"But if Mallory's alibi is verified, that lets her off the hook."

"Ah, but you're forgetting the boyfriend."

"You're thinking they could have worked together?"

"It's possible, isn't it? I mean, she could have given him a key to the house, plus the security code, then gone off on her shopping trip followed by the committee meeting while Zarnik did the dirty work."

"But," Carrie said, frowning thoughtfully, "that puts *him* on the hook. Wouldn't the police then be looking at him?"

"I would hope so. But I don't know how much interference Mayor Kunkle might be running. He might believe his niece is innocence personified. Or he might worry about *his* reputation suffering if she starts to look bad. He may have let her convince him her relationship with Zarnik is simply an art-related friendship."

Jo heard footsteps thump down the stairs along with

Dan's voice calling, "Hon, we got any more coffee?" Dan appeared, coffee mug in hand. "Oh, hi, Jo. Didn't realize you were here."

Carrie took Dan's mug from him and carried it to the half-filled carafe staying warm on its burner. Dan leaned casually against the counter as he waited, but Jo sensed his tension, seeing his hand grip the back of one of the chairs with knuckle-whitening pressure.

"Carrie and I have been trying to pull up murder suspects to replace Xavier," Jo said. "If you have enough coffee, Carrie," she added, "I'll take some too."

"There's plenty. Cupcake, anyone?"

Jo smiled and shook her head, as did Dan. He pulled a half gallon of milk from the refrigerator, poured some into his mug, then added two teaspoons of sugar, causing Jo, who took her coffee black, to wince at the sweetness.

"So," Dan asked, sitting down, "who have you come up with?"

Carrie and Jo alternated at filling him in. Dan nodded as he listened, but looked less than impressed. "Got a lot of ground to leap over between 'mad as hell' and 'murderous.'"

"Not any more than the police have for Xavier," Carrie protested.

"I'm going to work hard on closing the gaps," Jo said. "Have you had a chance to talk to any of Parker Holt's employees?"

Dan shook his head. "A couple, but all I got was the usual griping. Too much work, not enough pay, skimpy overtime."

"No tales of deep grudges?"

"Not yet, but I'll check with a few more, see if I can dig up anything."

Dan ran his hands through his hair, then scrubbed at his face. He looked at Jo. "Carrie's probably told you I'm losing jobs over this. With Holt's basement renovation to do, I had held off several other smaller jobs. Now they're all afraid to hire me until they know what's what." He paused, swallowed, and said, "This situation has to be cleared up, and fast, or we're in real danger of going under."

Carrie reached over to grasp Dan's arm. "It will be. It has to be."

Jo looked at her two best friends in all the world, her heart aching for them. It *will* be cleared up, she vowed, realizing as she did that she was promising to herself what she had been appalled to hear Loralee promise the Ramirezes just that morning.

Could she clear Xavier by finding out who really murdered Parker Holt? She wanted to, very badly. But would desire translate into success? Certainly it could at least translate into action.

Jo drained her mug and stood up. "I've got to go, guys. I've got a lot to do."

Chapter 14

Jo put down the phone at her shop desk. She waited for Carrie to finish with her customer, a knitting enthusiast who had just bought several skeins of beautiful, apricot-colored wool.

The knitters of Abbotsville had been flocking back to the shop all morning, word having spread that Carrie was back. Jo was grateful that any negativity from Dan's connection to Parker Holt didn't seem to have spilled over to Carrie, and wondered idly if there was something about knitters that made them more reasonable than others. Perhaps the rapid motion of their fingers acted like some sort of yoga exercise, calming their brains and making leaping to ridiculous conclusions less likely. If so, she'd like to see all of Abbotsville take up knitting.

And come to her craft shop to buy their wool.

After the woman exited the store amidst happy promises to bring back her finished sweater to show, Jo called over to Carrie. "It's all set."

Carrie replaced a knitting magazine, one of several her

recent customer had paged through, and headed over. "Zarnik's going to see you?"

"Two o'clock. He assumes I'm in the market for an expensive, original painting."

"And how do you suppose he got that idea?"

"Beats me." Jo shrugged and grinned. "All I said is that I had this big, empty space on my wall in need of something beautiful and unique. I didn't mention the many other big, empty spaces in my house that were in need of, oh, say, a decent chair to sit on, or a carpet to cover, or even certain empty shelves in my pantry."

"No use bombarding the man with details, right?"

"No use at all. But I still have a problem. Since Zarnik didn't seem to recognize my name, he hopefully thinks I'm someone with money to spare rather than the struggling owner of a craft shop. But I don't have anything to wear that will prolong that assumption when I go see him. No designer rags whatsoever are hanging in my closet."

"Then why not just go with rags? Do the Bohemian look that says, 'I'm so rich I don't have to bother dressing the part.'"

"Ah, good idea! Raggedy jeans, a few interesting layers on top, maybe scarves wrapped artistically. Plus those beaded necklaces and earrings I've been making lately for the workshops—they look a lot more expensive than they are. Oh! And I'll carry one of Sylvia's bags. I have a gorgeous one I kept aside for Ina Mae's birthday present to her daughter-in-law. She won't mind if I borrow it for a few minutes in my effort to clear Xavier."

At mention of Sylvia and Xavier, Carrie's face grew solemn. "I spoke to Sylvia this morning. The police want Xavier to come in again today for more questioning. I advised her to contact the public defender's office. I'm certain Xavier would qualify, financially."

Jo nodded. "That's good advice. I hope they follow it. Loralee said she'd get her church group to help them out in the food department." Jo stood up from her desk. "That leaves it up to me to find a strong reason for the police to look elsewhere."

She looked at Carrie worriedly. "I hope I can do it."

Jo knocked on the door of Sebastian Zarnik's studio. She had left Carrie to mind the shop after making numerous promises to be very careful, and made a quick stop at the house to assemble her "wealthy, but not flaunting it" outfit. She wasn't sure that what she had come up with would convince Zarnik, even with the piled-on costume jewelry, and only hoped he would be more interested in showing his art than in spotting holes—literally—in her costume.

Zarnik opened the door, and Jo found herself facing an incredibly attractive, thirty-something man. Although on consideration his features were actually unremarkable—average nose and mouth, high cheekboned face on a slim, six-foot frame—she realized his eyes made all the difference. Deep blue and thick lashed, they had focused on Jo's face as if it were precisely what he had longed to see all day. Possibly all his life. Jo understood Mallory Holt's attraction to him. The man was magnetizing.

"Mrs. McAllister?" he asked.

"Yes." Jo tore her eyes away from his hypnotic ones and glanced at his studio beyond. "Thank you for letting me come on such short notice."

"My pleasure." He seized her hand and drew her in.

Jo entered an artist's studio similar to the many she had been in, filled with canvases, paint, and paint-stained worktables, along with the debris of everyday living. She had never yet met an artist who cared about ridding his work space of food containers, empty tubes of paint, or just plain dirt and dust. It brought back strong memories of her life with Mike, though his debris had been pieces of metal rather than paint. She had protested often enough in those days when the accumulation got to the "wading" level. But living alone now in Abbotsville, she felt her much tidier home had the uncomfortable feel of emptiness, of the kind no mere things could fill.

Jo stopped short in front of an abstract painting that, in its shape and predominance of black and gray, reminded her of one of Mike's metal sculptures. She drew in a quick breath.

Zarnik mistook her reaction for admiration and moved closely next to her to gaze at it. "I call this one *Conundrum*. It's done in acrylics, which I've taken to lately. I find they give me more freedom of expression."

Jo had heard that phrase many times before and it still meant little to her. She had decided, though, to play the art novice with Zarnik and challenge nothing, so she merely nodded and smiled.

"Would you like a glass of wine?" Zarnik asked. "I have a very pleasant Merlot, or, if you prefer, a chilled bottle of Chablis."

"Merlot would be nice, thank you." Jo followed him to a small kitchen area and watched as he opened the Merlot and filled two glasses he had sitting there. She spotted a large, open box of tools on the floor beside some wooden frames and rolled canvas. "You stretch your own canvas," she asked, then instantly kicked herself for asking something that sounded art knowledgeable.

"Always." He handed her a glass.

Jo took a sip. "That's quite a collection of tools. It must be a complicated operation," she said, hoping to cover her misstep.

Zarnik smiled. "They're not all for my work. My landlord is unreliable on things like maintenance. I've gradually acquired tools for calking leaky windows as well as replacing a faucet or two."

Jo grinned. "I'll bet he's reliable on collecting the rent, though!"

Zarnik laughed. "You'd collect on that bet." He clinked his wineglass against hers. "To landlords!"

"To landlords!" Jo drank her wine, her thoughts flying to the Caribbean where her landlord might be, sipping his own wine and possibly counting his money from the sale of her building. To landlords, indeed!

"Do you have an image of the kind of painting you want?" Zarnik asked, leading her back to the first painting. "For that space of yours?"

"I'm trying to branch out," Jo said. "To move beyond the pretty picture that everyone chooses because the colors match their couch. I want something that will make me *think* every time I look at it." She shrugged and smiled, she hoped ingenuously. "That's my starting point, anyway."

"A very good starting point, I'd say." Zarnik turned a spellbinding look at her.

Jo dragged her gaze toward the black and gray canvas, examined it for a moment, then moved on to a more colorful piece. Zarnik followed closely enough that she could feel his breath near her ear. She made positive-sounding murmurs toward the colorful painting then continued down the line of several pieces, placed on easels or leaning against the wall.

"I'm planning a show, soon," he said. "Most of these will be packed up and shipped off before long, so you've come at a fortunate time."

"A show?" Jo said. "How exciting. Where?"

"The final arrangements are still being worked out, but it will probably be in Philadelphia." He mentioned a gallery Jo had heard of. She was impressed and wondered how this had come about. Zarnik's work was good, but to her mind not that good. Was the gallery owner a woman? she wondered. Someone who perhaps had been mesmerized by Zarnik's persona?

Zarnik offered the explanation himself. "Mrs. Lucy Kunkle, our mayor's wife, has bought one or two of my paintings. She has connections in Philadelphia."

Ah, Mallory's Aunt Lucy. Jo pictured Lucy twisting an arm of one of her connections, with Mallory in turn twisting her aunt's arm. "How wonderful of her to be so supportive."

"Yes, well, you know how it goes. The success of the local talent in turn reflects well on the town."

"Mmm-hmm." Jo sidestepped to a canvas that was covered in swirls of reds and yellows. "Lucy Kunkle is related to Parker Holt, isn't she? That man who was murdered recently?"

Zarnik stiffened a bit but nodded. "I believe she was. Did you know him?"

"By reputation only. Did you?"

"I've met his wife."

"Yes, Mallory. What a tragedy. It's all everyone is talking about lately. I understand she was with her aunt when it happened."

"Possibly." Zarnik gestured to the red and yellow canvas. "I haven't titled this one yet. If you're interested in it, perhaps you can suggest a title for it."

Jo tilted her head at the painting. "With those strong colors spinning about, I might call it *Turmoil*."

"Turmoil. Not bad. Would *Turmoil* fit your needs? Does it make you think?"

"Yes, but maybe not the right kind of thoughts. I'm not sure I need more turmoil right now, painted or not. Probably," she said with a smile, "something called *Resolution* would be a better choice." Jo moved over to a gentler piece, full of softly floating greens and blues. "This one brings to mind a day on the bay. Or maybe a field of grass blowing in the wind, with bluebells." She checked its title, which was *Aquarius*. "Oh."

"The thing about abstract art is that it can be anything you want it to be. Or nothing. It can be just paint. Or it can be beauty." Zarnik focused on her again with those eyes of his. Jo struggled to stay cool.

For that purpose, as well as to keep the subject on her

murder investigation, Jo turned away, saying, "No, now that I think about it, I was wrong about where Mallory was when it happened. She came *back* from an afternoon spent with her aunt, but she was actually at her club's committee meeting when it happened. To Parker, I mean."

"You may be right. I couldn't say."

"I only know because the police have been questioning just about everyone as to where they were that afternoon."

"Is that so?" Zarnik's smile was beginning to fade.

"Yes. Of course, it can't possibly help them. I mean, how many of us can say we were at a certain place and have friends or whatever to back us up with 'Yes, she was there. I saw her'?" Jo twirled the fringed end of the scarf she had tied as a sash about her waist. "Mallory, fortunately, had a whole committee of friends to verify where she was. I, on the other hand, was alone at the critical time, just as I'm positive half the people in town were.

"You," Jo continued, "were probably here, alone, working on your art. Am I right?"

Zarnik gave a small smile. "How did you guess?"

"It just proves my point," Jo said. "Alibis don't mean a thing. So it's a waste of time for the police to check for them. What they really need to look for is motive."

"Isn't that exactly what they're doing?" Zarnik said. "That handyman, I mean."

"Did he have a motive?" Jo asked. "I didn't see anything in the paper about a motive. What was it?"

Zarnik's thick eyelashes suddenly flickered. He must have realized that he had heard about Xavier's motive through Mallory Holt, but he clearly didn't want to admit this to Jo. "I might be wrong. I thought I'd heard someone say he had a connection to Holt, but I can't remember now what it was. Well, enough about this sordid subject. Have you seen anything displayed here that catches your interest? If not, perhaps we could discuss commissioning a work?"

Zarnik had just wriggled off her hook and put Jo onto

his own. Commission a painting? How would she get out
of that? Jo spotted a painting on the other side of the room
and pretended sudden ecstasy.

"Oh, isn't that one fantastic!" she exclaimed, rushing
over to it. The canvas was filled with squiggly lines of
bright colors, intersecting each other in a maze of spirals.
"I love it!" she cried.

Zarnik's smile returned. "I experimented with using
a paint spray gun for this. I think it turned out well."

Jo gushed for several minutes, spouting words she
rarely used such as "fabulous," "bewitching," and her least
favorite for its meaninglessness, "creative." Zarnik ex-
pounded on the difficulties he had run into with the process
and what precisely had been in his mind during the painting's development, then eased smoothly into its cost. Jo
suppressed a cough and managed to nod cooly as though
price were too coarse a topic to discuss. She continued on
for a few more minutes, changing her perspectives on the
painting often by backing up and moving from side to side,
then finally announced, "As much as I love it, I'm just going to have to sleep on it before I make my decision."

"I understand completely," Zarnik assured her. "But I
wouldn't wait too long if I were you. As I said, the show
will be coming up, plus one or two people have expressed
interest in the piece."

"Then I definitely won't take long." Jo thanked him profusely for his time and eased her way to the door.

Zarnik took her hand and fixed his incredible gaze on
her one last time left, and Jo found herself holding her
breath until the door finally closed behind her. She exhaled, pulled herself together, and headed toward her old
Toyota, which she had carefully parked around the corner
and out of sight. If she had learned anything at all at this
meeting, she decided, it was that Zarnik was an amazing
flirt. If Mallory Holt planned her future around him, Jo
wished her luck for the challenge it would be.

But she had also discovered that he had no clear alibi for the time Parker Holt was killed. Did the tools Jo had seen in his studio include wire cutters and strippers that would have been needed for the electrical trap? Possibly. Had they been used, though, for that purpose?

That question still remained.

Chapter 15

That evening, Jo pulled into the parking lot at Pheasant Run next to the blue Chevy Malibu that held Ina Mae and Loralee. Javonne stood waiting beside her SUV, and the headlights of Vernon's white pickup appeared in Jo's rearview mirror as it turned into the lot.

"Thanks, everyone," Jo said when they'd all gathered on the sidewalk. "I appreciate your agreeing to move our workshop over here tonight."

"No problem," Javonne said. "I've always wanted to see this place. This is my chance."

"Angie Palmer certainly set this up in a hurry," Loralee said.

"When I called this morning to suggest it," Jo explained, "Angie said the ladies we spoke to yesterday morning had been talking to their friends, who all immediately expressed interest, so she knew she had a ready-made group. Bringing you all here works great for me, for the time factor of doing one instead of two workshops, plus"—Jo grinned—"for the help I know you'll provide in the sleuthing department." Jo had updated them all on what she had learned recently. "Now," she said, "if everyone will please grab as much as they can carry from my car and follow me?"

The group gathered up boxes, then followed Jo in a line as she led the way through the front entrance of Pheasant Run and down its corridors. She couldn't help feeling like a mother hen with her chicks, especially on hearing Loralee let out occasional peeps when one of her smaller boxes slid atop her stack.

As they entered the Great Room, Jo saw that tables had been arranged at the far end for her workshop, and she headed there to deposit her pile on the largest, with her "chicks" following suit. Jo unpacked her bead boards first and handed them to Javonne to spread around.

"Oh, you're here!" Angie Palmer breezed through the door. "Great! I told everyone to show up at seven. Do you need anything more than what we've set up?"

"No, this looks perfect." She introduced Angie to her regulars, and by the time they'd all shucked their coats and begun opening up Jo's bead boxes, the Pheasant Run ladies had begun drifting in. Jo welcomed them, recognizing Loralee's friend, Betty, and her companions Donna and Celia, among a few others. She waved everyone to seats around the smaller tables and listened as the conversational noise level rose. Good, she thought. If this is a chatty group, the better to learn a few things from them. The only problem, though, was that Angie Palmer was still hanging around. Jo feared her presence might quash discussion of Pheasant Run's management problem with the late Parker Holt. She'd have to come up with a way to get rid of her.

"Everyone," Jo called out to get the group's attention, then tapped her pliers on the table and raised her voice to shout, "Ladies!" Several heads swiveled, and the group quieted down. Jo began her class.

"You each have at your place a bead design board. This is what you will create your necklace on." Jo paused as the women picked up their boards and examined them. "As you see they have three channels. That is where you will lay your wire, or wires if you decide you want a multistrand necklace. You will also have to decide on the length of your necklace. These bead boards, as you see, have lines and measurements marked on them. They will help you find your center as well as line up your beads in a nicely balanced way.

"The boards are flocked to keep your beads from rolling away on you. Plus you can use the handy pocket wells at the corners to separate your beads and to hold them."

The group was giving her their rapt attention, so Jo went on to explain about the various clasps they could choose from, and then held up a few sample necklaces to give them some ideas to start with.

"The cost of your necklace will depend on the particular beads you choose and the number of them. For instance, these plastic beads are very inexpensive but quite colorful and appropriate for a certain type of necklace, whereas the gemstones, especially the larger ones, get pricier. Then there's these Swarovski crystals, which are beautiful but will add to your cost. But you might be happy with a single, large stone strung as a pendant, with perhaps only a few smaller beads and spacers added to set it off. All of my bead boxes are labeled for price to help you estimate, but don't worry, I'll total it all up for you when you're ready."

The questions came then, all at once, and Jo did her best to answer them, explaining that she would help them individually with things like putting crimps at strategic points to keep beads in place, and attaching clasps. "Just holler when you need me." Considering the noise level the group had risen to earlier, she imagined the "hollers" would need to be lusty ones to be noticed, but she felt sure this group would manage.

The ladies milled about the circle of bead boxes, which

Jo had arranged by color. She listened to the hum of voices, as each dithered over which beads to choose, how densely to string them, what colors went with what, and so on. There were dozens of decisions to make, and Jo understood how overwhelming it could be to the first-time beader. She hovered nearby, pitching in with advice. Unfortunately, she noticed Angie Palmer also hovering closely, apparently just as fascinated as the other ladies, though not participating.

"Loralee," Jo heard Loralee's friend Betty ask, "have you decided on buying a condo?"

Loralee looked up from her bead board on which she had lined up several pink beads of various sizes. She shook her head. "It's a big decision."

"If you have any questions," Angie, whose ears had perked up, quickly jumped in, "I'd be more than happy to try to answer them."

"Thank you, dear," Loralee said politely, but turned back to her bead choices.

Vernon, Jo saw, had lined up an attractive set of beads on his board, a soft combination of beiges and browns, which he said his daughter Patty had requested. He settled down to begin stringing, and Jo demonstrated the crimping process to him with her needlenose pliers as several others of the class leaned over to watch.

Javonne brought her bead lineup over for Vernon's approval. "What do you think?" she asked. "Should I go with the blue and green, or stick with all blue?"

Vernon studied Javonne's beads a moment, then said, "The blue and green works, but I'd arrange them like this." He moved several beads around to make a new pattern, which, Jo saw, improved the look considerably. Javonne agreed, smiling broadly and thanking Vernon profusely. A few of the ladies who had turned to watch held their bead boards out to him, asking, "What do you think?" Vernon looked each over, giving a thumbs up or offering suggestions for improvement.

Jo grinned. It appeared she had an unpaid assistant with her. If Vernon continued to progress as rapidly in this craft as he had been, he might be teaching her a few things before long.

One by one, the ladies finished picking out their beads and sat down to work at assembling their necklaces.

"If this turns out," Donna, the thin, dark-haired friend of Betty's said, "I'll want to wear it to the Abbotsville Founders Ball on Saturday. I have a gray dress that will be perfect once it has something bright at the neckline."

"But Donna," Betty asked, "are they still having the ball? Mallory Holt was in charge of it, you know, as president of the women's club."

"Oh, I hadn't thought of that!" Donna looked stricken.

"Surely the ball has been all arranged before, well, before this other thing happened," said Celia, the woman Jo remembered as having overheard fights between Parker Holt and Pheasant Run's first manager. Celia held her own work-in-progress around her neck and judged it for length, pulling the wire tighter, then looser over her blouse.

"Yes, don't worry, Donna," Ina Mae spoke up. "I talked with Sally Robinson just yesterday. The ball is still on, despite Mallory's state of affairs."

Donna looked relieved, and renewed work on her beads.

"What's happening with that man they think did it?" A woman in a bright flowered top over raspberry-colored pants asked. "I mean that Hispanic worker. Have they charged him?"

Jo exchanged a glance with Ina Mae, not happy with the implied assumption of Xavier's guilt. Ina Mae spoke first. "No one's been charged yet. Obviously, the police don't have any clear evidence yet on anyone."

"How is Mallory holding up, anyone know?" This from Betty Kidwell, whose three-tiered, multibeaded necklace, Jo could see, was going to take her more than one workshop to finish.

The flowery-topped woman said, "My hairdresser told me that Lucy Kunkle told her Mallory is devastated and barely able to function."

Jo caught Ina Mae's eye again and knew what she was thinking. Mallory was functioning well enough to meet Sebastian Zarnik for lunch. But Ina Mae wisely remained silent on this point.

The conversation drifted to the topics of life insurance and Medicare, with Angie Palmer continuing to linger. At one point, just as Jo began to despair of getting anything helpful from the women, she noticed Ina Mae in close discussion with Loralee. Loralee shook her head—at what Jo had no idea—but then crept over to Vernon. Loralee put her head down close to her former butcher, speaking softly, and Vernon nodded and looked back at Ina Mae. Jo wasn't sure what they were up to, but in a minute or so, as she helped Betty choose a clasp, she found out.

"Jo," Vernon said, standing up, "I'm finished. When you have a moment, would you total up the cost of my materials?"

"Of course," Jo said, reaching for Vernon's board, which held a lovely two-tiered "illusion" style necklace in browns and beiges, its beads widely spaced and seeming to float on their near-invisible wire.

"Miss Palmer?" Vernon turned to Angie. "If you wouldn't mind, I'd be very interested in taking a look at your model condo."

"Certainly!" Angie cried. She popped up from an empty table on which she'd half sat, watching over the workshop. "Are you and your wife thinking of joining us at Pheasant Run?"

"Well," Vernon began, and Jo was left to imagine the tale he spun as he drew the woman away from the group. She glanced over to Ina Mae and Loralee, whose eyes danced. Mission accomplished, they seemed to say, and Jo smiled back.

After a moment, Ina Mae pronounced to no one in particular, "Angie seems to be a very capable manager."

"Oh, yes," Betty agreed, and several other heads nodded. "I have no complaints with her whatsoever."

"Pheasant Run is fairly new," Ina Mae continued. "Has she been here from the start?" she asked, already aware, of course, of the answer.

"No," several voices hastened to enlighten her at once. Celia's, being the strongest and highest pitched, prevailed. "The first manager was a younger woman. She was the one who sold Ralph and me our Blue Jay."

"Oh," a tiny-voiced woman piped up. "Was that the pretty blonde woman who first showed Jim and me around? She wasn't here when we came back for a second look."

"Yes," Celia confirmed. "Blonde, slim, liked to wear a lot of perfume."

"Uh-huh." Several heads nodded agreement.

"Poison," Celia said, then, noticing startled looks, explained. "I mean, that was her perfume. Poison."

"Oh!" Titters rippled through the group.

"You mentioned something the other day about problems between her and Parker Holt," Jo said. "What sort of problems were they?"

"Well," Celia said, drawing a breath as well as the group's attention, "all I know is several people overheard them arguing. My next-door neighbor, Elaine, told me she was passing by the office on her way out to her doctor's appointment—Elaine suffers terribly from psoriasis, you know—and she heard Heather—that was her name, Heather Bannister—say she was going to sue. Then a man who sounded very much like Parker Holt started laughing. Elaine said it gave her the chills, the sort of laugh it was. He said something like, 'You even think of doing that and I'll . . .' and Elaine couldn't hear the rest. But she thought it must have been some kind of terrible threat because next thing we knew Heather was gone and no lawsuit ever materialized."

The ladies of the workshop were silent as they took in this story.

"Heather Bannister?" Javonne asked. "I'm trying to remember. Is she related to the Prices who have the hardware store on Mulberry?"

The ladies exchanged blank looks until Betty answered, "Not her. It's her husband who's Ellie Price's nephew."

Javonne nodded. "That must be it." She looked over at Jo and smiled slyly, her eyes seeming to ask, "How'd I do?"

"Excellent," Jo said aloud, then added, "I mean, your necklace turned out beautifully, Javonne."

The ladies near Javonne looked over, oohing and ahhing.

Jo, however, looked over to Ina Mae and Loralee. *Excellent*, she telegraphed. *You all get an A*.

Chapter 16

As they returned to their cars, Jo thanked the ladies and Vernon profusely for their help. Vernon had told her that Angie gave him an enthusiastic grand tour of the facilities, but that he had put her off about bringing his wife to see it, claiming Evelyn wouldn't even consider downsizing from their three-bedroom house until he cleaned forty years' worth of junk out of his garage and basement.

"It's the truth," he said. "She's been after me to clean them out. Whether she'd be at all interested in moving after I do it is a whole different story." He gave a hint of a smile. "I might forget to suggest it to her."

Jo laughed. "You like having your work space, huh?" Vernon had nodded.

Another senior citizen, Jo thought as she drove away from Pheasant Run, who felt attached to his home. Loralee hadn't said much more about her own dilemma, but Jo was sure it was eating at her. She'd noticed Loralee pulling out a roll of Tums from her purse a few times during the evening, which was not a good sign.

Jo drove into her quiet neighborhood, which seemed even more still than usual on this starless January night. Everyone, she thought, was likely wrapped snugly in their quilts, either in front of TVs or in warm beds.

Jo pulled into her garage, lowered the door, and left her beading supplies behind in the car. She slipped past her small jewelry workroom, repaired from its damage of four months ago but sitting unused, and vowed she would find the time to return to her beloved metal craft as soon as this Parker Holt problem was cleared up. She entered the welcoming warmth of her kitchen, hung her jacket on a hook near the door, and dropped her keys on the counter. Glancing over at her sparsely furnished living room, Jo pictured Sebastian Zarnik's paint-gun creation hanging on the wall and smiled, thinking how the artwork cost more than what she had paid for the entire secondhand contents of the room. Hopefully, Zarnik hadn't picked up on that fact.

She considered fixing a quick cup of tea, but decided, after the fullness of the day, her wiser choice was bed. Not too many minutes later, Jo had begun pulling back the comforter when the phone rang.

"Jo?" a male voice asked, and it took her a moment to recognize it.

"Rafe?" She hadn't run into Rafe Rulenski, the director of the Abbotsville Playhouse, for ages—or at least a couple of months.

"Sorry to call so late. We just finished up with rehearsals. How's that kid doing? The one who fell into the pit here?"

Knowing Rafe, Jo suspected he hadn't really called because of Charlie. The man was not known for a deep interest in the "little" people around him. The obvious proof was that Rafe didn't remember Charlie's name. But Jo played along.

"Charlie's doing okay. He started back at school today."

"Great. Glad to hear it. So it wasn't too bad, huh?"

"A couple of cracked ribs. Painful but not life threatening. He'll be happy to hear you asked about him." Only four days after Charlie's accident, but oh well.

"Right. Say, are you doing anything Saturday night?"

"Saturday?" This was a surprise.

"Yes. Like to go with me to the Founders Ball? It's a dreary, dress-up kind of thing, but I have to go. I thought it'd be a little less dreary if you came along."

What a silver-tongued devil this man was. Apparently the best her companionship could do was make his night a little less dreary.

Rafe plowed on. "It's one of those 'the whole town turns out' functions. I've got to be there, talking up the playhouse and the support it deserves. Mallory Holt made me promise to show up, and if I don't she'll have my head."

"Mallory Holt will be there?"

"Uh-huh. I know, it's only a couple days after her husband's funeral, but she says she'll still be there. 'The show must go on' and all that. So, what do you say?"

Hearing that Mallory Holt would be there had suddenly made the ball tempting. "I'd really like to," Jo said, "but I don't have anything appropriate to wear."

"No problem. You could probably find something in the playhouse's stash of costumes. They'll fit almost anyone. I'm borrowing one of their tuxes, myself."

Jo grinned, imagining what her choices might be. Did she want to arrive at the ball dressed like Mary Todd Lincoln, or perhaps Lady Macbeth? Somehow, neither seemed quite her thing. "I'll see if I can dig up something, maybe borrow a dress from a friend. It sounds like an interesting night, Rafe. Thanks for asking me."

"My pleasure. I'll pick you up at eight."

Jo hung up and climbed under the bed covers. So she'd finally get to meet Mallory Holt on Saturday night. Who else, she wondered, might be there?

Rafe's words—*I'll pick you up at eight*—ran through her head, words she hadn't heard from a man in a long time.

"It's not a date, Mike," she said as she closed her eyes, somehow feeling the need to explain. "He simply wants me along as a distraction, and I'm only going for Xavier and Dan's sake."

Either Mike had nothing to say on the subject, or Jo fell asleep within seconds.

The next morning, Jo was helping a customer select papers for an ongoing scrapbooking project when Carrie arrived. Carrie greeted them both, and though she had sounded fairly upbeat, to Jo's more finely tuned ear the worries of the last few days were taking their toll.

"How's your boy doing?" the customer asked. The red-haired, pleasantly attractive mother of two was putting together scrapbooks of her children's individual achievements, both athletic and scholarly. Jo realized the older child, a girl, might be about Charlie's age.

"He's doing well," Carrie answered. "Thank you for asking."

The woman smiled and finished up with her purchases, chatting casually with Jo about how busy and active her family was and how she expected to fill many a scrapbook over the years. She thanked Jo for her help and took off. Jo turned to Carrie and, hoping to perk her up a bit, filled her in on her evening at Pheasant Run.

"I'd like to try to talk with this Heather Bannister today, if you don't mind holding down the fort here again."

"No, not at all. I'm so grateful for all you're doing. So you think this former manager could be a suspect?"

"She's worth looking at, anyway. Anyone who had a beef with Parker Holt is someone I want to learn more about. Has Dan had any luck talking with Holt's workers?"

Carrie shook her head. "He hasn't come up with a thing." Carrie sighed, and looked at Jo with shadow-edged eyes. "Dan went to talk with Xavier last night. He's worried—I mean *more* worried—about him."

"Did things go badly for Xavier at the police station yesterday?"

"Yes and no. They still haven't charged him, which is a good thing. But Dan thinks they're still convinced Xavier's the one. But there's something else."

"What?"

"Dan's starting to get the feeling, and he swears he can't put his finger on it as to why or what it might be, but he's wondering if there's something Xavier is holding back."

Jo flashed back to her talk with Xavier at the apartment and remembered having the same feeling. It had something to do with the way Xavier looked when he spoke about his time—the critical time—spent picking up groceries. Was he merely envisioning that hour, trying to come up with someone who might remember he had been there? Or was it something else?

"That's not a good feeling," she said.

"No," Carrie agreed worriedly. "Not at all."

Price's Hardware was a modest-sized store whose windows were packed with things like advertising posters, power tools, and mailboxes. From what Jo could see as she peered through the merchandise, the store currently had only two customers. She hoped they would leave soon and not be speedily replaced. She entered the store, and one or two heads turned to glance her way. Jo feigned interest in a chart of paint colors as she waited for a chance to talk to the owner.

She decided the older man behind the counter, discussing the merits of a certain snowblower with a heavy-set man, must be Jim Price whom she'd only glimpsed at

TJ's. Dark haired with graying temples, he appeared to be around fifty. He was perhaps five foot ten and looked fit, as though he actually used many of the tools he stocked and sold.

Jo caught sight of a younger man coming out of a back room and thought he must be Jim's son, Gary. She recognized the buzz cut and now caught a resemblance to his father in his broad jaw and thick brows. Gary looked barely twenty-one, if that old. Jo remembered the youthful emotionalism in his voice as he complained about the unfairness of Heather Bannister's situation. He clearly had a lot of sympathy for her problem. Whether she was truly deserving of it was something Jo hoped to find out.

The snowblower customer wound up the discussion with a declaration that he'd think it over for a while. The second man moved forward and laid his purchases—two boxes of nails and a roll of duct tape—on the counter, and paid for them with a minimal exchange of words. When he left, Jim Price looked over to Jo and called out, "Help you with anything, miss?"

"I hope so," Jo said, and walked over. She introduced herself, then said, "I understand you're related to Heather Bannister."

"Heather?" Price said, surprised. "She's married to my wife's nephew. Why?"

"I've been talking to someone who had a problem as an employee of Parker Holt. A sexual harassment, loss-of-job problem. Mrs. Bannister used to work for Parker Holt at Pheasant Run. I'd very much like to ask her about her experience there. I wondered if you could put me in touch with her."

Gary Price left a box of chrome faucets he'd been unpacking and came over to where his father stood, his face animated. "Is there a class action suit or something in the works?" he asked. "Are you a lawyer?"

"No, I'm not. I'd simply like to see if Mrs. Bannister ran

into problems similar to this other former employee. It may or may not be of any benefit to Mrs. Bannister, but it would help us."

"Heather was fired by Parker Holt and she didn't deserve to be!" Gary said.

"We don't really know the whole story, miss," Jim Price said, tempering his son's statement. "I got the feeling Heather was fairly embarrassed over whatever happened and didn't want to talk about it that much. I don't know if she'll want to talk to you, but maybe it would help her to know she's not alone. How about I give her a call and see what she says?"

"That'd be great."

Price went to the back room, and in a moment Jo heard the sound of his deep voice talking into the phone. Gary fidgeted as they waited, and before long Price came back out. He nodded and handed Jo a slip of paper with an address on it.

"She says you could come over right now if you like. She's been trying to sell real estate since she left Pheasant Run. But things are pretty quiet in January."

"Thank you. I appreciate this."

A man and woman entered the store, so Jo took her leave, Price nodding soberly, and Gary looking like he wanted to run out with her and follow along. Jo hated that she might be leaving him with a more hopeful expectation for what she was doing than was warranted, but she didn't see any way of clearing that up that would still allow her to meet with Heather. Her first responsibility was clearly to Xavier and Dan. If it turned out that Heather Bannister had a connection to Parker Holt's murder, Jo would turn her in without a second thought.

And Gary would just have to handle it.

Chapter 17

Jo found Heather Bannister's house without much trouble. A two-story colonial, it looked more expensive than what an average young couple could afford. Jo wondered if this particular couple had banked on Heather's higher paying job at Pheasant Run at the time of its purchase, and if her change of employment put their ownership at risk. Real estate could be an iffy career, particularly, as Jim Price had mentioned, in January.

Jo tapped the heavy, brass knocker on the front door, and a striking blonde woman in her late twenties answered.

"Jo McAllister?"

"Yes, hi. And you must be Heather?"

The woman acknowledged she was, smiled, and invited Jo in. She wore a blue cable-knit turtleneck that set off a perfect complexion and black knit pants that clung to her slim figure. Her blonde hair hung smoothly just below her chin in a cut that reminded Jo of a local news anchor—casual and chic.

"I was pretty surprised," Heather said, "when Kevin's

Uncle Jim called." She took Jo's jacket and hung it on a brass coat tree in the corner.

"I appreciate you're willingness to see me," Jo said, "and I want to make clear right away that I'm not a lawyer."

"But you had questions about my employment at Pheasant Run?" Heather led Jo into a living room decorated in pastels, with glass-topped tables and much light. A wedding photo dominated one of the side tables, showing a smiling couple beside an elaborate wedding cake. Heather gestured to one of the two sofas, inviting Jo to sit, and asked, "Coffee or anything?"

"No, thanks. I'm fine. To answer your question, yes, I wanted to know about your experience working for Parker Holt. I don't mean to be intrusive, but someone I know had a fairly bad experience in his employ, and I need to know if she was alone in that."

Heather crossed her legs, and one foot, clad in an ankle boot, bounced. "You know, I think I'd like something to drink. Come on with me to the kitchen. We can talk there." She jumped up and led Jo into a sparkling kitchen, one that didn't look much used, with black granite countertops and stainless steel appliances. Heather took a bottle of white wine from the refrigerator and pulled glasses from a nearby cabinet. She set one down in front of Jo, who had slid onto a tall stool on the other side of the counter, and filled it without asking, then filled her own.

Heather took a long sip from her glass, then set it down, staring at it. "My time working at Pheasant Run was enlightening, to say the least," she said.

Jo took a taste from her own glass and waited.

"I was doing a damn good job there," Heather said. "I came in when the place was just ready for occupancy, and those condos were 70 percent sold when I left in a year."

"Then why were you fired?"

Jo watched a series of emotions fly over the woman's

face, the mascara-coated lashes flicking and her highly glossed lips pressing tightly.

"Because I found out what Parker Holt was doing."

"What was that?"

"Misusing the condo fees, for one thing." At Jo's raised eyebrows, Heather elaborated. "It took me awhile to catch on. But one day I spotted the landscape crew that was supposed to be sprucing up the grounds of Pheasant Run taking off in their trucks with loads of shrubs and seed and stuff. When I asked one of the workers about it later, he said they had gone to Parker's house and worked on his yard. I drove by his house, and it was looking a whole lot better than it had before."

"Did you ask Holt about it?"

"No. I convinced myself it was a one-time thing and that he had paid them out of his own pocket. But then it was clear they were going there regularly, cutting grass, planting flowers, pruning. And things that were supposed to be planted on the condo grounds, weren't. I checked into it. Those shrubs and stuff were paid for by the condo fees. And the crew was getting paid from the same fund for the hours they spent at Parker's house."

Heather took another gulp of her wine. She leaned an elbow on the counter and twirled her glass on the granite countertop. "I finally asked him what was going on. He just blew it off and said not to worry about it. But I did worry about it, and I started noticing other things like the inflated cost for furniture in the Great Room and for the exercise equipment in the fitness area. I'm sure the difference went into Parker's pocket."

"So he fired you because you caught on to him?"

"Yes."

"But wasn't he worried you'd blow the whistle?"

"Oh, he took care of that." One side of Heather's glossy mouth pulled up.

"How?"

"When I threatened him with exposure, he threatened me right back, said he'd destroy my marriage."

"Your marriage? How could he do that?"

"You have to understand. Parker Holt has a reputation." Heather tossed her head, flicking the blonde hair off her face. "People here know he plays around. Sometimes he uses that to his own advantage. He threatened to tell my husband we had an affair. That all those evenings I worked late were evenings spent with him. And if I didn't keep my mouth shut, he'd claim I was just a jilted lover, trying to get even. I knew he'd make good on that threat. I couldn't risk it. I was afraid he could cook the books enough to cover his tracks. He had all the power on his side."

"Pretty rotten," Jo said.

"He was," Heather agreed.

She held up the wine bottle. "More?"

"So what did you think of her?"

It was early Saturday morning, and Jo stood in front of a mirror in Javonne's bedroom. Javonne's dentist husband was downstairs fixing pancakes for their kids' breakfast, and Jo had been invited to rummage through Javonne's closet for something to wear to the Founders Ball that night. Dresses lay scattered across Javonne and Harry's king-size bed, and Jo was filling Javonne in on her talk with Heather Bannister during the process of trying them on.

"I'm not sure," Jo said. She turned to see the back of the ivory-colored dress she currently wore. "Javonne, how did you accumulate all these gowns?"

"Oh, Harry has all these dental functions we have to go to, mostly in Baltimore, sometimes in Annapolis or D.C. You wouldn't think dentists were such party people, would you? We've gone to a couple of Founders Balls too but decided to skip it this year. Good thing too. With James's asthma acting up today, I'd hate to leave him. So," she said, repeating her question, "what did you think of Heather Bannister. Was she mad enough at Parker Holt to kill him?"

"She was mad, that was clear. Mad enough? I don't know. But she did have that threat of Holt's hanging over her, to ruin her marriage and her reputation if she spoke up about what he was doing."

"But she told you about it, so maybe she wasn't all that worried. Take that dress off, Jo. Ivory is just not your color." Javonne reached for the dress's zipper.

"Yeah, you're right," Jo agreed. "It's a gorgeous gown, but I look pretty sickly in it." She stepped out of the dress and looked over to the bed. "As far as Heather's telling me about Holt's threat, maybe now that he's dead and can't contradict her, she feels safe enough to talk about it." Jo picked up a red silk number with spaghetti straps. "Maybe I'll try this."

"I don't know," Javonne said. "I mean about that woman talking, not the dress. Go ahead and try it, though it might be—well, try it and we'll see. It sounds to me like Heather's maybe working hard to make herself look good and him look bad."

"But we already know from Sylvia what Parker Holt was like, so Heather's account of his threats seems credible to me. Well!" Jo looked at her reflection as Javonne zipped up the red dress. "Well," she repeated, grinning, "maybe not."

Javonne laughed. "I bought that not too long after Terrell was born and I still carried some pregnancy weight. Plus I was nursing."

"Yes," Jo said, holding up excess red silk at the bodice, "I can see that. Since I don't have the time—or inclination—to get implants, I think I'd better keep looking."

"Too bad, that was a good color for you." Javonne poked through a few dresses in the pile and held up a green chiffon. "What do you think?"

"I'm thinking I should probably consider that I'll need

to wear shoes too. Dresses we can adjust, but not shoes. I
do have a pair of black strappy sandals, and they wouldn't
go all that well with pale green. But I see something black
under there."

"Good point. Here you go." Javonne pulled out a long,
slinky-looking dress that had fluttery sleeves trimmed in
white. She helped Jo slip it over her head. "Anyway, I still
don't know about that Bannister woman's motive for
killing Holt. I mean, if it was to shut him up, why would
she go telling people like she did with you? Maybe there
was more to it—something she's not telling?"

"Quite possible. I did learn, however, that she doesn't
have a good alibi for that critical time period. She mentioned before I left that she's been sitting home alone every
day this week, working the phone and the computer for her
real estate sales efforts."

"Well, there you go. She had the opportunity. Jo, that
dress is *you*, girl! Va-va-voom!"

Jo saw that the black dress followed her minimal curves
closely, perhaps too closely. "Javonne, how did you ever
dance in this?"

"That was from my skinny period," Javonne explained.
"After I did Weight Watchers for a few months. Overdid it,
actually. Harry doesn't dance, so I just sauntered around on
his arm that night and showed off my fabulous figure."

"I don't know," Jo said, looking over her shoulder at her
reflection in the mirror. "This might be too tight."

"Yeah, it is a little snug in the hips. All you need, though,
is a good body shaper. Something to suck you in a bit. You
got anything? It'll smooth out all those, ah, ripples."

"I don't have one, but I could pick one up, I suppose." Jo
looked over the many dresses she'd already tried, lying re-
jected on the bed. This was the best of the lot, and if it took
that minimal investment on her part to get her to the ball
dressed appropriately, she could manage it.

"I guess," she said, "if I'm going to do any sleuthing tonight, a black dress would be the thing to wear. To be inconspicuous, I mean."

Javonne threw her an odd look but said only, "Right."

A knock on the door was followed by Harry's voice. "Is everyone decent?"

When both of them told him to come in, Harry opened the door. "I just need to get my . . . Wow!"

"Doesn't she look great?" Javonne asked.

"Yeah, terrific!" Harry smoothed back a stray hair on his nearly bald pate as he took in the sight of Jo in her gown. "I remember that dress, but I don't remember it looking quite that good!" Harry rapidly backpedaled. "I mean, ah, I don't, that is, didn't it used to have a big flower on it or something?"

"No, Harry, it never had a big flower on it!" Javonne said, looking at her husband mock sternly, her hands on her hips.

Javonne's oldest, James, came up behind Harry and peeked around him into the room. "Wow-ee!"

Jo and Javonne both burst out laughing. "I think," Javonne said, "that means the dress works. Have a ball, Jo."

Chapter 18

Jo heard the knock at her door, precisely at eight. Who knew that Rafe Rulenski was a promptness freak? Just when she could have used another few minutes. She scrambled to strap on her high-heeled sandals, fumbling with the buckles.

Jo had spent far too much time on her hair, something she hadn't done in a long time. The colorful bruises from that car incident of four months ago had long since faded, but her hairdo hadn't yet regained its balance. Parts of it were still growing out from what had been cut away for the stitches in her scalp, requiring her to struggle with curling iron and spray in an effort to produce some semblance of sanity to it. She ended up stealing a white silk camellia off of a work-in-progress wreath and using it as camouflage on her sparse spot.

"I'm coming," Jo called, then hustled from the bedroom toward her front door, finding movement to be, disconcertingly, a bit of an effort. That compression garment she'd picked up at Lily's to help her fit into Javonne's slinky dress turned out to be much sturdier than she'd realized. From what long-ago era had Lily stocked it? Comparisons to bone-constricting Victorian corsets ran through Jo's head. This was, she feared, going to be a long night.

"Well," Rafe said when she opened the door, "I guess you dug up something to wear all right."

"Just don't expect a lot of conversation tonight. I'm having trouble breathing."

"No problem," Rafe grinned. "I'll do all the talking." He glanced down at her feet. "You might want something to cover those," he said, pointing to her open shoes. "It's starting to accumulate."

"What? Oh my gosh," Jo said, looking past Rafe's shoulder to see snowy white flakes floating downward. "I never noticed. All I own are clunky galoshes. I can't wear them!"

"Suit yourself. But don't expect me to whip my coat over any puddles for you. It comes straight from the playhouse costume department and has to go back in the same condition."

"I'll be fine." Jo pulled Javonne's black hooded, street-length coat from the hall closet, grateful for its cozy lining of fake fur. At least she'd be warm from the knees up. Rafe helped her slip it on and they bustled out to his car, Jo carefully protecting her silk camellia from the snow with Javonne's hood.

"Ever been to the Bradford Hotel?" Rafe asked as he slipped behind the wheel of his several-years-old Miata.

"Is that where this is? No, I've never been inside. But I've driven past, and it looks regal."

"That's a good word for it. The place is close to a hundred years old. Built, I suppose, when Abbotsville was in its heyday, whatever that was."

Rafe put the car in gear and pulled off. "They use the entire downstairs area of the hotel for the ball, a regular rabbit warren of rooms to circulate through. Lots of polished wood and brass wall sconces and such."

"Sounds elegant."

"It makes a good setting," Rafe agreed. "Unfortunately, the cast of characters doesn't always live up to the scenery, but what can you do?"

Jo thought that neither she nor Rafe in their borrowed finery qualified as anyone who fit into a regal setting but wasn't too concerned about it. She was more interested in seeing Mallory Holt up close for the first time. And hearing what Holt's acquaintances might say about him once they had downed a drink or two.

Before long Rafe pulled up to the front entrance of the Bradford, an elegant, old-brick building with Tiffany-style windows. Jo wiggled her naked toes with relief as she saw a protective green canopy stretched out from its door, as well as valet parking in use. A doorman in quasi-military uniform loaded with gold braid reached down to open her door. Jo swung her legs out, and as she took the doorman's hand, she looked up to his face.

"Randy!"

Randy Truitt gave an embarrassed smile. "Hi. I mean, good evening."

"You're working here?"

"Just for tonight. They actually hired me to clear the snow. Then the doorman called in sick so I'm filling in."

"Well, you look really nice in that uniform."

"I feel kinda dumb. But the tips have been pretty good so far."

"Great. I hope you can keep warm enough."

"Yeah, I can go inside once in a while, as long as I keep the snow shoveled." Randy was already looking toward the next approaching car, so Jo moved out of his way and took Rafe's arm as he came around, passing Randy rapidly enough to avoid a tip.

"Let's head for the food table first," Rafe said. "I'm starving."

"Fine with me. But could you slow down a little, please? I'm a bit too constricted tonight for jogging."

"Oh, sorry." Rafe slowed and let another couple sweep past. "It's just that all the better stuff disappears first at these things."

"I understand. By the way, did I mention you look very nice tonight? You wear a tux very well." Jo meant it. Rafe had surprised her with his look of casual elegance, the "casual" coming from his perpetual day's growth of beard and the "elegance" from the actor in him having risen to carry his evening attire with aplomb.

"Thanks." Rafe brushed a few flakes of snow from his shoulder as he tossed off, "And you're not looking so bad yourself." They followed others into the Bradford and left their coats at the cloakroom, Rafe looking about and fairly sniffing the air for food aromas. "This way," he declared as he led Jo accurately to the room that held bountiful tables of every kind of food Jo could imagine, from fruits and cheeses to platters of meats, salads, and delicate sweets.

"Dig in," Rafe suggested, and immediately did so himself, grabbing a plate and proceeding to pile it high. Jo picked up a succulent-looking strawberry and took a bite out of it. The food was presented so beautifully that it was enough pleasure for her at this point to simply soak it up visually. She sauntered along beside Rafe as he moved from station to station.

"Wine, miss?" A ponytailed waitress in dark vest and slacks came up to her with a filled tray.

"Thank you," Jo said, and plucked off a glass of red wine. She sipped it, then reached for a square of cheese from a nearby tray of hors d'oeuvres.

Jo looked about at the slowly gathering crowd, not recognizing a soul so far. Many couples greeted each other, but the names she overheard didn't ring any bells. She heard music begin to play in another room.

Rafe rejoined her, holding a brimming plate and munching on a roast beef–crammed roll. "Is that all you've got?" he asked.

"I like to graze. By the way, Rafe, what play are you working on lately?"

Rafe took a moment to swallow, then said, "*Barefoot in the Park*. Sorry I couldn't ask you to do any jewelry for it. The playhouse put this on once, before I came, and everything we needed was in stock." Rafe was referring to the fact that Jo had put together the costume jewelry for the playhouse's last production—a tongue-in-cheek fairy tale that eventually ran into major problems.

"That's all right," she said. "I don't envision your present characters needing much jewelry. And I've got my hands pretty full for the moment."

"Mr. Rulenski! How nice to see you here." A dowager-type in black lace swept up to Rafe, towing a boy of about seventeen with a severe case of acne along with her.

Rafe set his plate onto the table behind him and smiled charmingly. "Mrs. Sinclair. Always a pleasure." He introduced Jo, and Mrs. Sinclair in turn introduced the young man who turned out to be her grandson, and who was "so talented! He's written a play which is simply wonderful. It's all about . . ." She paused. "What is it about again, Zachary? You can explain it much better than I."

Zachary launched into a description, as best Jo could understand it, of a group of teens, washed up on a desert island, who battle prehistoric monsters, are visited by outerspace aliens, and develop a new civilization infinitely better than what they had left behind. Jo watched Rafe's charming smile freeze in place as he nodded. "Well," he said, "that's quite imaginative!"

Mrs. Sinclair burbled happily, "I thought you might like to consider putting it on this summer. Wouldn't it be a wonderful way to draw in more of our young people?"

Jo listened with amusement as Rafe wriggled his way

out, suggesting Zachary's play would be much better served on the screen and how he should really think in terms of a Hollywood submission. "You don't want to waste a story like that on our kind of small-budget production. Speaking of which, have you considered, Mrs. Sinclair, becoming involved in our upcoming playhouse fund-raising event . . . ?"

Jo tuned out about that time and let her gaze wander the crowd once more. It stopped abruptly at a certain man, turned partially away—dark haired, tall—and she puzzled for a moment until recognition flashed. Lieutenant Morgan! Out of uniform and looking very nice in a dark suit. Was he with someone? Jo searched through the crush of people surrounding him, but she didn't see any woman who resembled his lunch date of last fall. Morgan suddenly turned in her direction and caught her watching him. He looked as surprised as she felt, perhaps more so, but he nodded courteously. Then his gaze moved toward Rafe, standing beside her. Morgan stood too far away for Jo to say for sure, but she thought she saw him frown. Finding herself growing a tad flustered, Jo refocused on the people she was with.

Mrs. Sinclair was saying something to her. "So nice to meet you, Miss Malachey." Jo smiled and considered butchering Mrs. Sinclair's name in turn, but minded her manners and wished her and her grandson a pleasant evening.

"Now you see why I hate these things," Rafe muttered once the pair had moved off. He retrieved his plate.

"You handled it like a pro," Jo said. "Which, of course, you are. Do you see Mallory Holt anywhere yet?"

"Mallory?" Rafe took another bite out of his roast beef sandwich and checked around the room. "There she is, in the purple."

Jo looked in the direction Rafe indicated with a wave of his sandwich, and saw a woman of perhaps forty, slim, brown haired, and attractive in a gracefully draping purple satin and velvet gown. She looked appropriately subdued, considering her recent widowhood, as well as thoroughly involved in the evening's event, moving from person to person like a hostess, which in a way, as president of the women's club and the ball's chief organizer, she was.

"You want to meet her?" Rafe asked. "C'mon." And before Jo could respond he took her arm and led her over.

"Mallory, sweet, you look amazing tonight."

Mallory Holt turned from a distinguished-looking couple she had been speaking to with a graceful apology. "Rafe! You made it after all. After leaving me in suspense all these weeks."

"You know I wouldn't miss it for the world, Mallory. Too much gold to be mined—for the arts, of course. May I introduce Jo McAllister?"

Mallory ran a rapid and speculative eye over Jo and her outfit, looking completely capable of identifying its designer and cost in milliseconds. Since the only thing Jo had paid for herself was her underwear and shoes, and assuming the woman didn't have X-ray vision, Jo withstood the scrutiny with confidence.

"How do you do?" Mallory held out her hand. "I don't believe we've met before, have we? Are you from Abbotsville?"

Rafe jumped in before Jo could answer. "Jo runs a little arts and crafts shop on Main Street. Isn't that where it is, Jo?" Jo had to agree, though she wasn't totally pleased with the dismissive "little" used to describe her shop. "She's also," Rafe went on, "done some costume-jewelry design for the playhouse, which is how we happen to know each other."

"Oh, really?" Mallory's smile dimmed a few watts.

"Yes. I'm fairly new to Abbotsville, but I love it here. And I'm very impressed with this Founders Ball. I understand you're responsible for it?"

Mallory laughed lightly. "I and about a hundred other

very hardworking people. Have you seen the decorations in the Jefferson Room yet? That's the room where our orchestra is set up. You, especially, would appreciate it, I'm sure. Our flower committee really outdid themselves this year."

"I'll have to take a look," Jo said. "I don't suppose that my former neighbor, Frannie, of Fantastic Florals had a hand in it, did she? I mean, since she had to close her shop after your late husband bought the building."

Mallory stared a moment, then shook her head. "No, I believe the committee worked with a flower wholesaler. That was unfortunate about Frannie's closing, wasn't it? But I've heard she's quite happy to be out of the retailing rat race now and delighted to have more time to spend with her family." Mallory smiled brightly at this.

"I've been trying," Jo said, smiling less brightly than Mallory, "to find out what's happening with my own building. I don't have a family to spend more time with and need to keep my shop running. Did the Holt Corporation buy it from my landlord, Max McGee?"

"Well . . ." Mallory seemed to be carefully forming an answer, but then a plump woman in pink satin hurried up and plucked at her sleeve.

"Mallory, there's a major problem with the bar manager. Can you come talk to him?"

"Yes, of course." Mallory excused herself with a gentle sigh over the never-ending demands on a Founders Ball organizer. "I'm so sorry," she said. "I'll have to get back to you on that. Or perhaps you could call the office on Monday."

Right, Jo thought. I'll want to do that and set myself up for the same runaround I got before. As Mallory turned away, Jo puffed her cheeks in frustration, feeling she had come so close to finally getting an answer. Or maybe not. Possibly Mallory was simply on the verge of giving a nonanswer, a nothing's-been-settled-yet kind of answer. Or she might not have known at all. Jo watched her hurry off, thinking how very poised and in control Mallory seemed.

She couldn't imagine a woman like that being happily married to Parker Holt. At least, not for long.

"I've got to talk to that man with the horrendous overbite over there," Rafe said, breaking into her thoughts. "He promised to look into getting us a discount on our program-printing costs. Want to come along?"

Jo looked where Rafe indicated and, spotting Sebastian Zarnik standing nearby, shook her head. "I think I'll go check out the decorations in the Jefferson Room, if you don't mind. I can meet you back here later."

"Right. See you then." Rafe took off, and Jo turned in the direction of the music.

As she rounded a corner, she saw two white-haired ladies, one tall, the other petite with their backs to her. The tall one was dressed in powder blue, and the short one was all in peach, both covered from chin to toe. Jo recognized them immediately.

"Ina Mae and Loralee, how nice to see you!"

The women turned, Loralee lighting up with particular pleasure. "Why, Jo! I had no idea you were coming tonight!"

"It was pretty much a last-minute thing."

"Wonderful to see you, Jo," Ina Mae said. "Javonne told me you were coming, but I hadn't mentioned it yet to Loralee. Javonne also told me about your visit with the former Pheasant Run manager."

"Oh! The woman who left after a blowup with Parker Holt?" Loralee asked. "Tell me about it."

Jo did, as well as clarifying a few details for Ina Mae.

"You know the woman's here tonight," Ina Mae said. "I ran into Celia when Loralee was powdering her nose, and she mentioned it."

"She's here?" Loralee glanced around, as did Jo.

"Yes, with her husband. But Celia wasn't able to point her out."

"I see her," Jo said. "She's the blonde over there near

the window, dressed in burgundy. The man next to her must be her husband." A good-looking man of about thirty stood close to Heather Bannister as both sipped from champagne flutes.

"Why, that's Kevin Bannister," Loralee said.

"You know him?" Ina Mae and Jo asked in unison.

"Yes, I met him years ago when he was helping his father with his tree-removal service. He was in college at the time, but it was summer break. What was he majoring in? Oh, yes, he was studying to be an engineer. An *electrical* engineer."

Ina Mae and Jo exchanged looks.

"Hors d'oeuvres, ladies?" The ponytailed waitress held a tray out to them, this one filled with luscious-looking bacon-wrapped shrimp. Jo took one, as did both Ina Mae and Loralee, thanking her politely.

"By the way," Loralee said before trying hers, "Xavier is here, in the kitchen. They apparently were short of help, and the poor man probably needs any work he can get right now."

"Did you speak with him?" Jo asked.

"No, he looked too busy. I caught his eye when the kitchen door swung open, and I waved. I think he's doing cleanup."

"Maybe I can talk to him later on," Jo said.

"Talk to who later on?" A male voice said at her shoulder, startling Jo.

"Why, Lieutenant Morgan, I hardly recognized you," Loralee said. "Are you having a nice time?"

"Yes, ma'am, I am, thank you," Morgan said. "And tonight I'm simply Russ Morgan, not lieutenant, since I'm off duty and therefore not doing any detecting." He threw Jo a significant look, and she suddenly found absorbing interest in her wineglass.

"Russ, such a nice name," Loralee burbled. "I have a

nephew named Russ. He was a darling child. Unfortunately, when he grew up, well, never mind. Doesn't our Jo look nice tonight, Lieu—I mean, Russ?"

"Yes, she does." Morgan gave Jo a look of a different type this time, and she felt her cheeks warm. "And I'm sure her escort feels the same way. Rafe Rulenski seemed to be looking about for you when I left the buffet area."

"He was more likely looking for another roast beef sandwich," Jo said.

"Is that who you came with, Jo?" Loralee asked. "How nice! I always liked Rafe. Didn't you, Ina Mae?"

"Perhaps this is our chance," Ina Mae said, "to ask Mr. Rulenski if he truly plans to put on that highly inappropriate play I heard about next season. Come along, Loralee." Ina Mae nodded to Morgan and left Jo standing with the off-duty lieutenant.

Morgan waited until the two rounded the corner, then turned to Jo to repeat his original question.

"Talk to who later on?"

Chapter 19

Jo popped the shrimp hors d'oeuvre she had been holding into her mouth, giving herself time to answer the lieutenant's question. The orchestra in the Jefferson Room began playing a slow tune, and several couples moved onto the dance floor.

"If Ina Mae were still here," she said, licking a finger, "she might protest that you should correctly ask 'to whom.'"

"All right, Miss Jo. To whom were you planning to speak later?"

"Xavier Ramirez. He's working in the kitchen tonight. Apparently he's taking any job available, since Dan's business has been suffering cancellations."

"I'm sorry to hear that."

Russ Morgan did look sorry, and Jo, who had been prepared to relaunch their argument of three days ago, relented.

"But," Morgan said, "I also noticed you talking with Mallory Holt a minute ago. I'm sure, though, that being the highly considerate person you are, nothing whatsoever concerning what we discussed in my office came up. Am I right?"

"Nothing at all," Jo acknowledged. "I merely inquired about the status of my shop's building, wanting to know if Parker Holt had bought it or not. Unfortunately, I didn't get an answer."

Morgan nodded.

"Is Mayor Kunkle here tonight?" Jo asked.

"I haven't seen him. Why?"

"Oh, nothing, except as mayor I would assume he'd attend. Plus, as Mallory's uncle he would naturally provide support for the ball she'd organized, wouldn't he? He certainly was very supportive of his niece the night of Holt's murder. I presume he was just as supportive when he came to see you immediately after I did, possibly to discuss the status of your murder investigation."

Jo's last statement ended on a questioning note, and she looked up at Morgan and waited. He returned the look, then grinned.

"Nice try. Tonight, though," his glance swept over her, "you don't quite fit my image of an investigative reporter." Morgan paused, then turned toward the buffet room. "If your escort is really more interested in the food than in being seen with a beautiful woman on the dance floor, he's a bigger fool than I thought. Would you care to dance, Miss Jo?"

Jo blinked. Dance? That was not something she'd actually planned on when she'd pictured the evening. Particularly with Russ Morgan. But it was a ball, after all. He was waiting for her response. Would she dance? Maybe the better question was *could* she dance? Would this supersnug cocoon of a dress allow her to dance?

"Yes. Yes, of course," Jo heard herself saying, and before she knew it she had set her wineglass down and was being led onto the dance floor. Morgan's arm circled her waist and hers reached for his shoulder. He didn't pull her too close, which she appreciated since she found herself feeling, for some reason, just a bit breathless. Which was ridiculous. They began to move in unison in time to the music, and Jo found herself smiling, liking the feeling, liking the scent of him. Had he actually called her beautiful? she wondered. Or had he simply thrown the word out there, aiming at no one in particular?

Other couples whirled about them, one middle-aged twosome looking quite proficient. Russ's dance steps, however, were basic, though firmly on the beat and nicely clear of her toes, which were no small virtues. Jo spotted Donna, the woman from the Pheasant Run beading class wearing her gray dress topped with her nicely done blue and silver beaded necklace, and she caught sight of Loralee at the edge of the room, beaming in her direction.

"The flower decorations really are beautiful," Jo said.

"Mmm," Morgan responded, taking a moment as though he had just realized there *were* flower decorations.

"You said you were off duty tonight. Does that mean the evening is purely social, or are you here semiofficially as a representative of the Abbotsville police force?" She wanted to add, "And are you here alone or with a date, possibly that very attractive woman whose cheek I saw you kiss?" but didn't.

"It's never purely one thing or another," Morgan said. "If people know who I am, I'm therefore representing the police to some extent."

"That makes it rather hard to relax, I imagine."

"Oh, I find ways," Morgan said with a smile.

It was a very nice smile, Jo thought. She seemed to be seeing more of it lately, and liked that. The music, though, which they had come in on late, ended and she didn't like that. Couples scattered, and Morgan led her off the dance floor. He seemed about to say something when, to Jo's consternation, Alexis Wigsley suddenly popped up.

"I *thought* that was you on the dance floor," she cried to Jo. "I told myself no, that can't be Jo McAllister, but it was! And Lieutenant Morgan! So you came together?"

"Ms. McAllister simply honored me with a dance," Russ said.

"Oooh," Alexis said simperingly, causing Jo to cringe. "I wanted to tell you," she said, moving closely to Jo, "remember that girlfriend of Randy's I mentioned the other day? She's here!"

"Excuse me, ladies," Russ said—unfortunately, to Jo's mind, taking this as his cue to leave. Did he believe she was bosom buddies with Alexis Wigsley? "If I see Rafe, I'll tell him where you are," he said, and Jo helplessly watched him walk away.

Alexis took hold of her arm and leaned even closer. "Lisa Williams. She's that waitress over there." Alexis pointed to the ponytailed food server circulating through the crowd.

"That's Lisa?" Jo asked. She glanced back to see that Russ had disappeared. "She came up to me once or twice in the buffet room. She seems nice," Jo said, wishing she could shake Alexis off her arm.

"She is!" Alexis agreed. "A perfectly decent woman, and there she is going out with someone like Randy Truitt! I took the opportunity to take her aside and have a little talk with her, explaining that for her own good she needs to drop him like a hot potato."

"You said that to her?" Jo asked, horrified. "Now? When she's working?"

"Certainly! And the sooner she takes the advice, the better. The man will only drag her down. Lisa may not be the brightest, or beauty pageant material, but there's no need to waste her time like that. Someone has to steer her away from trouble if she's not seeing it herself."

"She seems old enough to make decisions of that sort for herself," Jo said, stiffly.

"You would think so, wouldn't you?" Alexis said, clearly

not picking up on Jo's meaning. "But despite being, oh, way over thirty, she's clearly still thinking like a teenager, which is what probably got her into those few problems in the past. Like that one incident, for instance—"

"Excuse me, Alexis, I promised to get back to someone about this time." Jo made a move in the direction of the buffet room.

"Oh, certainly," Alexis said, but her fingers pressed into Jo's arm even harder. "But before you leave, did you know *that man* is here? The one the police have been questioning in connection with Parker Holt's death? I saw him myself, in this very kitchen!"

"What were you doing in the kitchen?" Jo asked, amazed at the amount of ground Alexis was able to cover.

"I went to speak with the chef, of course, to inquire if any of the foods contained MSG. Monosodium glutamate gives me terrible headaches, you know, all quite avoidable if the chef simply uses natural seasonings. Anyway, there this man was, working at the sink, scrubbing up pots. I can't imagine Mallory is aware of that, can you? Have you spoken to her yet?"

"Yes, and please, Alexis, don't say anything to her about Xavier being here. He's simply trying to earn a few dollars, which he needs badly, and Mallory doesn't need to know anything about it."

"Well, I don't know about that. But then again, Mallory doesn't seem all that concerned, does she, about finding the person who murdered her husband? I mean, she could hardly get Parker in the ground fast enough, and here she is flitting about, with that artist friend of hers here too. They didn't actually come together, you know, but they haven't been more than ten feet apart all night."

"You seem quite aware of everything going on here tonight."

Alexis took Jo's comment as a compliment, her eyes lighting up. "I've never been one to just stand in the corner and ignore the world around me. Life is just too fascinating! Oh, by the way, Jo, I've made progress on tracking down Max McGee."

"You have?" That was something Jo wanted to hear.

"Yes. I haven't learned exactly where he is right now, but I discovered he had a knee replacement recently. It was more difficult to go through than he had expected and he decided to treat himself to a vacation in the Bahamas. But I'm still working on precisely where and for how long."

"Great." Jo didn't ask how Alexis managed to get that far, and at the moment didn't really want to know. "Let me know when you find out."

"I certainly will. Now Jo," Alexis said, "I'd love to stay and chat, but I really can't." She released Jo's arm and began to move away, then stopped. "Oh, who did you say brought you to the ball?"

Feeling the woman deserved that little innocuous nugget in return for her work on Max McGee, Jo told her.

Alexis nodded, then looked across the room. "Well, there's Heather Bannister. And with her husband. How interesting. I wonder if Mallory is aware *she's* here?" And with that she hurried off, leaving Jo to breathe a sigh of relief and free to reconnect with Rafe.

She found him, not surprisingly, near the buffet table, chatting with an attractive young woman, his plate holding a fresh selection of edibles. He turned as Jo came up.

"Oh, there you are. Jo, I don't believe you've met Tara Miesner." The two acknowledged each other, and Rafe explained, "Tara is interested in trying out for one of our future plays."

Jo smiled and wished her the best of luck. She hoped for Rafe's sake that Tara worked out. He was in need of strong leading actors after what the playhouse had suffered last fall.

"Excuse me," Jo said. "I think I'll try a couple more things from the buffet." Jo's stomach had begun reminding her she hadn't eaten much before Rafe picked her up, and that the single strawberry and hors d'oeuvre wasn't doing it.

She took a plate and began filling it with various goodies—caviar, stuffed tomatoes, pasta salads—glancing around occasionally for any sign of Russ Morgan but not finding it. She wished she had managed to learn if he'd come with someone to the ball. Alexis would find out by the end of the evening, Jo was sure, but she had no intention of seeking the woman out to ask. Jo had just scooped up a forkful of pasta when she spotted Mallory Holt heading toward her. Mallory looked somewhat less hostessy than she had on their initial meeting, and Jo wondered what was up.

Mallory simply said, "Come with me," and drew Jo by the arm to a quiet spot in the corner of the room.

Jo assumed Mallory intended to finish their original conversation that had been interrupted, and so complied without protest. She was completely taken aback, therefore, when instead Mallory turned blazing eyes on her and asked in an ominously low voice: "What do you mean by pretending to be someone you're not, to get into Sebastian's studio?"

Uh-oh, Jo thought. Sebastian Zarnik had obviously spotted her and asked questions. Jo decided to play it cool.

"What do *you* mean? I never pretended to be anyone other than Jo McAllister."

"Oh, really? And do you intend to commission a painting from Sebastian? Or buy one of his finished works? Your little craft shop must be doing extremely well if that's the case."

"I appreciate art," Jo protested. "If Mr. Zarnik's prices were higher than I expected or more than I can afford right now, I at least enjoyed seeing his work."

"Don't tell me that! You misled him completely. I don't know what you think you're getting away with, but rest assured, you won't. Sebastian doesn't appreciate such tricks, nor do I."

Mallory paused ominously. "If you were at all worried," she said, "about your building having been bought, Ms. McAllister, your worries have just increased tenfold. I suggest you start looking around for a new shop location, and the farther from Abbotsville the better."

Jo felt her jaw drop.

As quickly as Mallory had spit that out, so did her face rapidly change from an expression of fury to one of total ease. "Yes, that would be wonderful, Ms. McAllister. Let's follow up on that. Delia!" she called to a woman passing nearby. "Just the person I was looking for. I wanted to ask . . ."

Mallory moved off without a second glance in Jo's direction, leaving Jo reeling from what had just slammed into her. Had Mallory Holt just threatened her? Was she saying that the Holt Corporation had in fact bought her building from Max McGee? Or was it something she planned to press for, now that Jo had angered her.

And what, exactly, was Mallory Holt angry about? Was it simply that Jo had wasted the time of her artist lover? Or was it that Jo had come too close to a murderous secret?

Jo realized she had been standing openmouthed, so she snatched a caviar-topped cracker from her plate and bit into it. She moved back into the crowd, and seeing Rafe still in close conversation with the aspiring actress, veered away, searching for a friendlier face than the one she had just encountered, or perhaps a bit of quiet, where she could pull herself together. She eventually found herself in the hotel foyer, which was empty at the moment except for staff. One of that staff wore gold braid and was blowing on his cold hands. She headed toward him.

"Getting warmed up?"

Randy Truitt looked up and nodded.

Jo peered through the glass in the hotel's front door and

saw the snow coming down steadily. Randy had done a good job keeping the immediate walkway cleared, but elsewhere she saw the snow had accumulated a few inches.

"Have you had anything warm to drink?" Jo asked. "If not, I could grab some coffee back there for you."

"That's okay. Someone brought a cup out to me." He smiled. "She's also gonna sneak out something for me to eat, but don't tell anyone."

That must be Lisa Williams, Jo thought. She wondered if Lisa had brought the coffee before or after Alexis Wigsley had her intrusive talk with her, and if she had mentioned it to Randy.

"I'm glad you're being looked after. Looks like the worst of your job is over, huh?"

"Nah, I'll be hopping again when people start to leave. Which might be soon if they're worried about the snow."

"Good point." Looking out at it once more, Jo wished she could have borrowed Javonne's supertraction SUV along with everything else. How, she wondered, would Rafe's aging sports car fare on the slippery streets?

Jo felt more than ready to leave the ball, but not just because of the weather. The thought of going back and having to see Mallory with her "gracious hostess" mask firmly in place was unnerving. But she needed to get over it. She had more work to do. Randy got a signal from a hotel staff person to return to his snow clearing, so Jo wished him well and headed back to the ballrooms.

Rafe, she saw, had been joined, in addition to Tara, by another attractive, possibly aspiring actress, so she changed direction, not interested in more theater talk. She decided to try for a word with Xavier—to see if he'd followed up on Carrie's suggestion to get a public defender, and to ask after Sylvia.

She slipped behind the buffet table and pushed through one of the swinging kitchen doors into a large room of stainless steel efficiency. Jo walked past warming tables and hanging pots, searching for Xavier, the noise and clatter of the ongoing work echoing about her until she spotted him at the far end of the room. She also spotted Alexis Wigsley and Mallory Holt hovering over him. Their backs were to Jo, but Mallory's words rang clearly.

"I'm appalled that this hotel, knowing what I've gone through so recently, actually hired this man to work at my ball!"

A managerial type in navy pinstripes stammered out placating phrases: "Extremely sorry—had no idea—a terrible mistake." A chef in a tall white hat stood to the side, hands on his hips, his face a picture of extreme annoyance.

Alexis Wigsley chimed in with, "Inexcusable, totally inexcusable. I was certain you'd want to know, Mallory."

The focus of all this, Xavier, stood quietly, looking miserably from one to the other.

Jo began to rush forward, but a kitchen worker, unaware of her presence, stepped back from his workstation with a large wire basket of clean plates, blocking her path. By the time she squeezed by, the pinstriped man had Xavier by the arm and was marching him out a back door.

Mallory and Alexis waited until the door slammed behind the two, then turned and headed toward the door Jo had just entered, Mallory flush faced and Alexis babbling on about having to watch everything like a hawk or heaven knows what would be slipped by a person. Neither seemed to notice Jo as they hurried by on the opposite side of a wide, center work island with tall kettles atop it, which was just as well. Jo felt as furious as Mallory presented herself to be, but with far greater justification, and she couldn't predict what might have come out of her mouth if Mallory had stopped at that moment. Jo willed herself to cool down and think.

Mallory's reason for ridding the hotel kitchen of Xavier's lowly paid presence was obviously that she suspected him of her husband's murder. But did she really? Jo wondered. Was she truly convinced of Xavier's criminality, or was it merely a smokescreen to cover a murderous plot of her own? Mallory hadn't been too upset over her husband's murder to meet with Sebastian Zarnik or to carry on "bravely" with the Founders Ball. And her outrage, as Jo had seen, could be turned on and off when it suited her. Pointing the finger at Xavier, who already had several fingers conveniently pointed at him, certainly aimed people away from looking too closely at her.

Mallory, Jo was learning, was a very clever woman, but had she been clever enough? Jo got a revealing look at her tonight. But a lot more, she was sure, remained hidden. How was she going to dig it out?

After taking a few minutes to regain her composure, Jo rejoined Rafe in the buffet area, finding him, for once, standing alone and with no mound of food in hand. He looked over at her approach and smiled just a bit guiltily.

"Sorry, I seem to have been neglecting you," he said.

"No problem. I've been having a very interesting time."

"Did you want to have a dance?" he asked with no discernable enthusiasm.

"Thanks," Jo said, "but I think I'd rather just stroll around and listen to the music."

Rafe obligingly held out his arm for her to take, and they wound their way through the crowd toward rooms neither had yet seen.

"So," Jo asked, thinking of the aspiring actresses, "will you be getting some good new blood for the playhouse?"

"That remains to be seen. Having played the second lead in a high school production of *Grease* doesn't automatically translate into working on a professional level." Rafe sighed. "Sometimes, though, I have to take what I can get."

Jo noticed Heather Bannister standing alone on the other side of the room, and followed the woman's gaze to see

Heather's husband, Kevin, putting in an order at the nearby bar. Suddenly Alexis sidled up to Heather, and Jo watched them talk, Heather looking not terribly pleased. Jo could sympathize and wondered what was being said.

"Ah, Rulenski," a male voice boomed. A tall, large-chested man stepped up to shake Rafe's hand. "I hear you're doing *Barefoot in the Park* next. Any room for the wife in it?"

As Rafe went into a diplomatic explanation of the sparseness of roles for the play and how they had already been cast, Jo glanced over toward the Bannisters and saw Kevin heading toward Heather, two stemmed glasses in his hands. He stopped abruptly, possibly on seeing Alexis, and veered off in another direction. Interesting, Jo thought.

Rafe was introducing her to the large-chested man, and Jo turned back to find her hand quickly swallowed up in his much larger one and heartily pumped up and down.

"Crafts, huh?" the man, whose name Jo had missed, said. "The wife likes crafts. I'll have to send her over. Where did you say your shop was?"

By the time Jo explained her shop's location and answered several follow-up questions, Alexis was no longer to be seen, and Kevin Bannister had delivered Heather's drink. The two looked to be in close consultation, and Jo could only guess as to its nature.

The large-chested man moved off, to be replaced by several others, all interested in Rafe's theater plans, and most offering suggestions for changing them. Mallory Holt was nowhere in sight, nor Sebastian, nor Alexis. Given their early-bird habits, Ina Mae and Loralee were likely tucked in their respective beds by now, and Jo began to long for the comfort of her own soft pillow as well.

When the last of a seemingly endless stream of theater enthusiasts took off, Rafe turned to Jo and asked, "Had enough?"

"Absolutely!" she answered, and they headed to the

coatroom to retrieve their wraps. They weren't the only ones, unfortunately, and they had to wait in a slowly moving line, then join a second line to wait for Rafe's car. Jo glanced around several times, wondering if Russ Morgan had left already, and if so, with whom, but saw no sign of him.

When the Miata was driven up, Jo and Rafe scurried out through the cold to it, and Randy Truitt opened the door for her to slide in.

"Thanks, Randy," she called out, her breath fairly freezing in place.

Randy only nodded, looking somewhat grim, and Jo supposed the pace might be getting to him, not to mention the cold. Her own toes had turned numb in that short run, and she hoped the Miata's heater would kick in rapidly.

Rafe, thankfully, drove off with care. The streets, despite evidence of having been plowed once or twice, were slippery, and Jo felt the car fishtail slightly on a curve. Rafe chatted on, though, seemingly more concerned with a few criticisms he had received that evening than with the driving conditions.

"That tall woman," he groused, "what's her name? Used to be some kind of teacher."

"Ina Mae?"

"Yeah. I think she'd like to see us put on a stream of G-rated Pollyanna-type stories. How does she think I'm going to get an audience for that kind of stuff?"

"From the families of Abbotsville, I suppose." Jo reached down to rub her chilled toes.

"Right. The families who stay home to watch their rented DVDs. They're not going to drag themselves to our playhouse. The people that do come want sophistication; they want mind-blowing drama, they want . . ."

Rafe ranted on about the supposed preferences of his audience, and Jo wondered when he had actually offered them such things at his playhouse? Not as long as she'd been in Abbotsville, which admittedly hadn't been very long.

They came to Jo's street, and Rafe groaned at the sight of its unplowed surface. He gamely turned into it, though, and bumping through high ruts, pulled up in front of Jo's house. He reached for his ignition to turn it off, but Jo stopped him.

"Never mind walking me to my door. There's no use you ruining your shoes."

"You're sure?" Rafe asked, unable to completely cover his relief.

"Absolutely. Thanks for inviting me, Rafe. It was a highly interesting evening."

Rafe grinned. "That's one way of putting it. Thanks for coming along."

Jo gritted her teeth and pulled off her sandals. It would be a frigid run in bare feet, but she couldn't afford to ruin her good shoes. She hopped out, holding Javonne's dress up knee-high, and made her way up the snowy walk as rapidly as she could manage. She knew she must look like a duck on drugs, but her appearance, at this point, was the least of her concerns. She waved to Rafe once she'd reached her door and had turned the key in the lock, then watched him drive off, after a worrisome but brief tire-spin in the snow, and sincerely hoped he'd make it home without trouble.

Jo dropped her shoes in her little foyer and made a mad dash to the bathroom to wrap her icy feet in a warm, fluffy towel. Once the feeling returned to her toes, she carefully removed her borrowed finery, returned her silk camellia to its wreath, wiggled gratefully out of her "corset," and flopped into bed to soon find images of her dance with Russ Morgan inexplicably weaving their way through her dreams.

Chapter 20

The next day, Jo arrived at the craft shop a half hour early, which, being Sunday, meant around 11:30. She had left word at Otto's for Randy to come shovel the snow in front of the shop, wishing she'd thought of mentioning it the night before. Who knew when he'd get her message? Charlie had taken care of her walk after the couple of previous snowfalls. But since he was temporarily out of commission, it looked like it was up to Jo, unless Randy miraculously appeared.

Bundled up in a parka, wool hat, and snow boots, Jo managed to clear the deep snow from her shop door to the curb, and a couple of feet or so on each side, before finding herself puffing. She decided that would do, that her doorway was at least minimally accessible, and set her shovel aside to open up shop. She had doffed her wet outerwear and was setting up her coffeepot when the phone rang.

"Jo's Craft Corner," Jo sang into the phone, pleased at the early sign of interest in her shop on this cold, quiet day.

"Jo!" Carrie's voice cried into her ear. "Did you hear about the accident?"

Jo's first frightened thought was for Rafe and his fish-tailing sports car. "What happened? Who was it?"

"Alexis Wigsley. Her car spun into a telephone pole over on Greenview Street. She's dead!"

"Alexis! Dead?" Memories of having seen and spoken with Alexis only hours ago rushed over Jo, making that difficult to believe.

"How awful! But how did it happen?" Jo asked. "Was she that reckless a driver? I know the conditions were terrible, but we're talking about town driving."

"Greenview is fairly steep," Carrie pointed out. "And it curves sharply near the bottom. But you're right. It does seem like she'd have to be going awfully fast. I don't know. Maybe we'll find out more. I'll be in as soon as I can get there. Did you have any trouble driving this morning?"

"Not once I got out of my driveway. Two wonderful neighbors with snowblowers helped with that."

"Great. I'll ask Dan to come clear the shop's walkway."

"No, don't, Carrie." Jo knew Dan would be able to pick up a few dollars clearing parking lots and long driveways with the snowplow attached to his pickup. There was no way she'd interfere with that. "I've made a decent dent in the snow, and someone's coming to finish it for me."

"All right. I'll see you soon, then."

Jo hung up, stunned at the news about Alexis. Knowing the woman, Jo figured she probably had stayed to the very end of the ball, letting the driving conditions worsen as she caught as much gossip as she could and caused as much trouble—Jo stopped at that thought. Alexis had certainly caused trouble, at the ball and on a daily basis. Could it possibly be . . . ? No, Carrie had described an accident, pure and simple. Unfortunate, but unforeseen.

Still, Jo couldn't shake an uneasy feeling. To distract herself, she began unpacking an order that had arrived the day before: silk flowers and greenery that needed to be sorted and tagged, then placed on the proper shelves in customer-friendly bins. She clicked on her radio for further distraction and dug in, finding, before she knew it, that half her job was done and that Carrie was stomping snow off her boots outside the door.

"Sorry it took me so long," Carrie said as she came inside.

"No problem. I haven't had a single customer yet."

"Everyone's probably waiting for the streets to clear a bit more. They'll venture out, little by little." Carrie headed for the stockroom to pull off her boots and jacket. "They'll want to talk about the latest bad news."

"I'm still floored by it myself. Not grief stricken, I have to admit, just stunned. But I hate for that to happen to anyone."

Carrie called from the back room, "Don't apologize for your feelings—they're honest. I suspect we'll hear too much insincere bewailing today. Most people have difficulty saying a bad word against the dead. But Alexis was a troublemaker, and that's the truth."

"That she was, and to the very end, I'm afraid," Jo said. When Carrie came out front, Jo told her about the scene she witnessed in the hotel's kitchen the night before.

Carrie scowled, shaking her head. "That's outrageous. As if poor Xavier didn't have enough trouble as it is. Do you suppose he even got paid for the work he put in?"

"I couldn't say. That manager seemed anxious to put on a big show of apology to Mallory. I doubt he worried much about what Xavier was owed."

Jo then told Carrie about Alexis's intrusive advice to Lisa Williams, and what had surely been a most unwelcome conversation with Heather Bannister. She skipped her own annoyance at Alexis's chasing off of Russ Morgan at the end of their dance, having decided, while thinking it over as she'd sorted through the greenery that morning, that he was unlikely to have lingered with her much longer anyway. Russ Morgan's sole purpose, she figured, was to warn her away from interference in the Parker Holt case. Once that was accomplished, he surely had more important people to talk with.

"And then," Jo continued, "there was Mallory Holt and her not very well-veiled threat to me." Jo described the scene that occurred after Mallory had learned about Jo's visit to Sebastian.

"Well, you had quite a jolly time last night, didn't you?"

Jo laughed. "It wasn't the senior prom, I'll admit." Except for that one, lovely, too-short dance, she mused wistfully.

The sound of stamping outside her door shook her back to business. "Our first customer of the day."

A large, well-bundled woman opened the door and walked in. "Well! That was an invigorating walk! Very few people have shoveled their sidewalks yet, but the snow-plows did a good job, so I walked in the street. Need to get a few things, including some scrapbooking papers for the project I'm in the middle of. Did you hear about poor Alexis?" the woman asked, bright eyes going from Carrie to Jo. "I've been absolutely heartbroken since Mary Louise called me this morning. Poor, dear Alexis."

Carrie caught Jo's eye as if to say, *And so it begins.*

The afternoon continued in that vein, the flow of people to Jo's craft shop increasing as the wintry sun grew brighter. Most bought craft items, some simply accompanied buyers, but all discussed Alexis Wigsley's terrible crash. Jo learned little more about the accident, other than that it had occurred at 12:30. Kimberly Costello told her that part, explaining that she had been up with her new baby and, living only one street over from Greenview, had heard the crash, though she didn't realize at the time what it was. But when sirens soon followed, she knew something bad had happened.

Ina Mae stopped in around midafternoon, complaining that her power-walking group had cancelled because of the snow.

"I thought I'd come out anyway," she said, "for some fresh air." As she began to browse through Jo's beading section, Ina Mae overheard two women commenting on Alexis's accident.

"She must have been driving terribly recklessly," the older of the two said. "I heard the damage to her car showed she was clearly traveling at a very high rate of speed."

Ina Mae spun around to contradict them. "Alexis would never have driven recklessly. She was an extremely cautious driver ever since a cousin of hers was killed over twenty years ago in a car accident."

"She was?" Carrie asked. "I didn't know that."

"Yes, it was a hit-and-run accident out on Route 30. The cousin was in a coma for days before succumbing. Alexis was quite shaken by it and wouldn't drive for months afterward. When she did resume driving, she was very careful."

The other customer looked like she didn't quite believe Ina Mae as far as Alexis's careful driving, but Jo knew her friend well enough to know she never made a statement she wasn't 100 percent sure of. Why then did Alexis's car show such high impact?

The answer came much later in the afternoon. All the customers had cleared out, and Jo was doing a quick mop-up of melted snow on her floor. The phone rang, and Carrie picked it up. Jo could tell it was Dan, and she turned back to her mopping, though her ears perked up when Carrie's tone of voice changed dramatically. When her friend hung up, Jo looked over for an explanation.

"That was Dan," Carrie said unnecessarily, her thoughts clearly still on what she had just heard.

"Is something wrong?" Jo asked.

"Alexis's car crash. We were all wondering about her driving speed? There seems to be an explanation."

Jo waited.

"Dan got this from someone at Hanson's Garage. They towed the car. They also saw a major problem."

Carrie looked at Jo with worried eyes. "Her brake lines were cut. It wasn't an accident after all, Jo. Alexis was murdered."

Chapter 21

Jo closed up shop at six and stopped on the way home to pick up a precooked chicken and fixings from the supermarket's salad bar, feeling too mind-boggled after what Carrie had told her to think of cooking. After she had her dinner and cleaned up, she brewed a cup of tea and settled on her living room sofa, prepared to kick off her shoes and mull over the events of the last two days. She didn't get beyond the first sip before the phone rang. It was Carrie.

"Jo, I'm at the hospital. Sylvia's here because she started having problems. Xavier's a wreck, and he needs someone to be with him, but I can't stay much longer. Dan's still out plowing parking lots."

"I'll be right down," Jo said. She set her tea down and rushed about to gather up her things, managing to pull into the hospital's parking lot within twenty minutes. A short time after that she was heading rapidly down the corridor to Sylvia's room.

"Jo, we're here." Carrie's voice came from a little seating alcove to the right, and Jo braked to see her friend sitting next to Xavier. Xavier's forearms were on his knees, his head hanging low, and as he lifted it up to look at Jo, it seemed to require much of his last remaining strength.

"How is Sylvia?" Jo asked, taking a seat across from the two of them.

"Her water started to break. They're afraid the baby might be born too soon. They're with her now." Carrie sighed. "I'm sure the stress brought this on. The police have been talking to Xavier again."

Jo nodded, not surprised. "Did they want to know what you did after you left the hotel kitchen last night?"

Xavier looked at her with eyes that had aged years since she last saw him. *"Sí."*

"Xavier," Carrie said, standing, "I have to go home now. Amanda's been running a slight fever," she explained, turning to Jo. "It's probably nothing, but I should be with her. I'll come by again in the morning, Xavier. I'm sure everything will be much better."

Xavier stood up with Carrie, and she patted his hand in farewell.

"Thank you, señora," he said.

Jo watched Carrie head for the elevator with her cell phone in hand, ready to check on her daughter the minute she left the building. Jo waited for Xavier to sit back down.

"I'm so sorry Sylvia's having problems."

"It's what Señora Brenner says. It's all too hard on her. It could be very bad for the baby."

To look at Xavier's eyes was heartbreaking, but Jo kept hers steady. "The doctors here are very good. Try not to worry. She's in good hands."

After a moment, Jo asked, "Did you get a lawyer to be with you when you talked to the police?"

Xavier nodded. "Yes. Mr. Merkle."

"Good. What did you tell the police you did after you left the hotel?"

Xavier sighed. "I tell them the truth. I drive around

awhile. I'm very sad to lose my job. I know Sylvia be very sad, and I don't want to tell her, so I drive."

Jo groaned inwardly. That wasn't good.

"After you drove around, when did you finally get home?"

"I'm not sure. I don't look at clock. Sylvia was sleeping, and I was quiet and get into bed without waking her. Maybe it was eleven, maybe twelve. I don't know."

"Did the police ask you if you had ever worked with cars?"

"*Sí.* I tell them I never work at a garage. But I know how to fix things. I have to. We can't afford to take a car to be fixed. If I can't fix, we don't have a car."

Xavier said it so openly, Jo was sure he had no idea of the deep hole he had dug for himself.

"Xavier, this is the second time you have no one to back you up as to what you were doing at the time of a murder."

"But I have no reason to kill anyone!" Xavier had raised his voice, and a nurse's aide pushing a cart of medical equipment looked over, startled.

Jo waited until Xavier had calmed, then said, "The police might think you had good reason to want Alexis Wigsley dead. After all, she caused you to lose your job by dragging Mallory Holt over to find you there."

Xavier shook his head vehemently. "No, no, no."

"But the worse problem is your connection to Parker Holt, which is probably the main reason they're also looking at you for Alexis's death. They're likely thinking one thing led to the other. You have, in their eyes, a very good reason for wanting Parker Holt dead, and you also had a very good opportunity. It's that hour after you left Dan and spent grocery shopping that's the sticking point. Is there no one you can think of that can back you up on that? No one who can give you the alibi you need?"

Xavier looked down at his hands, which were clenched tightly. He shook his head. "No one, señora."

"Are you telling me the absolute truth, Xavier? I'm

sorry, but I keep getting an uneasy feeling that you're leaving something out."

Xavier shot Jo a look, turned away, then turned back, stating grimly, "I didn't kill Mr. Holt. I didn't kill the lady last night."

"Mr. Ramirez?" A nurse in green scrubs stepped into the alcove. "You can see your wife now if you like."

Xavier jumped up. "Yes, thank you!"

Jo watched as he hurried down the corridor to his wife's room. She hoped Sylvia's pregnancy was stabilized and that their baby was safe. The Ramirezes had enough troubles to deal with.

As she saw Xavier disappear into the room, she thought about how he reaffirmed his innocence regarding Parker Holt's murder. His sincerity had been convincing. However, he hadn't answered her question concerning whether he had left anything out.

Xavier, she believed, had told her the truth.

But, she wondered as she stared down the hall to the room holding the Ramirezes, had he told her the *whole* truth?

Monday morning, Jo drove straight to the shop, having heard from Carrie that she was at the hospital once again and that Sylvia was doing well. Jo had stayed late the night before until both Xavier and Sylvia fell asleep, Xavier in the chair beside his wife's bed. She was glad that Carrie would be there to help them through whatever their next steps were.

As she turned onto Main she was greeted with the cheering sight of Randy shoveling the walk in front of the craft shop.

She pulled up even with him and lowered the window. "Randy, you got my message!"

"Morning, Ms. McAllister. Right. Sorry I didn't get here sooner."

"I'm just delighted to see you now." Jo drove into the small parking lot beside the shop, which thankfully had been plowed the day before, though the process had created a high ridge along the edge of Jo's sidewalk. She had feared she'd have to tackle that ridge herself if Randy didn't show up.

As she unlocked her shop door, Jo told Randy, "I'll get some coffee going. It should be ready in a few minutes." She went in and flipped on the lights, the first sight of her craft wares always making her smile no matter what else occupied her mind. She headed past her red Valentine's Day display near the front, the brightly colored silk flowers she'd worked on yesterday, and the beautiful array of scrapbooking papers, stamping essentials, and beads, shucked her outerwear to stow in the back, and set up the coffeepot. She could hear Randy's shovel scraping against the pavement.

The phone rang, and Jo picked it up, wondering if it might be Carrie calling from the hospital.

"Jo, it's Loralee. I hope I'm not calling too early?"

"Not at all, Loralee. Is anything wrong?" Jo had picked up a seriousness in Loralee's usually cheerful tone.

Loralee sighed. "I just wanted to tell you. I've decided to take a condo at Pheasant Run. The Cardinal, I think— the one-bedroom. That should be all I'll need." Loralee sounded like a fugitive who decided to finally turn herself in and face up to spending years in the penitentiary.

"Are you sure?" Jo asked.

"Yes, dear. I do so want Dulcie and Ken and the children to be nearby. It will be fine. And I'll be close by to many lovely people at Pheasant Run. There'll be lots of bridge games."

Jo didn't remember Loralee ever enjoying card games.

"And such convenience with the shuttle bus available. I won't need to drive much at all." ·

Loralee *loved* her car.

"And that lovely fitness room."

Uh-huh.

"I wanted to thank you, Jo, for all your help."

"I did very little, Loralee," Jo protested. And for what she did do, Jo felt guilty since it had edged Loralee toward an existence she probably wouldn't enjoy. But what could Jo do? It was her friend's decision to make. "I wish you all the best, Loralee. If I can help you with this transition, I hope you'll tell me how."

Loralee promised, then asked after the Ramirezes. Jo told her what she knew about Sylvia's condition and heard some life come back into Loralee's voice as her focus switched away from her own concerns. "I'll notify the ladies at church," she promised. "That dear couple won't have anything to worry about when they come home from the hospital."

"That's great, Loralee," Jo said, and wished that could really be true. Xavier and Sylvia might not have their meals to worry about, but there would still be a heavy cloud hovering over them, which the Ladies' Sodality could do nothing about.

"Oh, Jo, I almost forgot! You know that lovely candleholder you have? I admired it once when I was there, if you remember."

"The stemmed, glass bowl that holds a scented pillar candle?"

"That's the one. Would you put it aside for me, dear? It will make a lovely housewarming gift for Dulcie and Ken with a rose-colored candle in it, don't you think?"

What Jo thought was that Dulcie and Ken should be showering Loralee with gifts for the sacrifice she was making for them, not the other way around, but she said, "Of course, Loralee. I'll find a nice gift box for you too."

Loralee fluttered on with more thanks before finally ending the call. Jo went to find the candleholder, thinking, as she lifted it off its shelf, that it really was a lovely piece. Shaped like an oversized brandy snifter, it was designed to hold a six-inch pillar candle inside and could be easily trimmed with matching flowers or ivy at its base. She wiped a bit of dust from its foot, found a rose-colored candle that smelled like strawberries, and set the whole thing on her desk. She heard the coffeepot come to its final sputters and glanced out her front window. Randy looked to be finishing up on the walk, so she went to bring him in.

Jo leaned her head out the door and called, "Coffee's ready."

Randy, who had been scraping up the final crumbs of snow from the pavement, looked over. "Okay. Thanks. I'll be right there."

Jo went back to pour out two mugs and set them on the workshop table where she and Randy had eaten their lunch a few days ago. She heard Randy stamp off his boots, then cautiously open the door.

"Don't worry about bringing in the snow," Jo said. "My customers will be tracking it in all day. Come on back."

Randy did so, Loralee's glass candleholder catching his eye as he passed by.

"That's just like the one at Parker's house."

"It is?" Jo handed him his mug. "You've been there?"

"Yeah." Randy blew at his coffee and took a tentative sip. He pulled out a chair and sat down, opening up his jacket and pulling off his knit cap. "Some time last summer. Parker hired me to work on his yard. I remember that candle thing because I nearly knocked the darn thing off a little table near the back door. I could hardly see when I came in from bright sunlight to use the bathroom."

Randy took a hearty drink of his coffee. "That's good. First cup of the day."

Jo smiled and nodded. "For me too." She pulled out

a chair and joined Randy at the table. "So you did some landscaping for Holt? Were there others there too? Workers from Pheasant Run?" Jo realized she'd never checked on Heather Bannister's story of Parker Holt dipping into the Pheasant Run resources.

"Not when I was there. But I could see there had been work done there recently—new bushes and stuff with their tags still on. I was hired to spread mulch from a big pile. I remember thinking it was funny that whoever did the planting hadn't finished the rest of it."

Jo made a mental note to verify who *had* done the planting and where they'd gotten the plants from.

"So you worked there just that once?"

Randy shifted in his chair. "Well, that might have been the last time I was there. Parker threw a few odd jobs to me, off and on. We knew each other from high school."

"Oh, right, I guess he would have been about your age. Were you in the same class?"

"Uh-huh."

"What was he like then?"

Randy shrugged. "I only knew him from shop class." He grinned, remembering. "He wasn't much good at it. Funny in a way, seeing as how he turned into a big developer. Guess he was a lot better at getting other people to do the work, while he just added up the numbers."

Jo took a drink from her mug. "Some people have accused him of dishonesty. Did you see that in him then?"

"As I said, I only saw him in shop. Hard to cheat there. You either build the thing or you don't. You're not going to get someone else to do your work for you with the teacher right in front of you, watching."

"No, I suppose not."

The front door dinged, and Jo looked over to see her first customer of the day, a woman Jo remembered who had bought Jo's prepackaged key-ring kit. Was it just a week ago? It seemed, after all that had happened, more like months.

"Excuse me, Randy," she said, getting up to greet her customer.

The woman smiled. "That kit I bought here turned out so well, I came for another one, plus one for my daughter."

"Great, I'm glad it worked out." Jo led her over to where the kits were stacked.

As the woman sifted through the various choices of colors and styles, she said, "Wasn't that a shame what happened to Alexis Wigsley the other night?"

"Yes," Jo said, by then weary of hearing that same comment, which had been repeated often the day before. She heard Randy pushing his chair back and remembered she hadn't paid him yet for his snow shoveling. She excused herself from her customer and went to her cash register. Randy seemed to have forgotten his payment as well, as he continued on to the front door.

"Randy!" Jo called, and held his money out to him.

"Oh, yeah. Thanks." He took the cash and stuffed it into his pocket.

"Thank *you*," Jo said. "By the way, Randy, did you happen to notice when Alexis Wigsley left the ball Saturday night?"

"The police asked me that too." Randy pulled on his knit cap. "I can't say for sure. I think it was toward the end, but people were leaving in bunches because of the snow, and I was kept hopping."

"So I guess you didn't see if her car was acting funny or not?"

Randy shook his head.

Jo's customer brought two key-ring kits over to the counter, and Randy took off. As Jo rang up the purchase, she reminded the woman of the ongoing beading workshops, "In case you want to learn a few more beading techniques."

As she said it, Jo's thoughts went to her group of regulars and how she looked forward to meeting with them again. She wanted their help to make sense of all the bits and pieces of information she'd picked up over the last few days.

"I'd really like to do that," the woman said. "But with so many things popping up lately in my life, I'll be lucky if I manage to get to this new kit anytime soon. Can't hold on to too many strings at once, can we?" The woman laughed. "You just end up with a tangled mess!"

Jo nodded. How very true.

Chapter 22

Javonne was the first of the workshop group to arrive, and Jo handed her the black dress on a wire hanger, covered with a plastic dry-cleaner's bag, along with the coat she had borrowed for the ball.

"Thanks so much, Javonne. It was a great outfit for my undercover work."

"You had the dress cleaned?" Javonne protested. "Why did you go and do that? I'll never be that size again, so all it's doing is going back into my closet."

"I don't think I was that size, either, to tell the truth. I doubt I took a full breath the entire night."

"Then it was a good thing you didn't have to chase down any criminals, wasn't it?" Javonne grinned. "I'll just take this right out to the car and get it out of the way."

As Javonne left the shop, Ina Mae and Loralee entered, and Jo retrieved the glass candleholder from the stockroom, where she'd packed it carefully with tissue paper in its gift box.

"Here you are, Loralee," she said. "I added a rose-colored candle to it."

"Thank you, dear!" Loralee said, taking it. "This will look lovely on Dulcie's coffee table."

"In *your* living room," Ina Mae added with a sniff.

"No, it will be her living room then. I've had it long enough." Loralee said it with a smile that didn't quite reach her eyes. "I went to talk with Angie Palmer yesterday. She's drawing up the papers."

Jo struggled with what to say and settled on, "Pheasant Run will be lucky to get you."

Javonne breezed back into the store, accompanied by Vernon, and they all gathered around the workshop table, where Jo had already set out the boxes of beads.

"I thought we could work on a multistrand bracelet," Jo said. "It's a bit more complicated, so don't expect to finish it tonight. But the result, I think, will be a lovely piece and worth the extra work." Jo explained how beads of various sizes would be strung on five separate wires, all attached in a row to the end slide clasp. "If you make each string hold a different pattern of beads, you'll get a nice effect. Then we'll string a sixth wire, and wrap it loosely around the other five." She held up the sample bracelet she had put together and got a pleased reaction from the group.

The ladies and Vernon got to work, needing much less direction by then, their major problems being the choice of color and style of the beads.

"So, when you weren't busy sleuthing, Jo, did you enjoy the Founders Ball?" Javonne asked. Jo noticed that she watched Vernon closely as he chose his beads, having likely figured out if she followed his lead she couldn't go wrong.

"I think she enjoyed her dance with our lieutenant, didn't you, Jo?" Loralee asked with a teasing smile.

"Russ Morgan asked you to dance?" Javonne asked. "I *knew* that dress was the right one for you."

"I think he just wanted to make sure I wasn't harassing the mayor's niece," Jo said lightly, but she felt her cheeks warm just the same. She bent down to retrieve a runaway bead as well as cover her reaction. What she had said to the group was what she'd been telling herself, but it didn't keep her from wishing another social event was in the works that would bring the two of them together once again.

"As it turned out," Jo said, straightening and dropping the bead in its proper box, "Mallory was the one harassing me. Where was Russ Morgan then, I ask you?"

"Mallory Holt gave you trouble?" Ina Mae asked. "That must have been after we left you. What happened?" Ina Mae wrapped a piece of wire around her wrist to judge the length.

Jo told about facing Mallory's fury over Jo's visit to Sebastian Zarnik's studio, and the follow-up threat to Jo's craft shop.

"How very unfair," Loralee said, "to hurt someone in a business way over a personal disagreement!"

"It's been done before," Ina Mae said. "However, this might be more than just personal. She could be fearful because of what she and this Zarnik fellow cooked up regarding her husband's electrocution, and wants to scare Jo off."

"It sounds like a very real threat to me, Jo," Vernon said. He had been working rapidly and had one wire of his bracelet nearly strung. "It sounds like she was giving you notice."

"I know," Jo agreed. "I've had a couple sleepless nights over that, believe me. My only hope is that she was bluffing or simply voicing what she'd *like* to do. I don't know that the building's actually been bought."

"You're still unable to reach Max McGee?" Ina Mae asked.

"Unfortunately, yes. Alexis had tracked him down to the Bahamas, but not precisely where in the Bahamas. She was going to work on it."

Jo's words hung in silence as each of them, she was sure, considered the fact of Alexis's untimely death. Word had spread by now that her car had been tampered with. But by whom? That question remained. Javonne broke the silence first.

"Did the same person who killed Parker Holt also kill Alexis?"

"I think we have to assume so," Ina Mae said.

"Somebody who was at the ball?" Loralee asked. Her partially beaded wire lay limply in her hands as she looked from one to the other and got four nods.

"The police, of course, have zeroed in on Xavier," Jo said. She told them about her conversation with Xavier at the hospital and his lack of alibi once more, for a critical time.

"Why does that man do this to himself?" Javonne cried. "It's as if he wants to be sure he'll be the chief suspect."

"I'm sure he wasn't aware that a crime was being committed," Ina Mae said, "when he chose to be alone and unaccounted for. If he had been the person who cut Alexis's brake lines I'd think he might have arranged some sort of fake alibi."

"How much time would it take to cut through the lines?" Javonne asked.

The women looked to the sole man in their midst for the answer. Vernon cleared his throat.

"Probably not all that long. The perpetrator wouldn't have wanted to cut all the way through, since the brake fluid would then have emptied out altogether, and Alexis would have known her brakes weren't working long before she got to that hill on Greenview. So a small cut in the line that produced a leak would be what was wanted: a slow leak that might increase as she used her brakes so that finally the brakes would give out altogether."

"Would they need a special tool?" Jo asked.

Vernon shrugged. "Just a basic cutting tool you'd find in most toolboxes. Dike pliers would do it, or even a penknife. A lot of men carry tools around in the trunk of their car."

"Xavier told me he did his own car repairs. He probably kept such tools handy in case of a breakdown."

Vernon nodded solemnly. Jo knew what he was thinking: another nail in Xavier's coffin.

"We have to figure out," Jo said, "who else wanted Alexis dead."

"She wasn't well liked," Loralee said. "But I can't imagine who would actually murder her."

"Perhaps," Ina Mae said, "Alexis had come too close to Parker Holt's murderer through her snooping."

"But why wouldn't she have gone to the police if that were the case?" Javonne asked. She had gotten behind in her attempts to duplicate Vernon's bracelet and was starting to look a bit frazzled.

"Maybe she didn't know she was coming close," Ina Mae argued. "Maybe her murderer needed to stop her before she realized what she knew. Jo, who did you see her talking with at the ball?"

Jo thought back. "She was with Mallory, of course. She followed Mallory out of the kitchen after Xavier was fired."

"So Alexis could have let something drop to Mallory," Ina Mae said. "I can't picture Mallory working under the hood of a car, but I could certainly see that artist fellow doing it for her."

"Yes, I could too," Jo agreed. She remembered Zarnik's mention of having to fix things himself around the studio, and his handy-looking toolbox. "I also saw Alexis talking to Heather Bannister. Heather's husband avoided joining them, but I saw him in a huddle with Heather afterward."

"Hmmm. It would be interesting to know what they discussed, wouldn't it?" Ina Mae slipped a large black bead onto her second wire. "And he's an electrical engineer, I understand."

"Yes," Loralee agreed. "So he'd certainly know all about how to kill someone with electricity, as Parker was killed."

"I think I've missed something about Heather Bannister," Vernon said. "She's the former manager at Pheasant Run, right?"

"Oh, that's right," Jo said. "We didn't catch you up on everything." Jo filled Vernon in on her visit to Heather's home and how Heather explained her firing from her management job.

"So she claims Holt was threatening her with a lie about an affair?" Vernon asked.

"Uh-huh."

"Is Heather Bannister an attractive-looking blonde?"

"Yes, she is."

"About twenty-five, maybe five-five, hair down to about here?" Vernon held his hand at just below his chin.

"Yes."

Vernon cleared his throat. "Then I'm afraid she may have been the one telling the lie."

"What do you know?" The question burst out of all four women at once.

"Well," Vernon carefully crimped a bead near the end of his wire, "as you know, I had a standing rule not to repeat things I heard or saw at my shop. However, you all have convinced me of the need to break that rule." He drew a breath. "I do remember Parker Holt coming into my shop about a year ago to buy a couple of steaks. A woman was with him who I assumed at the time was his wife, particularly as she was clinging closely to him as he chose the meat. Something was said, I remember, about people being out of town, picking up some wine, and fixing a nice dinner for the two of them. Because I've since learned that Mrs. Holt is a brunette, I'm thinking this might have been Heather Bannister."

"So it sounds like she *was* having an affair with Parker," Javonne said. "And he threatened to tell her husband about it if she blew the whistle on him dipping into Pheasant Run's money."

"Or," Jo offered, "maybe it was the other way around. Maybe she was aware of what Holt was doing but looked the other way until he decided to end the affair. Then she threatened him with what she knew."

"So how would that lead to his murder?" Javonne asked.

"Well," Ina Mae spoke up, "perhaps he had built up her hopes for the future with grand promises, which, when they were broken, infuriated her. Or, perhaps her husband found out and was just as furious. He might not have been able to stand the thought of Parker Holt getting away with what he did, may have needed revenge, and murdered him."

Loralee shook her head in distress. "Poor Kevin Bannister. Did all his hard work and study lead to this?"

"It's still just speculation, Loralee," Jo said. "We'll need to find out what Kevin was doing shortly before Parker Holt's death."

"Time is running out," Ina Mae pointed out. "Xavier Ramirez is in imminent danger, I'd say, of being charged."

"And if Xavier goes to jail," Loralee said, her face wrinkled with worry, "it will be a terrible sentence passed on Carrie and Dan as well."

Jo nodded grimly. She had feared that from the very beginning. Dan's business would never recover from its association to murder.

The group grew silent, the only sound that reached Jo's ears being that of beads slipping over wire and pliers pressing crimps.

"Well, I'm sure, Jo, you'll figure something out," Loralee said, quickly turning positive. "You always do."

Jo watched in amazement as the others nodded in agreement. It was as though Loralee had predicted Jo would come up with a great new decoration theme for the next PTA party. She saw them turn back to their beading projects with apparently settled minds. *Hey, I'm not a miracle worker, guys,* she wanted to cry, *though I appreciate the vote of confidence. Plus at the moment I seem to be hitting a brick wall.*

"Any ideas, Mike?" Jo threw out that last silent appeal, realizing she hadn't spoken to Mike in a while. Nor had he sent down any messages from his heavenly cloud, or whatever, either. Not that she was convinced those messages had truly come from him. It was, though, a comforting concept at certain times of her life.

She watched Vernon wrap his final string of beads about the other five strands, producing a striking effect largely because of the beads he had chosen, and wondered who was going to be the lucky recipient of this creation. His wife Evelyn? His daughter or sister? Who would he gift with this bracelet?

A thought suddenly popped into her mind: *A gift opens doors.*

It did indeed. Jo smiled as she thought she saw a possible crack in that brick wall.

"Thanks," she telegraphed skyward, but didn't wait for a response. She was too busy wondering what kind of gift Mallory Holt would most enjoy.

Chapter 23

Jo stood on the front steps of the late Parker Holt's house, ready to lift the same brass knocker she had tapped only days ago. Was this a good idea? she wondered. What kind of response would she get when Mallory Holt opened the door, considering their last encounter? Had the woman acquired any large, vicious dogs?

Drawing in a deep breath for courage, Jo lifted the knocker and tapped it three times, hearing the sound echo inside the house. *One, two, three.* After a moment, she heard footsteps approaching, then the sheer curtain stretched over one of the sidelights twitched and an eyeball flicked into view. Mallory? Jo heard a lock turn and braced herself as the door before her opened.

"You!" Mallory Holt faced Jo. She was dressed in a gray suit and heels as though ready to go out. To Parker's office? She held the door half open. "What do you want?"

"Hello, Mallory. I came to apologize. You were absolutely right—I had no right to go to Sebastian Zarnik's studio and waste his time as I did. I'm sorry I upset you, especially with what's been going on in your life right now, and I've brought this little gift to make amends." Jo thrust the gift forward.

Mallory stared at the box. Jo had wrapped it simply but beautifully with one of her lovely scrapbooking papers topped with an exquisite bow of pink wired ribbon. Jo watched Mallory's struggle, her animosity toward Jo pitted against the lure of the gift. Her curiosity—her greed?—tugging hard.

"You didn't need to do that," she said cautiously, then stepped back and opened the door wide. She reached forward for the gift. "But it's very thoughtful. Won't you come in?"

Yes! "Well, just for a minute." Jo entered the foyer and followed Mallory's lead to the formal living room, not the cozier den where Jo had met with Russ Morgan the night of Parker Holt's murder. She remembered seeing Mallory rush into her house that night, as the emergency vehicles flashed lights in her driveway. Jo had felt a pang of sympathy for her then, as one widow to another. She had very different feelings about the woman now.

Mallory gestured to her to have a seat on the burgundy-striped sofa. Mallory perched on a gold velvet armchair and worked at her gift's tie. She pulled off the pink-washed paper and lifted the box's top.

"Ooh!"

Mallory lifted out the silk flower arrangement Jo had worked furiously to create the night before as she strained to remember the colors of Mallory's living room, arranging burgundies and golds along with dark greens and a bit of white for brightness.

"It's lovely," Mallory exclaimed.

"I hoped you would like it. I put it together from the flowers in my shop."

"You did this?"

Jo nodded, she hoped modestly.

"Well, thank you! It will be perfect in this very room." Mallory paused. "We did get off on the wrong foot, didn't we? Why don't we just forget about the whole thing, shall we?" Mallory set her new centerpiece down on the nearby end table. "I can see you're artistically inclined. That must be what drew you to Sebastian's studio."

"Absolutely!" Jo crossed two fingers surreptitiously and hoped her expression looked sincere. "I had heard so much about his work and was dying to see it. I only wish I could afford to buy one of his paintings."

"Yes, the price of his paintings has shot up astronomically, ever since Guy Paxton from the Paxton Gallery in Philadelphia spotted one of his pieces and invited Sebastian to do a show there."

Jo remembered how Zarnik had explained it—that Mallory's aunt, Lucy Kunkle, had connected him with someone she knew at the Philadelphia gallery—but smiled and nodded. "Well, talent has a way of rising to the top, doesn't it?"

Mallory agreed enthusiastically.

Thinking she had probably softened Mallory up enough and beginning to tire of the effort, Jo was ready to turn the conversation toward motives and alibis when the front door's knocker tapped. Mallory jumped up, saying, "That must be my aunt. I had thought you were her, actually, but a bit early." Mallory opened the door to a plump, white-haired woman wearing a stunning fur-trimmed, peacock blue coat and matching hat. They hugged, then Mallory's aunt held her niece out by the shoulders and looked intensely into her eyes.

"How are you doing, my dear. Is it getting any easier?"

"Yes, Aunt Lucy." Jo couldn't see Mallory's face, but from the tone of her voice she imagined a sad but courageous expression spread over it. Jo rolled her eyes.

Another hug, then the two women entered the living room. Mallory introduced Jo and showed her aunt the silk flower arrangement Jo had brought.

"Mallory's friends have been so kind!" Lucy Kunkle exclaimed. "There's been a magnificent outpouring of love for her in her time of distress. Of course it says so much about how beloved Parker was too."

Since Jo held no such emotions toward either Mallory or Parker, and highly doubted Parker's funeral had produced much of any kind, she struggled to look properly sympathetic.

"Aunt Lucy, I'll just be a minute." Mallory turned to Jo. "My aunt and I are meeting friends for lunch."

Jo knew that was her cue to stand up and politely leave, but she hadn't planned to be particularly accommodating today. "How nice," she said instead and turned to Lucy Kunkle. "At a local restaurant?"

Mallory paused for an instant, then turned and left the room, leaving Lucy Kunkle alone with Jo.

"Yes, at Hollander's. It has wonderful food, and it's convenient to the office. Parker's office, I mean. Though I suppose now I should call it Mallory's office."

"Mallory's taking it over?"

"Oh, yes. Isn't it amazing of her? She said she couldn't let the business just fall apart. There were too many people depending on it. So she's been going in almost every day now, having Parker's staff bring her up to speed."

That wasn't good news to Jo. It meant Mallory might really know what the corporation owned and what it did not, and the threat she had thrown out at the ball may not have been an empty one. Jo's heart sank, but she pushed that worry aside. She needed to focus first on who murdered Parker Holt and Alexis, for Xavier's sake.

A framed painting on the wall over Lucy Kunkle's shoulder caught Jo's eye. Recognizing the style, she said, "That must be a Sebastian Zarnik."

Lucy Kunkle turned to look behind her. "Yes, don't you love it? Such a talented young man. And so good-hearted too! Why, that terrible evening after Parker's—well, that terrible evening—Sebastian rushed over to ask what he could do for Mallory. He had been halfway to Richmond at the time, where he was going to meet with a gallery owner. But when he heard the news on the radio, he turned right around."

Interesting. Zarnik had told me he was working in his studio at the time.

"I remember seeing him at the Founders Ball the other night," Jo said, "but I never got a chance to talk with him. Did he leave early, do you know?" *Early enough, for instance, to find Alexis's car and cut her brake line?* "I don't remember seeing him toward the end of the evening. I know the snow began to worry many people."

"Well," Lucy said, frowning, "now that you mention it, I can't say I remember him being around later on, either, and Warren and I stayed to the very end. I do remember Nancy Hatfield asking me a question that I thought Sebastian could answer best, something about a certain artist that she'd seen discussed on a PBS show, but when I looked to see if he was nearby, I couldn't find him. I didn't go searching of course. Nancy's question wasn't all that urgent."

"Mallory," Lucy asked as her niece reentered the room wearing a chic black jacket over her gray suit, "did Sebastian leave the ball early?"

"Sebastian? No. Why do you ask?"

"Mrs. McAllister, here, was—"

Jo broke in. "Your aunt said she had looked for him to answer something that Nancy Hatfield needed to know, and couldn't find him. We wondered if he'd left early because of the snow."

Mallory looked at Jo with slightly narrowed eyes, then at her aunt. "Sebastian may have stepped out for a cigarette—an unfortunate habit he slipped into during a stressful period of his life and has been trying hard to stop. That may have been when you didn't see him, Auntie. But no, I'm sure he didn't leave early. He's originally from upstate New

York, you know. Snow would never worry him. Now," she said firmly, "it's getting late. We'd better be going."

Mallory turned to Jo as she briskly gathered up her pocketbook and keys. "Do you mind if we all go out the back door? It's easier for me to set the security code there."

"Not at all," Jo said, rising. "By the way," she began, wanting to keep the discussion on Zarnik, but Lucy Kunkle spoke over her.

"Oh, certainly, Mallory dear," she said. "I do hope you had the code changed since . . ."

"Yes, Auntie," Mallory answered, a tad impatiently, and turned to lead the way through her impressive kitchen and into the short hall leading to the back door, the same hall Jo had entered that night as she searched for Parker Holt. Loralee's glass candleholder, or rather its twin, sat on a small table, something Jo hadn't noticed that night as her attention had been drawn to the lighted basement stairs.

"How in the world," Aunt Lucy asked, apparently focusing on the same item, "did this delicate thing survive all the goings-on of that awful night?"

"One of the medics apparently moved it out of the way and into the kitchen," Mallory said. "That's where I found it, anyway, the next day." She opened the back door to usher out her aunt and Jo, then punched in the code on the keypad before stepping out herself.

"Thank you again for the lovely flower centerpiece," Mallory said, pausing beside the silver Lexus that Jo recognized from having seen it parked in the driveway that night. A second Lexus sat beside it, this one black, and Jo assumed it was Lucy Kunkle's. Lucy pulled open the passenger door of Mallory's car.

"I'm so glad you liked the arrangement," Jo said. "Since you are obviously a person of impeccable taste, I was specially concerned."

Mallory accepted the compliment with a pleased tilt of her head.

"I mean," Jo continued, gesturing toward Mallory's front yard, "just seeing how beautifully your place was landscaped, told me so much. Did you design it yourself?"

Lucy Kunkle called out the answer. "Yes, she did! I remember you sketching it all out, Mallory, shortly after you and Parker moved in. I was so impressed. Then Parker surprised you by having all the plants and shrubs delivered and put in lickety-split!"

"Wow," Jo said. "How lucky of him to find a landscape service that had everything you needed on hand."

Mallory's brow puckered. "Not everything. As a matter of fact, there were quite a few changes made from what I had originally planned. But Parker, it seemed, found a good deal—plants that were available at a very good price."

Jo nodded, wondering if that very good price was in fact no cost at all, such as shrubs that had been ordered and paid for by the Pheasant Run condo association? It sounded like it.

Mallory glanced at her watch. "We'd better be going, Aunt Lucy," she said, and moved briskly toward the driver's side of her car.

Jo watched as the pair prepared to take off, wishing she could slip into Mallory's backseat and keep the conversation going. Her surprise gift, though, had produced an interesting tidbit or two, and it had at least put the two of them on civil speaking terms. This would be helpful for the future when Jo hoped she could pry more from the not-so-grieving widow.

Lucy Kunkle called out several farewell pleasantries to Jo as Mallory put her car in gear and began to back away from the house. Jo headed for her own car whose shabbiness seemed magnified by its proximity to the two luxury vehicles. She consoled herself with the fact that her rusty bucket of bolts had at least been fully paid for.

And with honestly earned money.

* * *

Jo had left Carrie in charge of the craft shop with a promise to bring back lunch for them both. Her first impulse was to head for the Abbot's Kitchen, but she realized she wasn't all that far from TJ's, the restaurant where she'd encountered Heather Bannister's hardware-store relatives. TJ's did takeout, so Jo headed there to pick up something.

She was standing at the takeout counter, reading over TJ's menu when a ponytailed waitress walked by and smiled. Jo automatically returned the smile, thinking the woman looked familiar, and after a moment realized she was Lisa Williams, Randy's girlfriend, whom Jo had first seen Saturday night at the ball. Lisa must have been a temporary hire for that night, just as Randy had been. And Xavier.

Jo gave her order to the counter person—a Chinese chicken salad for Carrie and eggplant parmesan for Jo— then sat down on the small bench provided for waiting customers.

Business at TJ's was light this midweek afternoon. Jo watched Lisa deliver an order of salads and burgers to two mothers with toddlers in high chairs, the only one of several booths occupied at the moment. Lisa chatted for a few moments with the mothers, then deposited her empty tray on a stand nearby and wandered over toward where Jo sat, exchanging a friendly word on the way with a passing waitress. She pulled a pack of cigarettes part way from a pocket and walked to the front window as if considering stepping out for a smoke, but apparently changed her mind and wandered back.

Lisa smiled once more at Jo, then stopped. "You were at the ball Saturday night, weren't you?"

"Yes, I was. I thought I recognized you too. Aren't you a friend of Randy's?"

Lisa's face took on a slightly defensive look. "Yes, we're friends. Some people seem to think that's odd, but . . ." Lisa shrugged.

"Some people like Alexis Wigsley?"

Lisa looked surprised, but then she nodded, apparently accepting that of course Jo would know it was Alexis Wigsley. Slightly overweight and blunt featured, Lisa's age, Jo guessed, was late thirties. Her face already showed signs of fatigue, the ingrained kind that came from hard work that produced very few rewards. Despite this, there was an openness about her that made her very approachable.

"Yeah," Lisa said, grimacing. "Alexis Wigsley. I suppose she was only trying to be helpful and all. But it kind of upset me, you know?" She fingered the cigarette pack in her pocket.

"Alexis was out of line, talking to you like that."

Lisa smiled gratefully. "I know Randy's had problems in the past. But who hasn't? At least he's honest. He might not be a big shot like his old friend Parker Holt, but the only harm he's ever done was to himself, not to anyone else. I mean, look how Parker ended up. I hate to say it, but it's the kind of thing that only happens to someone who deserves it. Parker may have been rich, but he wasn't much else."

"That's pretty close to what I've heard from a lot of people."

Lisa moved over to the vacant hostess stand and began rolling tableware into napkins. On a slow day like this, and with plenty of napkin rolls already prepared, Jo thought Lisa probably wanted to appear busy as she continued talking.

"It was really nice for me that Randy was working there that night, you know?" Lisa said, pulling a basket of spoons closer. "I mean, I was able to go talk with him when I had a break, and seeing him looking so great in that uniform and all helped me get over all the nasty things Alexis said."

Lisa dropped a fork and bent to retrieve it. She seemed on the verge of returning it to its napkin before catching herself and setting it aside for washing. She smiled at Jo, and Jo couldn't help wondering what the decision would have been if she hadn't been sitting there observing. The takeout person showed up with Jo's order packed in a brown paper bag, and Jo stood up to pay for it.

"Well, enjoy your lunch," Lisa said. "I'd better get my tables cleaned up. My shift's over soon, and Randy's coming by to give me a lift to my sister's."

"Say 'hi' to Randy for me. Tell him the shelves he built for Jo are holding up great."

Jo was halfway out the door with her bag of food when she stopped and turned back, catching Lisa before she disappeared.

"You called Parker Holt an old friend of Randy's. You meant, didn't you, that they knew each other in school, not that they hung out together or anything, right?"

Lisa shook her head, surprised. "No, they were real good buds. All through high school. Funny, isn't it, how they ended up so different?"

Jo nodded slowly. Alarms had started going off in her head so loudly that she barely heard the crash of crockery coming from a dropped tray somewhere in the back.

Lisa cried, "Oh gosh," and hurried off, leaving Jo still nodding and saying to no one, "Right."

Funny.

Chapter 24

Jo sat in her car for several minutes, thinking, then finally turned on her ignition and pulled away from the curb. She had gone halfway back to the craft shop when she abruptly made a left turn to do a backtrack of sorts. Jo passed the turnoff for TJ's and continued on for a few minutes until she pulled up in front of Hollander's, the restaurant where Lucy Kunkle said she and Mallory were lunching.

"Good afternoon." A mustached man in a dark suit greeted Jo as she entered the foyer. "Do you have a reservation?"

"I'm looking for Mallory Holt's party."

"Of course." He turned to a woman who stood nearby clad in dark slacks and a white dress shirt topped with a red bow tie. "Mrs. Holt's table."

Jo followed the woman, who had picked up a menu and obviously assumed Jo was a late-arriving guest of Mallory's. They wound their way through widely spaced tables that were topped with vases of fresh flowers and seated several well-dressed patrons. Soft music floated through the air along with muffled conversations, but most of that barely reached Jo's consciousness. Her mind focused on the questions she wanted to ask Mallory.

"Ms. McAllister!" Lucy Kunkle looked up in surprise as Jo approached their table. She managed a pleased expression, unlike her niece, who only looked annoyed. The other two women, closer in age to Lucy than to Mallory, glanced up with interest.

The waitress immediately brought a fifth chair to the table, although Jo explained she didn't intend to stay. "I'm very sorry to interrupt your luncheon, but I have something important to ask."

"If it's about your shop building—" Mallory began, but Jo stopped her.

"No, it's nothing to do with that." Jo sat, deciding she'd be less conspicuous and could speak more quietly if she did. "Can you just tell me, was your husband a good friend of Randy Truitt's when they were teenagers?"

Mallory's eyebrows shot up, and Jo could imagine her thoughts regarding Jo's mental state.

"I'm not asking this idly, believe me. Was he?"

"Well, yes," Mallory admitted. "Parker did tell me they had been friends as kids. You know how it is," she smiled deprecatingly to her other tablemates, "when you're that age. I'm certain the draw was the fact that Randy had a car to drive. Parker's parents were terribly strict at the time about allowing him access to theirs."

"So Parker and Randy did things together, outside of school, I mean?"

"Yes. Why do you ask?"

"I'm puzzled because Randy told me he barely knew Parker, and only from having shared a single class together in high school."

"Well," Mallory said, laughing, "you can understand why, can't you? I mean, how could the paths of two former friends have diverged much farther? It must be humiliating.

But Parker, despite Randy's, ah, shortcomings, never forgot his old connection. He gave Randy jobs off and on, that is, when he felt Randy was sober enough to handle them."

Lucy Kunkle crooned softly, obviously adding the information to her long list of Parker's saintly qualities.

"Yes," Jo said. "Randy mentioned having worked on your new landscaping last summer."

"Did he? I really don't keep track of that kind of thing."

"He said he almost toppled the table in your back hallway when he came in to wash up, and nearly broke the glass candleholder you have on it."

"Not last summer, surely," Lucy Kunkle spoke up. "He must have been thinking of some time more recently. You only got that piece two weeks ago, Mallory, didn't you? From the women's club—in honor of your first year of presidency."

Jo suddenly remembered Sharon Doyle having come into her shop shortly after Christmas looking for a gift item and buying one of the two glass candleholders Jo had in stock, the second going only recently to Loralee. Sharon hadn't mentioned at the time who the gift was for. Once again Jo was amazed at what a tangle of connection things in Abbotsville so often turned out to be.

"Yes, you're right about when I got that gift," Mallory said to her aunt. "However, I don't recall having had work done at the house since then. But"—she shook her head impatiently—"who can remember every little thing. Was there anything else, Ms. McAllister?"

Jo stood up. "No, that's all I need. Thank you." She vaguely heard Lucy Kunkle imploring her to stay and join them, with faint echoing murmurs added by the other two women at the table. A social lunch, however, was the last thing on her mind as she made her way out of the dining room. The bright sunlight Jo encountered as she stepped outside would have normally been cheering on a midwinter's day. But all she was aware of was the cold.

* * *

Jo slowly pulled away from Hollander's and headed back
to the Craft Corner. Traffic was light, which was fortunate,
since she drove on autopilot, her thoughts far beyond traffic lights and stop signs.

Had she been focusing in the wrong direction all this
time? she wondered. Had Parker Holt's murderer—and
Alexis Wigsley's—been right under her nose? Fixing her
shelves? Clearing her walk? Or was she overreacting to the
lies she had just caught Randy in? They were certainly
nothing that would hold up in a court of law. A lie about
how well he knew the victim, plus one concerning when he
had last been in the victim's house? What did they, in actu-
ality, add up to?

The thing was—Jo braked as she realized the traffic
light before her had turned red—why would Randy need to
lie at all unless he had something to hide? Jo supposed it
was possible that, as Mallory claimed, Randy simply hated
to invite comparisons between his life and Parker's, and so
had denied their past connection.

But Jo couldn't buy that. Randy's general history was
well known in the town. He must have been aware that Jo,
though new to the area, would have eventually learned at
least the basics of his background. So pretending little connection to Parker Holt, Jo felt, must have sprung from guilt.

Randy surely knew that Xavier was strongly suspected
by the police, and that Carrie and Dan were suffering severe damage by association. Jo's concerns, he would have
seen, would clearly have been for her friends. Randy may
not have been aware of the extent of Jo's investigations, but
he would have realized she was someone to be careful
around.

But his lie about when he was last inside the Holt's house
was, for Jo, the most incriminating one. Randy's comment
on the glass candleholder, she figured, must have slipped

out before he realized its possible significance. When he did, he clearly tried to cover by changing the time he had nearly broken the piece. Except he unwittingly trapped himself by not knowing how recently Mallory acquired the candleholder.

Jo sighed deeply. She had liked Randy, had felt he had potential for getting his life back on track. She would never have thought him capable of murder. What had derailed him so completely? Neither of the murder victims were sterling characters, but what about them could have drawn such violent actions? She arrived at Main Street and gradually braked as she approached her shop's parking lot. Jo signaled for her turn, then slowly drove in, feeling as weighted as if she were the one carrying her car instead of it carrying her. Uncovering the dark side of a liked and trusted individual, she was finding, was not a particularly satisfying coup.

Jo parked next to the Craft Corner's building and she opened her door. Engrossed with her dour thoughts, she stepped out, then remembering her lunches, leaned back for the paper bag. As she did, a voice spoke chillingly close to her ear: "Just stop there."

Jo felt the pressure of the knife before she saw it. She froze, then turned her head slightly to see Randy inches from her, his breath puffing into her face. He pressed a very large, very lethal-looking knife against her side.

"Be quiet, or I'll have to use this," he warned, and reached past her into the car, grabbing her keys from the ignition. He gripped her arm tightly with one hand, the other holding the knife, and jerked her toward the battered pickup that Jo had failed to notice as she pulled in, parked as it was beyond a large van.

"Randy—" she began, but he showed he meant what he said by pushing the knife into her jacket enough that she heard its nylon fabric pop.

"Just move," he repeated, and Jo did.

Randy pushed her toward the passenger's side of his pickup, Jo's eyes searching the lot for someone, anyone, who could help, but without success. He yanked open the door and shoved her forward.

"Get in," he said. "All the way over."

Jo climbed up and into the truck, then scrambled awkwardly over the console to get to the driver's seat as Randy pushed, while at the same time gripping her tightly. Randy took the passenger seat and pulled his door closed.

"Drive out onto Main," he said, his knife still pressing at her side. "And don't try to signal anyone or I *will* use this."

"Where—" Jo began, the knife instantly stopping her. Her foot fumbled for the pedals, which were out of reach until she yanked the seat forward. Then she turned the ignition and put the truck into reverse.

When Jo turned her head to look back, she got her first full look at Randy's face. It wasn't the face of the man she knew, the man who had come to her shop that first day, nervous and grateful for the promise of a job. This was the face of a total stranger. Though the features hadn't changed, the person behind them definitely had. The fear Jo had felt from the first, suddenly tripled.

"Turn right," Randy said as they approached the street. He held the knife against her with his right hand and gripped the collar of her jacket with his left. Jo checked in each direction but could see no pedestrians who might notice them and help her. The drivers of the few passing cars kept their eyes on the road ahead of them, Jo and her captor apparently catching no attention. She turned the truck onto the street and pulled away from the Craft Corner, feeling her heart sink with every inch of road she put between her and all reasonable hope of aid.

Jo drove up Main, staying, at Randy's orders, within the speed limit, while at the same time her mind raced, searching for a means of escape. Any scenario she came up with, though, ended with the high probability of her blood fatally spilling over the inside of the truck, so she drove on, hoping against hope that she'd still find a way out of this.

Jo drove straight when Randy told her to and turned when Randy told her to turn, gradually suspecting where he was taking her. This was confirmed when they pulled onto her street. He told her to slow down as they approached her house. Banks of snow lined the curbs, but the laughing children that had so recently played in them, building snow forts and tossing snowballs, had gone off to school, their parents most likely away as well at their jobs. The street was empty of both neighbors and traffic, and Jo turned into her driveway without, she feared, a single eye witnessing it.

Randy switched the knife to his left hand and fumbled in his pocket. Jo glanced over to see him pull out her automatic garage-door opener, which he must have snatched from her car's visor when he grabbed her keys. He pressed the button to raise the garage door, and when it reached its top, grunted, "Go." Jo did.

As Randy closed the door behind them, Jo stared forward, hearing the noisy clang behind her as the door hit bottom. It sounded like the clang of a prison door, which was what her once-cozy home had just become—her prison. But what was her sentence to be?

Life, or death?

Chapter 25

Randy got out of the truck and raced to the driver's side. He yanked Jo out and dragged her over to the connecting door, unlocked it with her keys, then pulled her into the kitchen. Randy stopped, glanced around, then dragged her through the small kitchen into the living room. He pushed Jo onto the sofa as he remained standing. It was a relief for Jo to at least have that knife out of her side, but it flashed menacingly as the steel caught the sunlight beaming through her windows.

"Don't move," Randy warned. He lurched over to the nearby windows to pull her blinds closed, after first checking the window locks, until Jo sat in murky dimness. He then did a rapid run-through of the other rooms of her small house—her bedroom, the spare, and her bathroom, all mere steps from where she sat—before returning to the living room. He sank into a chair facing her.

"Randy, this is crazy and you know it."

"Shut up!"

Jo noticed for the first time that he was sweating. Beads

of it had formed on his forehead despite the cold temperatures outside. His eyes twitched nervously as his gaze darted about the room, and the heel of one foot bounced against the floor. He pulled a small whiskey bottle out of his jacket pocket, uncapped it, and put it to his lips. He evidently had been drinking from it already, as he tipped it high for a final swallow.

"Randy, this won't solve anything. You're only making it worse."

"What do you know about making anything worse?" he shouted. "I've killed two people already! I can go to the chair for that. Do you know that? One more won't change anything. But you're the only one who knows I killed the other two. I get rid of you, I'm home free. You're my only problem."

Jo waited, giving him time to calm a bit. What was his plan for getting rid of her? Did he have a plan? His edginess suggested he hadn't formed one yet. If she could keep him talking he'd have less time to come up with one. She quietly asked, "How did you know I'd figured it out?"

Randy stared at her, scowling. "Lisa. I went to pick her up and she told me about you asking questions. She told me what she said about Parker and me being friends." His mouth twisted contemptuously. "Friends—hah!"

"Parker wasn't a good friend to you? I mean back then?"

"Parker was a leech. A 100 percent, effing, blood-sucking leech."

This was good; he was talking. Jo needed to keep him going. "You mean Parker used you?"

"Yeah, he used me. Just like he used everybody his whole life. Only I was too dumb back then to see it."

"You were a kid, then, Randy. Kids don't pick up on things like that. Not right away."

Randy scowled at her. "Maybe. He was scum, though."

"But there's more to it, isn't there? You didn't kill Parker because he made you feel used. What did he do to you?"

Randy's foot began bouncing again. He got up and began pacing Jo's small living room, the knife gripped tightly in his hand.

"You got any beer here? Anything to drink?"

"No, I don't." Jo knew there was an unopened bottle of wine in one of her cupboards, a birthday gift from Carrie and Dan, but she didn't mention it.

He stared at her as if searching her mind, then said, "Shit!" He pulled out his whiskey bottle, tried for a few last drops, then threw it across the room. He got up and walked to a front window, pulling the drapery aside an inch and looking out, then went to Jo's back door, whose window looked out into her backyard, and did the same. No one knew they were there, so what was he expecting to see? His fear, Jo suspected, was probably as great as her own, but for different reasons.

Randy returned to his chair and sat down, holding his knife across his lap.

"You want to know what Parker did to me? Why I killed him? I'll tell you. You'll see why he deserved it." He looked past her and his gaze turned inward, to the past. His voice took on an odd, deadly tone.

"We used to go out in my dad's old Chevy," he said. "It was a piece of junk, but it rode, and that was all we cared about. Parker didn't have wheels—his folks were too tight—and I did. I shoulda known that was the only thing that mattered to him, but all I knew was I was having the kind of fun I never had before and that was great.

"Then one night, Parker was home on spring break, his first year at college. We went out and got some beers. We'd driven around thinking we might pick up a coupla girls, but that didn't work out. So Parker starts asking stuff like how fast would that Chevy go. He's daring me, you know? Like, 'Think it'd make a hundred before it shook apart?' Things like that. I'd been working on it, replaced a few parts, and that kinda bugged me 'cause it was like he was saying I hadn't made the car any better. So to prove him wrong—and I wasn't thinking too clear with the beer and all—I drove out to Route 30, which I figured would be pretty empty then—and I revved it up."

Randy stopped, wiping sweat out of his eyes. Jo waited, sitting as still as she could, not wanting the slightest rustle of her jacket's nylon fabric to distract Randy. After a moment he resumed his story.

"The Chevy was doing good. I got up to eighty, ninety, and it was running smooth. Then, out of nowhere, this car pops up, I dunno, from some side road or something. I *swear* I didn't see it until it was too late. I tried. I swerved, but I clipped him on the side, hard, and ran him off the road."

Randy's voice had become shaky.

"I kept on going, at that speed it was all I could do to stay on the road. But the other guy—I heard later it was some kid coming home from working late at Burger King—he lost control and flipped over into a ravine.

"I started slowing down. I was going to go back. But then Parker says, 'What're you doing? Keep going! You're just gonna get us in big trouble! Don't worry about him. He'll be okay.' I was scared, I couldn't think straight so I kept on going, and got home, and hid the car in the barn hoping I could fix the damage to it before my pop saw it."

"Was the other driver killed?" Jo asked, guessing as much.

Randy nodded, rubbing his free hand over his face. "Not right away. He died in the hospital."

"But they never found out it was you?"

"No. Parker said I should keep my mouth shut, and I did. He said I'd go to prison if I turned myself in. It wasn't long after that my pop had his tractor accident. I kept the Chevy hid in the barn. I didn't even have time to fix the damage on it. I was scared, 'cause the paper kept printing stuff about how they were still looking for the hit-and-run driver, and putting in stuff about this kid that was killed, how his family was all broken up. It was pretty bad. Then my mom got sick, and I had to get her taken care of."

Jo could imagine the turmoil Randy had gone through. Still a kid, with no one to advise him but Parker Holt, who had his own reasons for keeping Randy quiet.

"You sure you don't have any beer?" Randy suddenly asked. Not waiting for an answer, he went into the kitchen and threw open Jo's small pantry door. Seeing nothing besides cans of food, he turned to her cupboards, flipping open doors until he found the wine bottle. He grabbed it, saw it had a cork, and pulled open a drawer, rustling noisily through it.

"Where's a damn corkscrew!" he shouted.

Jo told him.

Randy shuffled through Jo's kitchen tools, then finally found what he wanted. He brought it over to Jo, thrusting the bottle and corkscrew toward her, still holding his knife. "Open it."

Jo peeled away the foil wrapped around the top of the bottle and worked at the cork with the screw until she was able to ease it out. She held the bottle up to Randy, and he grabbed it and gulped, tipping the bottle upward with his free hand.

Jo watched from her broken-springed sofa as Randy paced about the room, taking swigs of her wine. Was the alcohol needed to handle the pain of the memories he had dredged up? What else, though, would it do to him? Finally, he stopped drinking and held the bottle down at his side.

"What did Parker do during this time?" Jo asked, wanting to get him back to his story.

Randy's lip curled contemptuously. "Parker went back to college. I thought—I hoped—I wouldn't see him again. But he showed up near the end of summer, wanting money."

"He asked you for money?"

"Not asked. He *wanted* it. He said I owed it to him for keeping quiet about the hit-and-run. I gave him what I had. I thought that would be the end of it."

"But it wasn't, was it?"

"He kept coming back, every time he was back in town from college. I owned the farm by then and I guess he thought I was raking it in, but I wasn't. I was barely holding things together with the mortgage, the taxes, the help I had to hire." Randy exhaled loudly. "There were piles of loans on the farm equipment, and then there was my mom's medical bills. But Parker didn't care. He kept coming back. Finally I told him I was bled dry. I just didn't have anything to give him anymore. That's when he said yes I did." Randy sank into the chair and stared at Jo.

"He wanted your farm, didn't he?"

Randy nodded, his eyes sunken.

"I didn't have much choice. Parker, he made it sound like he was offering me a good deal, like he was taking something off my hands that was going to go under anyway. He was paying for the farm, not taking it outright from me, so it was supposed to be great that I'd have money in hand to do whatever I wanted. Trouble was, all I really wanted to do was run the farm. But I signed the papers and took the check and left."

Jo didn't ask how much Parker paid Randy. She was sure it was much below market price.

Randy picked up the wine bottle and guzzled more of its contents. "I took off for Atlantic City. I had the crazy idea I could triple my money and maybe come home and buy the farm back and make a go of it."

"I guess that didn't work, huh?"

"Stupid idea."

"But you came back?"

"Yeah, I came back, eventually," Randy said, pain showing in his face. "I go to look at the old place and what do

I see? Houses going up and roads going in and a big sign calling the whole thing 'Holt Meadows.' Holt Meadows! He didn't even have the decency to keep the Truitt name on it."

"That must have been tough to take."

"And suddenly Parker's a big shot in town, married to the mayor's niece, and moving into a big house of his own."

"And hiring you to do odd jobs for him," Jo said, adding, "which you did," she pointed out. "So what tipped you over the edge, Randy? What was the final straw?"

Randy stared at the floor awhile, seeing what, Jo couldn't imagine, then downed more wine, coming near the end of it. Jo waited, wanting to know, but wanting, mostly, to keep Randy talking. Talking, not thinking. She asked again. "What tipped the scales?"

He continued to stare at the floor. "That day, I was working on the Schillings' front lawn, cutting up a tree for them that had fallen halfway down. Their place is right next to Parker's big house. I was there a coupla days, actually, cutting up the wood, stacking it up, hauling away the brush, and the whole time I'm seeing Parker coming and going in his flashy, expensive car. And I'm seeing the home improvement guys bringing in stuff to make his big, expensive house even better, seeing his wife go out in her fur coats and diamonds. And I'm thinking the whole time how Parker got his run on making all that money because of my farm. *My* farm." Randy raised his eyes to Jo.

"And he couldn't even call it Truitt Meadows. He had to name it Holt Meadows, like *his* family had owned it all those years."

Jo understood how in Randy's eyes that may have been Parker's worst crime—erasing Randy's family name from all connection to their land.

"So," Randy went on, "that second afternoon, I saw the two guys who were working there take off early. Parker's wife was gone, and I figured he'd be showing up in an hour or two like before. I had heard one of the workers that first day call out the alarm code to the other as they were getting ready to leave—dumb of them, but they didn't know I was listening—and as soon as they took off I went over and got in the house and wired up the trap.

"I'm good at things like that," Randy added with a certain pride. "Parker, he liked to look down at me, but he wouldn't have known how to do what I did. I knew when he'd reach down to pick up that crowbar, even if he saw the wire running from it, he wouldn't figure out what was going on."

"So that was why you killed Parker," Jo said, hiding as best she could the chill she felt at Randy's eerily calm recitation of his steps toward the murder. "But what about Alexis Wigsley, Randy? Why did you kill her?"

"Wigsley?" Randy looked reluctant to turn his thoughts in a second direction, as though he preferred to linger on his satisfying removal of a long-hated enemy. Then he scowled, possibly remembering his feelings against the town gossip.

"She always watched me like a hawk," he said. "She knew it was me that run her cousin off the road."

"Her cousin?"

"Yeah, the kid coming home from his Burger King job was her cousin. Every time I ran into her after that, she was always giving me the evil eye, like she's trying to trip me up, find some way of getting the goods on me."

Jo doubted Alexis suspected anything of the sort of Randy, but was merely watching him as she did everyone in town. It was Randy's guilty conscience that had seen things otherwise.

"Always watching me," he continued, "even after all these years. And she saw me working in the Shillings' yard that day, and came to your shop just to let me know that."

Jo remembered Alexis barging in the day the craft shop was closed, as Randy was rebuilding Jo's shelves. Alexis *had* mentioned seeing Randy at the Shillings', but was it in any kind of threatening way? It hadn't sounded that way to Jo; to her, it had come across only as Alexis's usual babble tumbling out to demonstrate how aware she was of every-one's comings and goings. Except she probably wasn't the least bit aware of what she had actually seen—a man plan-ning murder. All Alexis likely saw was a handyman cutting up a tree, and had probably cared only about how much the Shillings were paying him.

"You killed Alexis because you thought she would turn you in?" Jo asked, thinking how incredibly easily one mur-der led to another to cover one's tracks. Randy was right in that one could hang for the first murder alone, so what was there to stop him from more? What would stop him from killing Jo?

Randy stared at Jo, his face darkening, his fingers flex-ing in their grip on the knife. "She told Lisa," he said, "that she should break up with me."

"Oh! Yes, I knew about that. Alexis shouldn't have done that."

"Lisa's the one good thing's happened to me in twenty years, and she wanted to take that away from me."

"Lisa wouldn't have left you Randy, just because of what Alexis said to her."

Randy slapped his knife hard against the wooden arm of his chair. "How do you know that? Tell me! How do you know that?"

Jo jumped at Randy's outburst. "I—I—" she stuttered, not knowing what to say that could calm him down. He glared hard at her, waiting. Then the phone rang.

Chapter 26

Jo turned to stare at the phone sitting on the end table beside her. She looked back at Randy.

"Don't touch it," he warned.

It rang, two, three, four times, then her answering machine clicked on. They both listened to Jo's recorded voice inviting the caller to leave a message. The phone beeped, then Carrie's voice came through.

"Jo, are you there? I tried your cell and it wasn't on. Where are you?"

Jo pictured her cell phone tucked into the purse that had been left behind in her car. The sound of her friend's voice wrenched at her, contact with her only inches from Jo's hand but totally out of reach.

"A couple customers have asked things I can't answer," Carrie continued. "Are you coming back soon? Call me."

The phone clicked off. The silence in Jo's living room hung heavily. Jo feared Randy might be thinking, as she was, of her car, sitting in the parking lot beside her shop.

How long before someone recognized it and mentioned that to Carrie? How long before Carrie found it herself?

Randy could be thinking they had to get out of there. But to where? If he had known where to take Jo from the first, he wouldn't have brought her here to begin with. This had been the only place he could think of in his rush to get hold of her. A stopping point. Possibly he had thought to stay there until dark, when it would be safer to be on the road again.

Randy had been drinking, Jo reminded herself. He might be struggling to keep his focus. Perhaps she could help keep it muddled.

"I just remembered," she said. "I might have a small bottle of Kahlua around. It was part of a gift basket someone gave me for my grand opening."

"Kahlua? What's that?"

"A liqueur. It's coffee-flavored, and kind of sweet, but it's alcohol. Shall I try to find it?"

"Alcohol? Yeah, sure." Randy got up to stand next to Jo. "Go get it."

Jo stood up, unzipping her jacket, which was making her feel over heated, but keeping it on. "I'm trying to think where I put it. It might be mixed in with everything in the pantry."

She moved toward the kitchen with Randy following closely. Jo opened her small pantry and peered into it, hoping she really *did* have a bottle of Kahlua, since the memory of exactly what had happened to it had grown dim. She could feel Randy's breath on her neck as she moved aside cans of green beans and jars of mayonnaise and pickles, then looked behind boxes of pasta, packages of soup mix, and cartons of microwave popcorn. Finally, a dark bottle with a foil label came into view.

"Here it is."

Randy grabbed for it and stared at the bottle. He seemed

to be having difficulty reading the label. He shoved it back at Jo and said, "Open it up."

Jo removed the foil wrapper from the top, then twisted off the bottle's cap. She handed it back to Randy, not bothering to offer a glass.

Randy tasted the Kahlua and grunted. "It's like syrup," he complained, but he downed a sizeable amount of the contents.

Jo watched, also keeping an eye on the hand holding the knife. Had it relaxed at all? Not any that she could tell. What else could she do?

Suddenly Randy banged the Kahlua bottle on her kitchen counter, hard. "I have to get out of here! They're going to come looking for you soon."

Jo jumped at the noise, aware that he had said "*I* have to get out of here," not "we." Was that his plan, then? To kill her there?

"No one will come here, Randy. I never come home in the middle of the day. Carrie knows that. She'll keep checking around town."

Randy began to pace the small kitchen. "They'll come. They'll come. I gotta do it. I gotta get out of here." He stopped at her kitchen door and peered through the glass at the edge of Jo's curtain. Then he turned around and stared back at Jo, his knife blade twisting in the air.

"Randy, you can't kill me."

Randy stared silently at her.

"I have to."

"I know you think you have to, but it won't help you at all, Randy. I'm not the only one who will figure out you killed Parker. Killing me won't mean you're home free. It will only be one more death on your conscience."

Randy snorted. "Conscience? What's that? You think I have a conscience anymore?"

"Yes, I do, Randy."

"Well, you're wrong, lady. I left it back on Route 30."

"I don't think you did, Randy. I think you still feel very bad about killing that boy, even though it was an accident. It's too bad that Parker Holt was with you that night, egging you on and twisting your thoughts. He pushed you into that first bad decision to keep going, but I think you've suffered over that night ever since."

Randy was silent.

"One bad decision led to another," Jo said, "didn't it? It's what got you here. It's time to stop, Randy. Too many people have been hurt. You can't undo what you've already done, but you can stop adding to it."

"I get rid of you and it's over," he said.

"But it won't be, Randy. There'll always be one more, and one more. Is that the way you want to go on? You killed Alexis thinking she would be the end of it, didn't you?"

Randy didn't answer.

"And it wasn't. There'll be someone after me, then someone after them. Is that what you want?"

"I can leave town tonight, take Lisa with me. It'll be over then."

"Is that fair to Lisa—life with someone always looking over his shoulder? And what about the man you'd be leaving behind? The man who could be charged with Parker's murder? Can you leave him to be sent to prison for what you did?"

Jo thought she saw something flash in Randy's eyes. Was it the smallest touch of regret?

"He's an innocent man," she said, "with a young wife whose baby will be born any day now. Can you do that to him? To his young family?"

"What do I care about that?"

"But you do, Randy. You do. You're not such a monster as you think you are."

Randy reached for the Kahlua bottle and gulped at it. He raised his knife and waved it at her, signaling to Jo that she should walk back to the living room. She hesitated, then moved forward, preceding him and half expecting to feel steel against her neck at any moment. Had she reached him at all? Or had she been talking to an already dead soul?

Randy didn't strike, and Jo made it back to her sofa, with quivering knees but alive. She sat down.

"You can end this now, Randy," Jo said, quietly.

Randy stood over her. He raised the hand holding the Kahlua and put the bottle to his lips, drinking up the remaining contents.

"I've had one hell of a shitty life, haven't I?" he said, wiping his mouth, his face twisted with disgust.

"It's been pretty tough," Jo agreed.

"All I wanted was to farm," he said. "Grow things, hold on to the land. And I couldn't do it. I couldn't hold it together."

"You might have, if you'd been allowed to."

"I should have killed Parker right off. Got him off my back right away."

"That wouldn't have been the answer."

"No? Would I be where I am right now if I got rid of him right off? A bum, without two nickels and ready to kill one of the few people who treated me with any decency?"

"You might have your farm, but if you'd killed Parker back then your life wouldn't be much better. You'd be as haunted as you are right now, always running from your conscience, thinking everyone who looked at you could see inside to what you had done."

Randy flopped into the chair he had occupied before. He sat, staring dully and silently at Jo. She could only guess what was going through his mind. After what seemed like several minutes, he spoke.

"I made a footstool for my mom once. I was only twelve. It was the first thing I ever made like that. I fitted the legs to it, sanded it, stained it. She told me it was the best footstool she'd ever seen."

Jo nodded, not knowing what Randy was leading to.

After another period of silence, he said, "My pop and me, we were talking about buying a few more acres to expand the farm. He asked me what I thought we should plant on it. He asked *me*." Randy's eyelids flicked briefly. "I told him I thought we shouldn't go with corn but that soybeans were looking good that year. So that's what we were going to do. Plant soybeans on the extra acres."

Jo waited. Why was he telling her this? The silence grew heavy, and Jo could hear herself breathing. Short, rapid breaths. Then Randy spoke again.

"Just before my mom died," he said, his voice having gone hollow, "she said she wanted me to find a nice girl to marry, and have kids. She wanted me to name one of them after my pop. Bill. His name was Bill."

Jo nodded, venturing a small smile. She waited again, but Randy had stopped. He didn't seem to be looking at her anymore, but looking *through* her. Finally, he stood up. Jo held her breath as Randy moved toward her, but then he continued on. He wandered about the room, touching things absently.

He moved over to one of the windows again, pulling aside its curtain an inch and peering outside. But Jo didn't sense the same urgency, the same anxiety he had had before, pushing him. There seemed to be a strange calm settled on him, and Jo didn't know what that meant. She began thinking of what she could do to defend herself should he suddenly come at her with that knife. But, as in the truck, everything she thought of seemed hopeless. She might be able to fight Randy off for a time, but ultimately she knew he had all the power.

He turned from the window, then crossed the room, moving past her again to her front hallway. She heard him enter her bathroom. Jo sat for a moment, confused, poised for action but not knowing what that action should be. Randy hadn't warned her to stay put, hadn't seemed to even be thinking of her, but most important hadn't taken the receiver of her cordless phone with him. Would she have time to call for help?

Before she could think any further, Jo heard a groan, then a noise as if something had dropped on her bathroom floor. Something heavy. She jumped up.

"Randy?"

Jo suddenly knew what had happened and rushed to the bathroom. The door was closed.

"Randy?" she called, and getting no response pushed at the door. She couldn't open it more than a few inches. Something pressed against it on the other side, holding it. She pressed harder, looking down at her bathroom's black and white checkered tile. When she saw red slowly seep over the squares, she moaned.

"Oh, Randy."

Jo ran to her phone and punched 9-1-1.

"Please get an ambulance over here right away!" she shouted.

Chapter 27

Jo realized she was clutching her middle, holding her arms wrapped tightly against her stomach. Was it because of what she pictured about Randy? Was she mentally trying to keep his blood from spilling out by holding her own in? She tried to relax but found it impossible.

The ambulance arrived, and she waved the paramedics into the house, rushing through an explanation of what she thought had happened. Then she backed away to give them room to work, hearing them shout commands, back and forth, their radios crackling, and hoping against hope they had come in time.

"Come on, guy, stay with me," she finally heard one say, and she collapsed into the chair Randy had so recently occupied. He was alive. At least there was that. But alive for how long? And for what? What was Randy's fate after that?

A stretcher was brought in and soon wheeled out with Randy bundled onto it, hooked up to an IV as well as other instruments Jo could not identify. As the team took him out to the ambulance, one paramedic, a burly man with a kind face, approached Jo.

"What about you? Are you all right? Do you want to go to the hospital?"

Jo shook her head. "I'm okay."

"How about calling someone? The cops will be here any minute, but you should have someone with you."

Jo looked up at him. Before she could respond, a deep voice at her open front door answered for her.

"She'll have someone with her."

Russ Morgan came in, flashing his badge and dismissing the paramedic. As he approached, Jo stood up, feeling suddenly unsteady. She took a step toward him, then wavered and fell against his chest. He wrapped his arms about her, and she could feel his head shaking back and forth.

"When," he asked, "are you going to start trusting us to do our job?"

"Right now," she said into the wool of his jacket. "I'm putting this whole thing in your hands as of this moment."

"About time."

"The coffee will be ready in half a sec," Carrie said to the small group gathered in her family room.

Jo looked around at the four who had shown up on the Brenner doorstep one by one, wanting to assure themselves that Jo was in fact all right: Ina Mae, Loralee, Javonne, and Vernon. An hour or so earlier, Carrie, horrified to learn what had happened, had instantly closed up shop and rushed to Jo's place. Jo, by that time, had given her full account of the ordeal to Russ Morgan, who then relinquished her to Carrie, after first exacting a promise from Jo that she would stay at Carrie's house and allow herself to be fussed over. It wasn't a difficult promise to make.

"Take a seat, Jo," Ina Mae said, patting the sofa cushion

next to her. "You shouldn't be on your feet. You've gone through an extremely stressful time."

"Yes indeed," Loralee agreed. "I still think they should have taken you right to the hospital."

"The hospital staff," Jo said, "had more important things to attend to besides patting my hand."

Ina Mae nodded. "Randy Truitt. He did do some terrible things, but I can't help feeling bad for him."

Loralee grew teary eyed. "If we'd only known what he was going through. Here we all thought Randy had brought his problems on himself. If we'd only realized what Parker Holt was doing to him from the beginning."

"From what Jo's told us, Randy wasn't exactly guilt free back when it all started," Javonne pointed out. "He did cause that boy's death by his reckless driving."

"But from what I understand," Ina Mae said, "he wouldn't have been driving that way at all if it weren't for Parker. Which just goes to show how important it is to choose one's companions wisely when in your teen years." Ina Mae looked over her glasses toward Charlie as she said this. Charlie, who had wandered to the doorway from the kitchen, did a rapid backpedal, bringing the first, small smile of the evening to Jo's lips.

"I could kick myself," Vernon said, "for not stopping in at your craft shop this afternoon. I had parked in your lot and thought of doing just that since Evelyn asked if I'd make her another set of earrings for a wedding that's coming up. But I put it off, thinking there was no hurry, and I was eager to pick up a book that Jim Wald ordered for me. A how-to-do-it on making wine at home.

"Anyway," he continued, "if I'd gone into your shop, Carrie would have said something about you not being there and I could have told her I'd seen your car in the lot."

"If I'd only stepped outside myself," Carrie said, "I'd have seen Jo's car and known something was wrong. Especially with the lunches you bought for us, Jo, sitting right there on the seat."

"Who steps outside for a breath of air in the middle of January?" Javonne asked reasonably.

"Indeed," Ina Mae agreed. "It was all most unfortunate that Randy managed to pirate you away, Jo, when everyone around was preoccupied with their everyday doings."

"You got that right," Dan said, carrying a steaming mug into the room. He had obviously helped himself to the first of his wife's fresh brew, and Carrie popped up with a mildly exasperated look at her husband.

"Let me get the rest of you some coffee," she said.

Javonne followed Carrie into the kitchen to help.

Dan stepped aside to give them room, seemingly oblivious to his faux pas, and finished his thought. "People might as well have blinders on when they're busy running errands. My own huge mistake was letting that Truitt guy overhear the alarm code for Parker Holt's house."

Jo reassured him. "Nobody would expect that someone would be listening to them on the other side of the bushes. Besides, if he hadn't chanced to hear that, I suspect Randy would have come up with some other plan. Attack Parker in his driveway, perhaps."

"Maybe," Dan acknowledged. "But then it might not have looked so bad for Xavier."

"Xavier!" Loralee cried. "Does he know what happened? Is he aware he's off the hook?"

"We've called him," Carrie said, bringing in a tray of filled coffee mugs and setting it down on the low table. Javonne followed, carrying cream and sugar, napkins and spoons. "He was so relieved! I could hear tears in his voice. Did you hear that too, Jo?"

Jo nodded. "I did. I spoke to Sylvia too. She's on bed rest, you know, which must be awful, but her only complaint was that she couldn't rush over to give me a great big hug."

"What a dear person," Loralee said. "I'll have to stop in and see her. I'll take a nice big cake that they can celebrate with."

"I want to see them too," Jo said. "I still have something to talk about with Xavier."

Carrie gave Jo a look that said she understood what she meant, but said nothing as she began passing out the coffee to the group.

Chapter 28

Three days later, Jo stood looking out the window of her shop. Carrie had gone to the back room for a box of knitting needles in order to restock the rack out front. Things had finally quieted down after a blizzard of news-hungry customers on the first day she'd reopened, and Jo was relieved to feel that things were returning to normal, although what "normal" was, was becoming hard to define. "Quieter" was probably a better word. She thought about her visit a couple of days earlier to Xavier and Sylvia.

Since Sylvia was on bed rest, Xavier had brought Jo into the bedroom, where they'd pulled up chairs close to Sylvia's bed, each holding a mug of coffee that Xavier had made. Sylvia sipped at the water she kept on the table beside her.

"We are so grateful," Sylvia said, holding out her hand for Jo to clasp. "If it weren't for you, Xavier would be in jail."

Xavier had added his thanks, emotion choking most of his words.

"I'm happy this ordeal is over for you," Jo said. "And I'm delighted to see you looking so well, Sylvia. Obviously you've been sleeping much better lately. But there's still something bothering me, and I hope, Xavier, you can clear it up."

"Yes, señora, whatever I can do for you."

"The police kept hammering at you for several reasons, but a large part of it had to do with your lack of alibi for the critical times surrounding the murders. I believed you from the first, Xavier, that you were innocent. But I also felt you hadn't told me the whole truth."

Xavier looked over to Sylvia and she nodded. "Tell her," she said. "Jo deserves to know, after what she has done for us."

Xavier heaved a great sigh. "Yes, you should understand, señora." He drew in a breath. "It was Sylvia's cousin, Miguel."

"Her cousin?" Jo asked, confused. "What do you mean?"

"Miguel, he was here illegally. Sylvia and I, we have our papers. We do it the right way. We will be American citizens very soon if all goes well. But Miguel, he could not wait. He want to come right away, make money. So he come, even though we warned him not to do it, and he got a job working with chickens on the Eastern Shore.

"Then he was warned the INS was coming, that they were going to raid the plant where he works. He had to get out of there right away or he be in jail. He could not even go back to the place where he was living. He call us for help."

Sylvia broke in at this point. "It was me who begged Xavier to help Miguel. It was very wrong, I know, but Miguel is my cousin! How could I turn him away?"

"The day Mr. Holt was murdered," Xavier said, "after Mr. Brenner and me we finish work and quit early, I did not go to grocery store like I say. I go to pick up Miguel and take him to my friend's house outside of Annapolis to stay for a few days." Xavier looked earnestly at Jo. "This was very dangerous for both of us, for my friend and for me. Helping Miguel hide is not right thing to do, we both know that. It could get us in much trouble. I could not tell police where I was when Mr. Holt was killed. My friend, who was very good to help, would go to jail. Maybe sent back to Mexico. I could not do that to him."

"And Xavier too," Sylvia added. "He would be in trouble because of what I ask him to do."

Jo nodded. Truly stuck between a rock and a hard place. Xavier's loyalty to his friend, though, might have cost him much more than his citizenship. "Where is Miguel now?" she asked.

"He's on his way home, back to Mexico, señora. We gave him what little money we had so he could go, but we said we would not help him anymore to stay."

"We're so sorry we had to lie about the grocery store," Sylvia said, looking genuinely distressed.

"Miguel put you in a very difficult situation," Jo said, though thinking they had made some unfortunate decisions themselves. "But thankfully it's over now. I'm glad you cleared that up for me."

Sylvia and Xavier had both looked so relieved that she wasn't angry, Jo was happy to soon change the subject to the much more neutral one of Sylvia's possible future handbag production.

Carrie's voice startled Jo back to the present as she called from the stockroom, "I think you'd better order some more Valentine paper." She stuck her head out the door. "And we're getting low, it looks like, on certain beads. You might want to check them over."

"Yes," Jo said. "I meant to do that, before, ah, things got in the way. Thanks for reminding me."

Carrie brought her box of knitting needles to the front and set about filling up the rack. As Jo started to turn away from the window, she spotted Loralee coming down the street toward the shop. The warmer temperatures of the last few days had melted away much of the snow, and Loralee looked to be fairly bouncing down the cleared sidewalk, moving with a liveliness that Jo hadn't seen in her friend in quite a while. Jo smiled, wondering if the reason for that cheeriness might be connected to the conversation Jo had had with Lucy Kunkle the day before.

Lucy had called Jo, full of concern for her well-being as well as gratitude. "You took such a huge burden from our dear Mallory," Lucy said. "She never admitted it, but I'm sure that not truly knowing who had set that awful trap for Parker was a terrible strain on her. You've given her closure, Mrs. McAllister." She had gone on to say how she and the mayor were in her debt and that Jo had only to ask and they would do whatever was in their power to repay her. Jo had begun to politely wave away the offer when she suddenly had an idea, which she shared with Lucy. She hoped, soon, to learn if what she had asked for had in fact been within Lucy and Warren Kunkle's power.

"Isn't it a lovely day?" Loralee sang out as she pulled the craft shop door open.

"Hi, Loralee," Carrie called from her knitting area. "It certainly is. What brings you here today?"

"I wanted to tell you that I've just been to see your husband," Loralee said, her eyes dancing.

"Dan? That's nice, but whatever for?"

"To discuss a project." Loralee set down her large tote and waited for Jo and Carrie to draw closer.

"What project is that?" Jo asked, hoping she was guessing correctly.

"Building a mother-in-law suite on my house!" Loralee clapped her hands. "Isn't it wonderful! I got the news yesterday and could hardly believe it! The zoning board has reconsidered. They're allowing me a variance so I can have the addition put on that I wanted."

"That's wonderful, Loralee," Jo said, mentally rejoicing over the power of politics. The Kunkles had come through!

"I'm so delighted. Dulcie and Ken will able to move to Abbotsville, and we'll all be close by, and I'll have my little garden to work in."

"And your car to continue to drive," Jo added, knowing what that meant to Loralee as well.

"Indeed. And," Loralee said, turning to Carrie, "Dan said he can definitely build it within my budget—the money I *won't* be spending now on a condo at Pheasant Run—and he can get started almost immediately. All we have to do is work out a few details."

"That's wonderful," Carrie said, her eyes shining, and Jo knew she was thinking about Dan finally getting work to do after so many projects had been cancelled.

Loralee must have been thinking of that too, since she said, "I wanted to be the first in line for Dan's time. I know, now that this murder thing is all cleared up, that his old customers will be flooding back."

"Well, they certainly might, once they see you're trusting him enough to hire him."

"Trust!" Loralee cried, flapping a hand dismissively. "Trust is a given. I wouldn't invest this amount of money with any other man besides Dan. And with Xavier, of course, helping. Which reminds me, Jo, I've been to see Xavier and Sylvia, and we talked, among many other things, about their baby-to-be. Did you know it's going to be a girl?"

"No, I didn't." Jo smiled.

"Yes, the doctors did a sonogram while Sylvia was at the hospital to make sure things were okay, and that's when they found out. And," Loralee said, her eyes dancing once again, "guess what they plan to name her, now that they know."

Loralee was certainly in the mood for announcements today. "What, Loralee?" Jo asked, happy to play along.

"They want to name her Jo!"

"Oh! Wow!"

"That's terrific," Carrie cried.

"Isn't it? Actually, it'll be Jovita, which will satisfy Sylvia's mother, but they will call her Jo. I told them they couldn't have come up with a more perfect name."

"Maybe," Carrie said, throwing Jo a teasing look, "they'd like to use Jo's full name. The one that's actually on her birth certificate."

"What's that?" Loralee asked. "I always assumed Jo was short for Joanne."

"No," Jo said, tossing Carrie a warning grin, "but we don't need to go into that. Jovita is lovely. They'll be much happier with that."

"Well—" Loralee began, looking like she *did* want to go into that, but happily for Jo the Craft Corner's door dinged as Javonne walked in.

"Hi, all!" she called. "I saw you heading here, Loralee, so I thought I'd pop in and catch everyone up on something I just heard."

"Isn't Harry's office open today?" Loralee asked.

"Oh, yes, which is exactly where I learned this. Harry has a break between patients, so I'm taking the chance to run over to the school to drop off James's lunch, which he left behind on the kitchen counter this morning.

"Anyway," Javonne drew a breath, "Sue Doyle was getting her teeth cleaned this morning. She lives right across the street from the Bannisters, and she says Kevin's moved out, and she's pretty sure they're heading for divorce."

"Oh, my," Loralee said, shaking her head.

"Well, Heather wasn't guilty of murder," Carrie said, "but from what you told me, Jo, she wasn't exactly innocent."

"No, Vernon pretty much confirmed that she and Parker had been having an affair. She tried to pretend to me that it was all a false threat on Parker's part, as she must have pretended to her husband. But apparently he stopped believing her."

"The truth always comes back to bite you," Javonne said.

"How sad," Loralee said. "But I suppose it could have been worse. At least neither of them is heading off to prison."

"No, there's that," Javonne agreed. Her face turned somber. "How is Randy? Has anyone heard?"

"He's out of intensive care and slowly recovering," Jo said. "Of course, he's under close guard at the hospital— both for suicide watch and because of the murder charges."

All four women fell silent, contemplating the grim future that lay ahead for the former handyman.

The phone rang, breaking the spell, and Jo moved to answer it.

"Jo's Craft Corner," she said.

"Mrs. McAllister," a male voice said, "I understand you've been trying to reach me. This is Max McGee."

"Max! At last!" Jo sank onto the tall stool behind her counter. "How are you? Did you get my messages? Please, tell me what's going on with this building!"

Javonne waved, pointing at the brown bag in her hand that she still needed to deliver to her son, and took off.

"My, my, my," Max's voice said into Jo's ear. "Hold on, there. That's a whole lot of questions, young lady. First of all, I'm fine, thank you. That dag-blasted knee of mine was more trouble than it was worth, but I'm walking on it again, so there's that."

"I'm glad to hear it," Jo said, holding her breath.

"And I did get your messages, eventually. The phones were down for quite a while where we were on the island. Not that service was all that good when they were up and running. But Rose and I went there to get away, and we certainly did."

"Uh-huh," Jo said. She rolled one hand in a speed-it-up motion, her frustrated glance catching Carrie's, who had picked up on Max's name and watched anxiously. Jo feared Max might next go into a description of the island and their accommodations, but he finally got to what she was dying to hear.

"That Holt fellow, he tried like the dickens to get me to sell my property up there. Kept upping the offer, throwing in perks, you name it. But I didn't like the sound of it."

Jo's heart leaped with hope.

"So I told him no, I wasn't going to sell."

"You did!"

"I sure did. If I'd known it was going to cause you some consternation, I would have told you about the whole thing. It just didn't occur to me that you'd ever hear a word about it. The discussion was just between him and me. I thought that was the end of it."

"Frannie had to close her floral shop because her landlord sold to Holt. That's how I first heard about what he was doing."

"George Miller sold? Well, he was looking to get out for a while, from what I understand. He probably was just waiting for someone like Holt to come along. But don't you worry, young lady. If you want to renew your lease, I can have the papers sent over to you right away."

"Yes, I certainly do, Max. I will sign that paper the minute I get it. And thank you so much for calling. You've pretty much made my day."

"Glad to be of service," Max said, a chuckle in his voice.

Jo hung up her phone and threw up her arms. "I can stay!" she cried.

"Oh, thank goodness," Carrie said.

Loralee smiled widely. "Wonderful! Dear Max. I knew he wouldn't let you down." She gathered up her tote and patted Jo on the arm. "I'm delighted with your news, but I'm afraid I have to be going. There are a million things on my to-do list. I'm so happy for you, Jo. We all want you to be here for a long, long time."

She gave Jo a hug, then one to Carrie, and took off, leaving two happy people behind.

"Well," Carrie said, "what's the first thing you're going to do, now that you know your shop is surviving?"

Jo grinned. "The evil side of me is tempted to call Mallory Holt, stick my tongue out, and say, 'Nyah-nyah.' But I won't."

"No, best stay on the good side of a woman like that. You never know."

"It will be interesting to see what *she* does next. Will Sebastian Zarnik be a part of her life? And will she stay in Abbotsville and run Parker's corporation, or chuck it all to follow Zarnik wherever his career takes him?"

"I don't see Mallory as much of a follower, do you?"

"Not really, but . . . well, we'll see. As to what I'm going to do, I want to sit down right now and design the best little necklace I can for my namesake-to-be, baby Jo Ramirez."

"Lovely idea. Maybe something that can be added to as she grows?"

"That's what I was thinking."

Jo happily headed to her desk to begin sketching. A customer came in who was interested in yarns, and Carrie and she launched into a detailed knitting discussion, which Jo tuned out as she turned on her creativity. Pleasant thoughts kept intruding, though, including the look on Carrie's face when she realized Dan's business was getting back on track, as well as Loralee's as she shared her rezoning news. Max's phone call, of course, had settled in two minutes the worry that had hung over Jo for several days, and Jo sighed, feeling a deep satisfaction with her life as it stood at that moment of that day.

There wasn't anything, she felt, that could make her feel any better than she did right then. Then the phone rang, and, seeing Carrie still occupied, Jo picked it up herself.

"Jo?" asked a male voice she instantly recognized. "This is Russ Morgan."

"Russ," Jo said, her own voice suddenly a bit wobbly.

"How are you?" The only contact she had had with Russ after that awful afternoon at her house had been through messages given to Carrie. Jo, within hours, had experienced an overwhelming fatigue that might have been more emotional than physical and had slept an unprecedented—and embarrassing—eighteen hours. The messages from Russ had only been polite inquiries as to Jo's well-being, but Jo had greatly regretted missing them.

"I wondered if you might be free tonight?" he asked. "There's a great little place just outside of town I thought we could go to for dinner."

Jo smiled foolishly at the phone and realized she had been wrong. Here she had thought she couldn't feel any better than she had a moment ago.

But suddenly she did.

Make a Special Key Chain

*(See one version of this beautiful key chain
on www. maryellenhughes.com.)*

1. Attach a small split ring to a key ring.

2. Run a six-inch-long wire through the split ring and bring both ends together.

3. Put a crimp on the double wire, close to the key ring.

4. String three or four large beads of your choice over your double wire.

5. Add a crimp after the last bead, then add your charm.

6. Run your wire ends back through the crimp and beads to finish off.

Designed by The Bead Shack of Crofton, Maryland
www.3sistersandabrother.com.

Beading Tips

1. Correct handling of jump rings: open the ring by curling one side toward you with pliers and close it by curling the same side back (away from you) until both ends meet. Never try to close by pinching both sides of the jump ring.

2. When making a floating (illusion) necklace, make sure there is an even amount of space between each pattern of beads. Crimp before and after the bead pattern with a .8-mm crimp (size #1) to keep in place.

3. When curling the loop of a head pin for an earring, be sure to close it completely against the pin so that your earring wire will not slip off.

About the Author

Mary Ellen Hughes is the author of *Wreath of Deception,* the first of the Craft Corner Mysteries, as well as two other mystery novels and several short stories. A member of Mystery Writers of America and the Chesapeake Chapter of Sisters in Crime, she has long been fascinated with both mysteries and crafts and enjoys being able to combine them. A native Milwaukeean, she presently lives in Maryland with her husband, Terry. You can visit her website at www.maryellenhughes.com.